PATRICIA WENTWORTH

Born in Mussoorie, India, in 1878, Patricia Wentworth was the daughter of an English general. Educated in England, she returned to India, where she began to write and was first published. She married, but in 1906 she was left a widow with four children, and returned again to England where she resumed her writing, this time, to earn a living for herself and her family. She married again in 1920 and lived in Surrey until her death in 1961.

Miss Wentworth's early works were mainly historical fiction, and her first mystery, published in 1923, was *The Astonishing Adventure of Jane Smith*. In 1928 she wrote *Grey Mask* and gave birth to her most enduring creation, Miss Maud Silver.

BOOKS BY PATRICIA WENTWORTH

Available from Harper Paperbacks

THE
ALINGTON
INHERITANCE

Patricia Wentworth

HarperPaperbacks
A Division of HarperCollins Publishers

HarperPaperbacks   *A Division of* HarperCollins*Publishers*
10 East 53rd Street, New York, N.Y. 10022

A trade paperback edition was published in 1990 by
HarperPerennial, a division of HarperCollins*Publishers*.

Cover illustration by Paul Cox

First HarperPaperbacks printing: August 1996

Printed in the United States of America

HarperPaperbacks and colophon are trademarks of
HarperCollins*Publishers*

10 9 8 7 6 5 4 3 2 1

CHAPTER 1

Jenny sat forward in her chair. It was eight o'clock in the evening. She sat leaning forward, her elbow on her knee, her chin in her left hand, her brown eyes, big and mournful, now fixed on Miss Garstone's pale face, now taking a quick glance round, as if to see the other presence that was so plainly in the room. There was a candle shaded by two propped books on the chest of drawers a little behind the bed. It was a cottage room, oddly shaped, with the thatch coming down to just above the little windows.

Miss Garstone lay in a narrow bed, her head raised by pillows, her arms neatly laid down by her sides, her face as pale as if she were already dead. She had not moved since they had brought her home that morning. She had not moved and she had not spoken. The doctor had been and gone. Miss Adamson, the village nurse, had been there all day. Now she had gone home to get one or two things she would need for the night.

"It's not likely she'll come round at all. And there's nothing to be frightened of, Jenny."

Jenny said, "No—" and then, "I'm not afraid."

"Well, I won't be long—not longer than I can help." Her footsteps went away down the narrow stair where you could not walk quietly however hard you tried, because the stairs were all twisty and they had never had a carpet on them since they were first built three hundred years ago.

As the sound of Miss Adamson's feet on the stairs died away and the other sounds of her going ceased, Jenny drew a long breath. Miss Adamson had been very kind, but she would rather be without her. As this was the last time she and Miss Garstone would be alone together, that gave her a solemn hushed feeling. She looked at the quiet white face with the grey hair parted neatly in the middle, and the clean white nightgown coming up to the chin and down to the wrists, and she wondered very much where Miss Garstone was. Was she asleep? And if she was asleep, did she dream? Jenny herself nearly always dreamed when she was asleep. She did not always remember her dreams, but she always knew that she had dreamed. Sometimes she remembered what the dreams were, sometimes they were just out of sight, sometimes there was no remembrance.

She mustn't think about her dreams, she mustn't think about herself. She wondered what could have happened to Miss Garstone on that lonely bit of road. Every day for as long as Jenny could remember, or nearly every day, Miss Garstone had got on her bicycle and gone off to the village. If she had not things to do for herself, there was always plenty to do for Mrs. Forbes who lived in the big house.

Jenny didn't wonder about Mrs. Forbes, because she was one of the people to whom she was so much accustomed that she hadn't to think about her. If you have always known someone and they are always there, you don't think about them, you take them for granted. Mrs. Forbes was always there, and so were her little girls Joyce and Meg, and her grown-up sons Mac and Alan. There was a lot of difference between them in age. That was because of the war. Mac and Alan had been born in the first years of Mrs. Forbes' marriage, and the two girls came after the war, so that the boys were quite grown-up and the girls were only nine and ten. They were all part of Jenny's life. She hadn't any relations of her own. When Mr. Forbes died she felt as if she had lost an uncle. He was always nice to her in a vague, absent-minded sort of way. He had been a very absent-minded sort of person. He had always struck Jenny as being only half there. Sometimes she wondered where the other half was. But the half that was there was always vague and kind.

Miss Garstone had always been there, too. Jenny called her Garsty. She was energetic, kind and industrious, but quite unsentimental. It was very strange to see her lie all day and never stir at all. Jim Stokes who worked for Mr. Carpenter had found her at twelve o'clock when he came whistling home to his dinner. She had done her shopping and started home, but she had not got farther than half way. There were the marks where the bicycle had run off the road. What had made it run? Nobody knew. If it was a car, it hadn't stopped to pick her up—it hadn't stopped at all. And Miss Garstone hadn't moved after she had fallen. She had lain there amongst the dusty trails of blackberry at the side of the road with her broken bicycle in the ditch beyond her, and no one to say what had happened.

Jenny had got as far as this when Miss Garstone moved. Her eyelids quivered and then opened. Her eyes looked out, looked all round the room, and then closed again. It was an unseeing look. Jenny's heart beat faster. She said "Garsty—" in a hushed sort of way as if she was calling to someone who might hear her but who mustn't be disturbed. The eyes opened again. This time they saw. She said in quite a strong voice,

"Jenny—"

Jenny said, "Yes?"

"I've been hurt."

"Yes, but you'll be all right now, Garsty."

"I—don't—think—so—"

Jenny stretched out her hand and took the pale hand nearest her. Miss Garstone had always been proud of her hands. They were her one beauty and she cherished it. They lay on the bed, the nails even and shining, the fingers a little curved, lying there quite empty. Jenny took the hand that was nearest to her. It felt slack and weak and empty. She said, "Oh, Garsty, Garsty!"

The eyes opened. Miss Garstone's voice came again. She seemed to be continuing something that she had been saying in the dream in which she walked. She said, "So it all belongs to you. You know that, don't you?"

"Don't worry about it now, Garsty."

Miss Garstone shut her eyes, but she was not at peace. The hand that was under Jenny's kept on moving. It was like something that was trying to wake up and couldn't quite manage it. Jenny's hand closed on it warmly.

"Don't. Don't try, Garsty. It's bad for you. You mustn't. Another time when you're better—"

The eyes opened again. For the first time the head moved. A very slight movement. It said, "No." She lay quiet, her eyes open, fixed on Jenny. Then she spoke in a thread of a voice.

"Did I say it?"

"I don't know."

"It's—so—difficult. I—must—tell—you. I oughtn't —to—have—kept it—from you. I never meant—to— go—without—telling you. It seemed—best—at the time. Your mother—" She stopped. "She was Jennifer Hill. Your father—your father didn't know—he didn't know about you—that you were coming—I don't think he knew—but Jennifer never said. He was Richard Forbes—Richard Alington Forbes. Alington belonged to him. But you know that—I didn't keep that from you—everyone knows it." The cold hand under Jenny's warm one twitched and turned.

Jenny said quickly,

"Don't worry yourself, Garsty. Oh, please don't!"

"I must." The two words came out quite clearly and strongly. They were weighted with a deep earnestness. After them she fell silent. It was like watching someone drift. Presently she spoke again.

"I ought not to have done it. At first I wasn't sure. And there you were, just a tiny baby, and your mother dead and she didn't tell me anything. If she had told me—I wouldn't have—let her down. Oh, I wouldn't! Do you believe me—because it's true—"

"Of course I believe you. Oh, don't trouble yourself."

The pale lips said, "I must—" on a failing breath. She was silent again. After what seemed like a long time she spoke in a faint voice. "I didn't think there was anything more—not till you were seven and Mr. and Mrs. Forbes had been here all that time. I was talking to a friend of mine, and she said, 'There's a way you can be quite sure, you know. If there was a marriage, it will be at Somerset House.' Did I tell you about the letter?"

"No. Never mind about it now."

Miss Garstone took no notice. She went on in that whispery voice which was like the trees sounding in a little wind, or something that you heard in a dream. She said,

"About the letter—it was in that little chest of drawers. It's there still—I put it back—I didn't want to read it. But you're their daughter—you have the right. It was the only letter she had from him, because they were together. She was in the W.R.A.F.'s—you know that. He was killed before he could write again.

His plane was lost. He went out on—what do they call them—a reconnaissance or something like that—and he didn't come back. He didn't come back—" There was a pause. The eyelids fell. The room was very quiet. The minutes went by.

Then very suddenly the eyes were open again.

"I only saw the one sentence—just the one—but it made me think. I couldn't get it out of my head. You see, he called her 'My wife—my precious wife'—there, at the end of the letter. I couldn't help thinking if they were married, then the house was yours—it was all yours."

It didn't penetrate. It was just something that the pale lips were saying. Jenny couldn't believe it. The hand which held Miss Garstone's was steady. Her mind shut all its doors. She couldn't believe it at all. She said,

"If they were married, she would have said."

"I thought of that—I thought he felt that way about her. But it couldn't be true—it couldn't really be true—"

The thought came into Jenny's mind, "Why couldn't it?" Before she knew what she was going to do she heard herself saying,

"Why couldn't it be true?"

Miss Garstone looked at her. She made an effort that moved her head a little, and she looked at Jenny.

"I knew you would ask me that some day."

All at once there seemed to be a tingling in the air between them.

"I knew it. Now it's come. I wasn't brave enough—I couldn't face it. I can't die without telling you—I never went to Somerset House—I was afraid—"

"Why were you afraid?"

"I loved you so much."

Jenny's heart melted in her.

"Oh, Garsty!"

"I thought—it was all wrong—I can see now. I thought if I said—and if it was true—that they were married—I thought—"

"Don't trouble now, Garsty."

"I must—there's so little time—"

"Tomorrow—"

"I haven't got any tomorrow. I never went to Somerset House—they would have taken you away from me. I couldn't bear it—it was because I loved you so much—" The lids came down again. There was a long silence which gradually became peaceful. Then suddenly the hand under Jenny's twitched and pulled. The eyes opened.

"You were born—here in this room. She came back—Jennifer came back. She never spoke. They weren't here then, you know—Mrs. Forbes and the boys. The house was empty—because of course it belonged to him, and if she was his wife and he was dead, then it belonged to Jennifer and to her baby. Only she never said—she never said anything. She would sit all day by the window. What I told her to do she did. She wasn't ill—not in body—but she was like a person in a dream. I had this cottage and we stayed here. The Forbeses came—because he was the heir. Mrs. Forbes came down and had a talk with me. She said it was stupid to stay on here—but I said 'Jennifer has no people and she has no money—but I've got this cottage—it's my own—no one can turn me out.' She saw I meant it, and she didn't say any more. Jennifer never roused at all. When her time came and you were born it was all easy. But she died that night—"

There was a long pause. When Miss Garstone spoke again there was a difference in her. She did not speak to Jenny. The eyes that she opened did not see her. They were fixed on someone else. Jenny had the feeling that if she could turn her head she would see who that someone was. She could not see, but she knew what Garsty saw. There was a presence in the room. She didn't know whether it was the presence of death or of life. She saw Garsty smile and say something, but she did not know what she said. And then in a moment it was over and Garsty was gone.

CHAPTER 2

Miss Adamson was away for an hour. She would not have been so long, but she met a number of people, and of course they all wanted to know about the accident and about how Miss Garstone was, and what with telling them and their saying how dreadful it was, and how shocking to think that anyone would run a woman down and not see if they had killed her, the time just slipped away. Then she had to let herself into her cottage and feed her cat and get what she wanted for the night, and it all took time. She hurried all she could, and then she made haste back along the lonely stretch of road where the accident had happened, and round the corner past the gate into Mr. Carpenter's farm, and then on to where the light shone from the window of the room where Jenny was watching. On the other side of the road was the empty lodge of Alington House where the Forbeses lived.

Miss Adamson felt a momentary twinge of resentment. She wouldn't have said that she got on well with Mrs. Forbes. She made it her business to get on well with everyone, but try as you will, if you've got a feeling you've *got* a feeling, and in her inmost heart Miss Adamson knew that she had a feeling about Mrs. Forbes. She didn't stop to think about it, but it was there as she put away her bicycle in the shed and walked up the dark garden path to go in by the kitchen door. Put into words, it would have been something of this kind—"She's always here when she's not wanted, and come the time when she might be some use she's away. Not that I suppose she'd have put her hand to anything if she'd been here." The thought was in her mind, if words did not clothe it.

She opened the door into the kitchen. There was a lamp burning here. She went through. There was no light in the front passage or on the stairs. The house was very still—it was very still indeed. There ought to have been some sound. The thought went quickly through her head. A little shiver went over her. She called up the stairs, "Jenny, I'm back!" and there was no answer.

Miss Adamson caught at herself. If anyone else had behaved like this, she would have known what to say about them. She couldn't believe that it was she herself, Kate Adamson, who stood at the foot of the stairs and was afraid to go on. She knew very well what she would say if it were anyone else.

In the room above her Jenny still held the cold dead hand. It had very little warmth to lose. She couldn't bear to let it go. She was glad to be alone. She was glad that there had been no one there except herself to see that look on Garsty's face. It was the look of someone who sees into reality. She would never forget that she had seen it. When the voice called to her from below it seemed very far away. She began to come back, but slowly. Even when the door opened behind her she did not turn.

Miss Adamson came into the room and stopped. For a moment she had nothing to say. She saw Jenny sitting forward holding Miss Garstone's dead hand in hers. She saw Jenny's face in profile, quite calm. She had rather the look of someone waking from a dream—waking, but not quite awake yet. Miss Adamson's eyes went to Miss Garstone's face. It had changed very little since she had seen it last, but she knew at once that she was dead.

There was a silent moment. No sound at all in the little room, and outside the wind that had been blowing gustily was still. As Miss Adamson stood there with the open door in her hand she heard the car. She could hear it quite plainly. It tooted twice at the entrance gate, which was just across the road, and turned in. Time was when the lodge was occupied and one of the children would run out and open the gates for the carriage to pass. But that was a long time ago. The carriage had given place to a car, the lodge stood dark and empty, and the gates were always open.

The sound of the car died away and was followed by a puff of wind. It shook the latched windows and made a rushing sound about the house.

Miss Adamson pulled herself together with a jerk and came into the room.

"Oh, Jenny my dear—" she said.

Jenny turned very slowly. There was only one thought in her mind. She said,

"It isn't true. It—it can't be true—not Garsty—"

Mrs. Forbes drove on to the house and beyond it. She put the car away, drew a long breath of the something accomplished something done sort, gathered up her parcels, locked the garage, and made her way to the front door. It was open, and Carter stood there peering out.

"Oh, ma'am," she said, "—oh ma'am, I'd have managed to keep it from them, because that was what I thought you'd want. But oh dear, what a dreadful thing!"

Mrs. Forbes was not paying very much attention. Carter was an emotional creature—it didn't do to take too much notice of her. She came into the lighted hall and began to undo her coat. The lamp in the ceiling shone down upon her and showed a very handsome woman. Not young—she owned to being over fifty, but she was very well preserved. Her two boys had been born with only a year between them when she was twenty-eight, the two little girls not for fourteen years, during which time Major Forbes had been in the Army—though what use he could possibly be, she never pretended to understand. When he did return he was even more absent-minded than he had been before he went. He was Colonel Forbes now, that was all there was to it. He slipped easily enough into the life of the village, was on terms of politeness with his wife, of vague affection for his children and for Jenny. He had died unobtrusively two years before, and his eldest son Mac reigned in his stead.

Carter continued to obtrude her excitement.

"Oh, ma'am," she said, "you could have knocked me down with a feather—you could indeed! I don't know when I've had such a turn! Right at our door as you may say!"

"What are you talking about, Carter? Not the children?"

Carter was at once shocked and impressed by the calmness of her voice.

"Oh, no ma'am! Oh my goodness, no! I couldn't have met you like this if there had been anything wrong with them."

"Well, what is it?" Mrs. Forbes was a carefully controlled woman, but the control was wearing thin. "For goodness sake, Carter—what's the matter with you? If you've got anything to say, say it! Oh, I got that stuff for Meg and Joyce—it will make up very nicely, I think. I'll go down and see Miss Garstone about it in the morning, or she can come up here. Yes, that'll be best."

"Oh, ma'am, you don't know—Miss Garstone won't never make no more dresses! Not a shred of hope—that's what the doctor told Mrs. Maggs when she asked him. She'll go out tonight or in the early hours, he said. Miss Adamson—"

Mrs. Forbes turned. She had reached the foot of the stairs, but she turned and came back.

"What are you talking about?"

Carter had her handkerchief out. She sniffed and choked a sob.

"It's Miss Garstone," she said. "Went into the village this morning same as she has time out of mind and nobody thinking anything about it, and when Jim Stokes come home at noon he found her—"

"Found her?"

"Yes, he did, poor boy, and it was a shock to him. He didn't try and move her, but he biked back to the village—he's a sensible boy—and they fetched Dr. Williams and Miss Adamson and they brought her home. And Miss Adamson she stayed with Jenny."

Mrs. Forbes stood where she had turned. It was a shock. She stood there assembling all her force to meet it. Then she said,

"The children don't know?"

Carter hesitated to avert, if possible, the cloud of anger which she could see sweeping up.

"Oh, ma'am, it wasn't me—it wasn't indeed! Mrs. Hunt she looked in to give me the last news, knowing I'd be interested. And Meg she come peeping round the door in the middle, and what Meg knows Joyce will know, there's no getting from it. And it isn't as if you could keep it from them—"

"Oh, be quiet, Carter!" Mrs. Forbes struck in with a sense of resolute strength. "I gather that the children know. I must go down there at once. It's a nuisance— I've just put the car away, but it's not worth getting it out again. I may be bringing Jenny back with me—I'll see. Get the bed made in the little room next the children's. Oh, and be on the lookout for the telephone, because I'll ring up when I know what's happening." As she spoke she came down the hall and picked up a flashlight from the table. As she finished speaking she was already at the front door. A moment later it fell to behind her with a resounding clang that echoed through the house.

Two little girls sprang from the top of the stairs and raced down them. They each put an arm round Carter and tugged her out of the hall and into the study.

"She's gone down there!"

"She said she was going!"

"We heard her, so you needn't mind saying!"

"Is she bringing Jenny back?"

"She said she was going to!"

"Jenny will have to come if she says so!"

"Oh, yes, she'll have to come!"

They hung on Carter and hopped while they spoke. When she tried to make herself heard they pulled her round and round about.

"I've got to get her bed ready. Meg—Joyce—leave go of me! I've got to get on. Oh my goodness—what's that?"

They froze where they stood, two little girls in white nightgowns with plaited hair, and Carter elderly and fat, all three of them possessed with the same fear. There was a dead silence. Everything in the house seemed to hold its breath.

Meg moved first. She whirled about and stamped with her bare foot on the carpet.

"You made it up! You pretended to hear something."

"Did you? Did you, Carter?"

"No, I didn't. You children will be the death of me.

I'm sure I thought I heard your mother. And if it wasn't her, we may be thankful, for she'd never understand the plague you children can be. You're not like it with her, and I don't know why you should be like it with me. Off to bed and no more nonsense!"

Mrs. Forbes stood in the dark and waited for her sight to clear. In a moment she had decided not to put on the lamp, and had begun to cross the open space before the house. It was not really dark. There was a moon behind those clouds which hurried in a wind she could not feel. She saw the racing clouds, and they meant no more to her than a rising wind that might or might not bring rain.

She entered the darkness of the drive. Her finger went out to the switch of the lamp and stopped short of it. No, she could manage. She kept her thoughts on finding her way. Time enough to think what she would find on the other side of the road when she got there.

She came out through the open gateway and crossed the road. There was a light in Miss Garstone's bedroom. Then it was true. She did not know that she had doubted it until that moment. If it was true, how did it affect her—and hers—the boys? She saw them suddenly, vividly, Mac—and Alan. But her mind was on Mac, her thought was full of him. He must be safe—safe. She opened the door of the house and went in.

Mrs. Forbes walked up the crooked stairs with her firm step. The door of Miss Garstone's bedroom stood open. She saw what there was to be seen—Jenny and Miss Adamson and Miss Garstone, and two of them were alive. And the third was a dead woman. Curiously enough, she didn't know whether that was a bad thing or a good one. It meant a change, but there are always changes. How the change would work out, she didn't know. Something rose up in her fiercely. She would see to it that the working out should be as she had planned. She spoke Jenny's name and came forward into the room.

"Jenny—"

Jenny turned. She wasn't crying. Mrs. Forbes would have thought it more natural if she had been. She said, "She's gone," and she said it quite steadily. Miss Adamson would have shared Mrs. Forbes' thought if she had not seen what she had seen and what she would never forget—Jenny's look when she came in and found her alone with her dead. No one who had seen that could possibly think anything except that Jenny had been so far with Miss Garstone that it was difficult for her to realize that she was gone, difficult for her to come back.

Mrs. Forbes took command. She said all the right things, and there wasn't the least bit of reality in what she said. Not to Jenny. Not to Miss Adamson either. She felt her dislike of Mrs. Forbes more keenly than she had ever felt it. It almost got the better of her and made her say something that she wouldn't be able to explain away afterwards. And yet when it came to thinking it out she was surprised at herself, because really Mrs. Forbes had done nothing to make her feel as she had felt. Thinking it over afterwards, Miss Adamson was astonished at herself—she really was.

It was Jenny who made the move. She said suddenly, "We can't talk in here—Oh, we can't. She doesn't hear us, but—" She left it at that and walked out of the door. They heard her step go down the crooked stair.

"She's upset," said Mrs. Forbes. "I suppose it's natural. I'll take her back with me, and you can get on with what has to be done here."

"And never a word to ask me whether I minded staying!" said Miss Adamson to herself.

CHAPTER 3

Jenny's spurt of independence did not last. She packed the suitcase with Mrs. Forbes standing over her.

"Your toothbrush, Jenny—and the toothpaste—and what else?"

"My face-cloth," said Jenny in the obedient voice of a little girl.

"That's right—put them in. Do you use a hot-water bottle?"

Jenny stood quite still and stared at her. The pupils of her eyes were larger than usual. It seemed to her that Mrs. Forbes' voice came from a long way off. It seemed to her as if she was floating in the air. It was with a great effort that she could come down and touch the things she needed.

The voice went on. It was Mrs. Forbes' voice. It said things like "You'll need your bedroom slippers, and your dressing-gown, and your night things. That dress you've got on will do to wear again tomorrow. Now your brush and comb—and that, I think, is all."

Jenny placed all the things in the suitcase neatly.

When they were walking up the drive together Mrs. Forbes asked her whether she had had anything to eat. She had to stop and think about that before she answered. Everything seemed so long ago and so far away, but when she got down to it she remembered that she and Miss Adamson had had tea at five o'clock, and that Miss Adamson had made her eat an egg. It felt like a long time ago—a long, long time. Garsty was alive then. It felt as if she had come a long way from the kettle boiling and Miss Adamson speaking cheerfully. It was a long, long way, and there was a gap in the middle of it which she could never cross over.

Mrs. Forbes asked her question again, "When did you have anything to eat?" and this time Jenny answered it.

"At five. We had tea. Miss Adamson boiled me an egg."

"Then you had better get straight to bed," said Mrs. Forbes briskly. "Carter can bring you up a cup of hot milk."

They came into the lighted hall. There was neither sight nor sound of the little girls, only Carter stout and flurried.

"I've brought Jenny back with me," said Mrs. Forbes. "You've got the room ready? Now just get her a cup of hot milk, and she'll be going to bed at once. She's had a trying day. Miss Garstone is dead."

The words went with Jenny and up the stairs into the little bedroom which she was to have. Mrs. Forbes threw open the door, put on the light, and said in a clear, firm, practical voice,

"Now, Jenny, no fretting if you please. We'll talk things over tomorrow. Get into your bed and go to sleep. I told Carter to give you two hot bottles."

Jenny stood in the middle of the floor and looked unseeingly at the door which had closed behind Mrs. Forbes. She was still standing there when it opened again. Carter stood there with a cup of milk and a piece of cake on a plate beside it.

"Oh, Jenny!" she said. "Oh, my dear, I know how you feel indeed, for I was just your age when my mother went, and I'm sure Miss Garstone's been a mother to you, hasn't she? You never remembering your own mother and all. And how should you when she died the day you was born, poor dear. But I'm sure you favour her something quite out of the way. Now you drink this up, and you eat the little bit of cake, my dear, for it'll do you good."

The kindness came in amongst Jenny's scattered thoughts and gathered them together. She crumbled the cake and drank the milk, sat when Carter told her to sit, and stood when Carter told her to stand. She was vaguely aware of her clothes being taken from her and her shoes and stockings being removed, and of Carter's soft country voice which never stopped talking but always said kind comforting things.

In the end she went into the warm bed, the clothes were tucked round her, the window thrown open, and the curtain drawn back. Did Carter actually say, "God bless you, my child"? or was it an echo of something she felt—and knew. . . .

The light was gone. There was a little moonlight outside. Jenny slept. She slept without a dream or any conscious waking. There was an enfolding sense of comfort and peace. That was all, and it was enough.

She came back gradually to morning light and her strange bed. Those were the first of her thoughts. The light had the hushed look which means the early morning. She waked and remembered, but even as the memory flowed into her mind there was a whispering sound on either side of her.

"You're awake at last."

"We thought you would never wake up."

"We've been sitting here as quiet as mice."

"We promised ourselves we would."

"But you're awake now, aren't you?"

"Oh, darling, *do* be awake!"

Jenny put out bare arms and stretched them. Somehow the arms became entangled with two plump little forms in teddy-bear dressing-gowns. They finished up, Jenny scarcely knew how, in the bed with her, one on each side, their arms about her neck, their little cold noses burrowing into a cheek on either side.

"We were frozen, but we waited till you were awake," said Meg on the right.

"Oh, yes—we promised ourselves we wouldn't wake you up. And we didn't, did we?" said Joyce. She wiggled her cold toes into a warm chink as she spoke.

Jenny sat up and hugged them both. The little warm bodies and the little warm ways of them were just what she needed. They brought her back to an everyday world.

"Nearly half past six," said Meg. "At six we came in, and you weren't awake, so we waited very patiently."

"We didn't make a single sound," said Joyce "—not a single one."

"And what we want to know is, have you come to stay—are you here for good? Because we want you—don't we, Joyce?"

"We want you dreadfully," said Joyce.

"And we've got it all fixed up," said Meg on her other side. "Joyce isn't supposed to go to school, or to do very much in the way of lessons—not since she was ill, you know. And first of all Mother had the horrid idea of sending me to school and keeping Joyce here with a governess. And you were to be the governess—lucky Joyce! But then she thought again. And this time she thought of having Joyce like a drip round her neck all the time, and she decided not to do it."

"Oh, Meg!"

"Well, you know what you are without me to brisk you up and keep you in order."

"Oh, Meg!"

"It was all arranged," said Meg, nodding.

Jenny had an odd mixture of feelings. It was so exactly like Mrs. Forbes to plan all this and not to say a word to her. Had she just gone on her own way and planned it all without a word to Garsty, too? Perhaps she hadn't gone quite as far as that. Perhaps Garsty knew. But how did these children know? She said,

"Nonsense!"

"It isn't nonsense," said Joyce, and Meg said,

"Didn't you know?"

"What I want to know is how you knew anything about it."

"You can't keep things from us. We always find them out," said Meg. "And this time—*this* time we were playing at being mice in the drawing-room, and Mother came past with Mac, and she said, 'I've decided not to send either of the girls to school for another term. That girl Jenny can come in and teach them. As a matter of fact she might just as well come and live in.' And Mac whistled and said, 'Garsty won't let her.' "

"And then they went away. We sat ever so still and held our breath, and they went right away. Wasn't it fortunate?"

"We stayed like mice without a single twitch until they had gone. We thought we should have *died*," said Joyce.

They both shuddered.

CHAPTER 4

The next few days were got through as days of that sort are got through. You have to live them, and know them, and feel them, and when they are over you have to get on with the business of living again. It was all rather like a dream. The disturbing thing was that Miss Garstone's sister suddenly appeared on the scene. Miss Garstone had met her once a year. She was ten years the younger of the two, and there was a certain dreadful likeness which made Jenny feel angry. But the younger Miss Garstone was hard and dictatorial where her sister had been patient and kind. She disapproved of Jenny and made no bones about it.

"Let me see now, you're seventeen, aren't you? Well then, we must find you a job! What could you do?"

Jenny was thankful to be able to say, "I have a job."

The sharp grey eyes looked her over.

"Indeed? Will it keep you? What is it?"

"I'm to be governess to the two little girls at Alington House."

"Oh. Well, that's quite suitable. As you know, under my sister's will made twenty years ago everything comes to me."

"Yes, I know."

Her thoughts went back a week to Garsty talking— "I really ought to see about making a will, Jenny. It doesn't do to put these things off too long. If I died tomorrow, you'd have only the hundred a year that Colonel Forbes left you. No, I must make an appointment with Mr. Hambleton and get it all fixed up. I can't leave you very much because I haven't got very much to leave, but if you've got something at your back it does make all the difference. I'll make an appointment with Mr. Hambleton and get it all fixed up." But she hadn't made the appointment, and next day she had been killed.

Jenny's eyes had been heavy with tears as she remembered dear Garsty. She helped Miss Garstone's sister to sort and pack the things she was going to keep. There were not a great many. Garsty's sister was a mistress in a big school. Most of the things were to be sold. Jenny remembered the little chest with her father's letter in it. She asked for it, and was met with a cool, suspicious look.

"Why do you want it?"

"There's a letter in it from my father to my mother."

"How do you know?"

"Garsty told me when she was dying."

The hard grey eyes looked at her. The hard voice said,

"You may look and see if it is there. We will go up together. If there is a letter from your father there you may have it, but I should say you would be wise not to count on finding it. If my sister was dying when she spoke of it, it is quite likely that she imagined the whole thing."

Jenny said nothing. She kept herself from speaking, because if she were to say anything at all she would say too much.

They went up the narrow twisting stair, Miss Garstone ahead, as if she were afraid that Jenny might come upon something and keep it.

"I mustn't," said Jenny to herself "—I mustn't think of her like that. She doesn't know me, and I don't know her, but she must have known some horrid girls to think like she does."

They came into the room where Garsty had died, and it wasn't like the same room at all. The bed had been stripped and taken to pieces. It stood up on end now between the two little windows, and Jenny kept her eyes from it because it looked so strange and she remembered sitting on the bed when she was very small indeed and learning to count on her fingers and toes. Against the opposite wall there was a chest of drawers, and on the top of it, right in the middle, there was the little chest which held the letter. Jenny went to it at once.

"She said it was in here—that's what she said."

"Well, you can look and see if there is anything there, but don't be disappointed if there isn't."

Jenny went up close to the chest of drawers and stood there. The little chest had two small drawers at the top and three below. It was very well made with beautifully turned ivory handles. But Jenny was not thinking of that. She drew out the two top drawers first. The right-hand one had some pink beads in it, and the left-hand one was empty. Jenny put them down carefully. Her hands were steady because she made them be steady, but her heart was not steady at all—how could it be?

The top long drawer was full. It had in it all those things which Jenny had fashioned with her unsteady childish fingers for Garsty's birthday and for Christmas. The next drawer was full of them too. But in the bottom drawer there was only one thing, a photograph frame with a picture of a laughing baby in it—Jenny at two years old.

And that was all. There was no letter from her father to her mother. There was nothing more at all.

"Well, are you satisfied?" said Miss Garstone.

Jenny was putting the things back.

"Yes—it's not here." She turned and looked straight at Miss Garstone. "If it turns up anywhere, you will let me have it, won't you?"

She expected a quick response, but she did not get it. Miss Garstone bit her lip and actually hesitated.

"Well, I suppose so," she said at last. "But if it does turn up, I advise you to burn it straight away, and without reading it. That's my advice, but I suppose you won't take it."

No, she wouldn't take it. It was too much to ask of her. She did not make any reply out loud. In her own mind she said secretly and firmly, "It's mine. And what I do with it is for me to say. Not for you, or for anyone else."

Miss Garstone remained looking at her for a moment or two. Then she said,

"I don't approve of keeping things—I've seen too much of it. But that's a thing you'll have to find out for yourself, Jenny. If you want to, you may have that little chest of drawers and the things in it."

Jenny turned round, her hands clasped, the colour high in her cheeks. She couldn't speak. Miss Garstone looked at her with disapproval—and something else. She didn't quite know what the other thing was. She tidied it away quickly and wouldn't let herself look at it. She told herself that she despised sentiment, and that girls were full of it and shouldn't be encouraged. She said briskly,

"Well, that's all, I think. If you want the chest of drawers you had better take it to Alington with you, then it won't get mixed up with the things that are to be sold."

Jenny said, "Oh, *thank* you." She didn't know how she got it said. It was somehow so difficult to speak, and Miss Garstone had turned round and gone briskly out of the room before she had done more than say her "Oh, *thank* you." She picked up the little chest and held it tightly, tightly. It wasn't just a little box with drawers in it. It was her life with Garsty—the whole seventeen years of it.

Miss Garstone was to go away that evening. She was to go back to her school, so they said good-bye at the door of the cottage. At the last moment she did a thing that surprised her. It really surprised her very much. She put out a hand and stopped Jenny at the front door.

"There's just one thing—" she said.

Jenny stood still.

"What is it, Miss Garstone?"

"It's not my business—I know that," said Miss Garstone. "But my sister was very fond of you, and I just want to say—" She stopped and broke off. What did she want to say? She didn't know. She was behaving like a fool. She took up her words again with a feeling that they were not her words at all.

"I just want to say that if at any time you don't want to stay with the Forbeses, I shall be very pleased to do anything I can to help or advise you for my sister's sake. I should like you to feel that I don't say things that I don't mean. Good-bye."

Miss Garstone did not shut the door at once. She stood with her hand on the knob and watched Jenny cross the road and pass into the grounds of Alington House.

CHAPTER 5

Jenny walked slowly up the drive. It was done. It was finished. It was all over. She was starting a new life. There wasn't any letter which would change everything for her. Poor darling Garsty had just imagined it. It was silly of her not to have thought of that for herself. And there were Miss Garstone's eyes too. . . . But she was glad about one thing. No, there were two things to be glad about. Miss Garstone had let her look for the letter her own self, and just at the end she had been quite astonishingly nice. "Quite human," said Jenny to herself, and with that she came round the last corner of the drive and caught her breath. Because there at the front door stood Mac's little red car, and that meant that Mac was there, and perhaps Alan, too. In the back of her mind was the thought, "They wouldn't have come down in time for the funeral. It wasn't so very clever to come down the same day." Because the funeral had only been that morning, and it would have been better to let a day or two go by.

There was anger in her as she had that thought. Didn't he care what people would think? And the answer was plain enough. It was no, he didn't, he didn't care a jot. What he wanted to do he did. What the village thought about him didn't matter at all. He could get away with it.

As she came across the hall, Meg darted at her and caught her wrist.

"Ssh—they've come! Did you see the car? Mac and Alan—they've both come! I do think they might have got here in time for the funeral—don't you? I said so to Alan, and he pinched my arm and said, 'Shh!' I expect I've got a black and blue pinch mark on it, and if I have—" She paused dramatically.

Jenny could not help laughing a little.

"What will you do?"

Meg hopped on one leg.

"I don't know, but I'll think of something. When I'm in bed and there's nothing to disturb me. Oh, what have you got there? What is it—may I see? Oh, it's a little chest of drawers!"

Jenny nodded.

"Yes, it was Garsty's. Her sister gave it to me. It—it was very nice of her."

"Well, she's got everything else," said Meg in a tone which dismissed Miss Garstone with finality.

They were half way up the stairs, when Mac came down them. As always when she saw him again, he made the same deep impression on Jenny. He was so terribly good-looking. He took after his mother, but where she wore her good looks with an air of being disillusioned, in him everything was heightened by a most visible air of enjoyment. And why wouldn't he enjoy his life? He had looks, and health, and youth, and an adoring mother. And he had Alington.

He came down two steps at a time with both his hands out.

"My poor little Jenny!" he said in his warm voice. "I was just coming down to dig you out of the Garstone woman's clutches. I hear she's a terror."

It was the old trick. When she was with him she forgot everything she had been thinking about him. He had only to smile, to say two words in his sympathetic voice, and she stopped thinking. And that wasn't right. That was just glamour. Like the fairy stories. Life wasn't a fairy story, it was real—not fairy gold which had turned into withered leaves when you took it out and looked at it next day. And these thoughts were together in Jenny's mind. They made a strange confusion there. And then, before she knew what she was going to say, she spoke. She heard herself speaking.

"Why didn't you come down in time for the funeral?"

She saw the flash in his eyes which meant that she had made him angry. He stood there a couple of steps above her and looked down at her. There was an antagonism between them. For the moment it was stronger than the attraction which had always been there and was sometimes very strong.

He gave a little laugh.

"My dear Jenny! Not really in my line, you know—not funerals! But I'll come and dance at your wedding if you ask me."

"I shan't ask you," said Jenny. The confusion in her had melted into a steady flame of rage. She looked up at him with a burning look, and then passed him by and was gone.

Mac was rather taken aback. Jenny had always been easy. Too easy really for his taste. This change lent interest to her. So he wasn't going to have it all his own way? Well, so much the better.

Jenny went on to the top of the stairs, where Meg was waiting for her.

"Were you quarrelling?" she asked. "You sounded as if you were."

Jenny laughed. It was an angry little laugh. She felt angry. She looked angry. She also looked astonishingly pretty, but she didn't know that. She tidied her hair, washed her hands, and put the little chest of drawers down on the middle of her big one where she could see it from her bed. Meg was very much interested.

"Oh, what a darling little chest of drawers! Is it yours? May I look at it? Is there anything in it?"

"There are the things I made for Garsty for her birthday and for Christmas when I was a little girl. I'll show you sometime. Not now."

"It's a baby chest of drawers! It's got a bow front, and it's got darling little ivory handles too! Oh, I do love it! Don't you?"

Jenny said, "Yes." It was just the one word, but there was something in it that stopped Meg's chatter.

They took hands and went down to the schoolroom, where Joyce was curled up in the sofa corner with a picture book and Alan sat strumming at the piano. He wasn't as tall as his brother, and he certainly wasn't as good-looking. He was, in point of fact, very much like his father. Jenny was struck with the resemblance as he swung round to meet her.

He said, "Jenny—" in a moved tone, and then, "I was so s-sorry—I really was."

She said, "Thank you," in a little voice. There was a warm feeling at her heart—there always was for Alan.

And then Meg broke in with "She's got the darling-est little chest of drawers from Garsty! She brought it home with her just now! It's all round in front, and it's got the dearest little ivory handles on it!"

Joyce scrambled down off the sofa.

"I want to see it! I want to look! Where is it?"

"It's in her room on the chest of drawers!" Meg called back to Jenny, "I won't let her touch it till you say we may," and was gone.

"I'm so s-sorry, Jenny," said Alan. He only stammered when he was upset, so she knew that he really meant it.

Jenny said, "I know. But it's no good talking about it, Alan—it's happened." And then the door opened and Carter came in with the tea.

"What are you doing here, Mr. Alan?" she said, putting down the tray.

"I'm going to have tea with the children."

"Oh, no, you don't. You will have tea in the drawing-room with Mrs. Forbes and Mr. Mac. This is schoolroom tea this is, and not for grown-up young gentlemen like you are now and have been these four years past. Get along with you, for I heard the mistress calling you, and she won't be a bit pleased if she finds you here!" She turned to Jenny. "Will that be all, miss?"

"Yes," said Jenny. "Thank you very much, Carter."

Carter turned and went out of the room. Alan took a couple of steps towards the door, and came back again.

"I'd better go if they're expecting me," he said, and paused, hesitating. And went.

Jenny turned round to the table and sat down.

CHAPTER 6

Mac and Alan only stayed for a bare twenty-four hours. Mac was two years down from Oxford and in process of becoming a barrister. Jenny was still not quite sure how this giddy height was to be attained, but she had very exciting visions of Mac scintillating with talent and good looks, sweeping all before him in some spectacular trial. This was when she wasn't angry with him, when he charmed, and she let herself be charmed. It had not got very far. He had kissed her once when she had a tray in her hands and couldn't stop him. She hadn't wanted him to kiss her—not like that. She had very nearly dropped the tray, which she wouldn't have been carrying if Carter hadn't come over queer just as she was going to take it in. Mrs. Bolton, the cook, didn't carry trays—she was very firm about that. And Mary, the house-parlour maid, who didn't live in but came up from the village, certainly wasn't going to do anything about it when it was her afternoon off and she was going with her young man to the pictures. Jenny had come out of the dark passage which led to the kitchen, and he had taken her by surprise. At the time it had just been fun, but when she remembered, it hurt. But then everything did hurt now. She didn't want the touch-and-go game, the here-today-and-gone-tomorrow kind of thing that had been fun in the past. She wanted something she could lean on and trust. There had been Garsty for that, and now there wasn't Garsty any more, and she wanted Garsty—oh, how she wanted Garsty!

She didn't think a great deal about Alan. He was a boy, just down from Oxford. Quite a nice boy if he could get over being so afraid of his mother—and of Mac. He was very like his father to look at. She wasn't so sure if he was really like him. She had been very fond of Colonel Forbes, and she had been aware of something in him which she missed in Alan. Colonel Forbes had not so much given way to his wife as stood out of her way. More and more as the years went on, he had avoided her, not in the way of offence or bad temper, but where their opinions differed—well, he made a point of not being there to be differed from. And more and more he had withdrawn into his library.

Jenny used to come in by the window and talk to him. He was a wonderful friend to have. He knew a tremendous lot about birds, and beasts, and all the country things. She loved him very much, and she had grieved terribly when he died. Alan was grieved too, but not Mac. And not Mrs. Forbes. "She doesn't mind a bit. I know she doesn't," she had said to Garsty when they came home after the funeral. "Jenny, you shouldn't say that—you can't judge." That was Garsty all over. She was so *kind*, even to the people who had no kindness in them—and you can't go farther than that. She remembered her own outburst—"How can you say she minds, when she's got her hair so beautifully done!" Well, it was a schoolgirl's judgment, but when she looked back on it Jenny was quite sure that it had been a true one. When people are broken-hearted they may see that their hair is neat, but they don't bother about whether it's becoming.

She thought that Alan had cared—she hoped that he had. He was abroad when his father died, and she didn't see him for three months. Mac didn't care, or only just a little. But then Mac was different. Jenny didn't explain to herself why she thought of Mac as different. That other sense which came from she didn't know where stepped in and told her that he didn't care.

She believed that sense, but she didn't analyse it. It lay under all her thoughts of Mac, but she didn't often look that way.

She settled easily enough into the routine of the house. It wasn't so very different from what she had been accustomed to. Until she left school she had bicycled the four miles into Camingford every morning and bicycled back at tea-time. After that she had spent her days at Alington helping to nurse Joyce when she was ill and teaching Meg. She didn't want to do anything else. She was quite happy. She had been head girl at her school, but she didn't want to go on to college. She was quite content to look after Meg and Joyce, and to see the boys at week-ends. That they came home much oftener than they used to did not strike her at all. She took it quite naturally. But now there was a change. Living in the house, things struck her that she hadn't noticed before. Or perhaps "struck" is the wrong word. There was nothing as definite as that. It was just that, the strangeness having worn off a little, there was something left that hadn't been there before. She couldn't get nearer to it than that.

As the second Saturday came round, Meg and Joyce began to wonder openly whether Mac and Alan would come down for the week-end.

"They don't ever come two weeks running," said Meg.

"They did in the summer."

"That was on a special occasion. I remember it quite well. It was for Anne Gillespie's birthday party."

"August's a stupid time to have a birthday. Everyone's away."

"Mac and Alan weren't away."

"Perhaps that's why she was born then."

"When?"

"In August, stupid!" Joyce made a face and put out her tongue.

"I'm not," said Meg with dignity. "And it's very vulgar to make faces like that."

"Who says it is?"

"Mother does."

"Oh—"

Jenny thought it was time to interfere.

"Who'll get to the elm tree first?" she said in a laughing voice, and the three of them raced away over the lawn to the big elm which creaked so horribly in winter, and which the gardener, old Jackson, always said was only biding its time. "Nasty trees, ellums," he would say. "No one ought to have 'em in the garden. Churchyard trees, that's what they are, and there they may bide for me. That 'ere tree ought to come down, miss. If I've said it once I've said it fifty times for sure."

"Well, it's no good saying it to me," said Jenny.

Jackson looked at her. He remembered her mother. "Features her proper," he thought, "but more of a way with her."

It rained in the afternoon, so they didn't go out. The little girls were going to have tea with their old nurse, Mrs. Crane, who lived with her daughter just on the other side of the village. They kept on going to the windows and looking out to see if it had stopped raining.

Mrs. Forbes came in and gave orders that they were not to go unless there was a reasonable probability of their getting there dry.

"It doesn't matter so much about their coming back, but they must get there dry," she said in her sharp, imperious way. "I shall be out in the opposite direction so I can't take them—I'm going to the Raxalls. You'll be going with the children of course."

Jenny hesitated.

"Well, I thought if you didn't mind I'd stay at home and let Carter go. She's such friends with Nanny."

"Oh, yes—I'd forgotten. Well, if they can get there dry they can go."

She was gone again without waiting for an answer. It wasn't her place to wait for answers. She gave an order and it was carried out, as she knew it would be when she gave it.

The rain was slackening off, when the door opened and Mac and Alan walked in. Meg and Joyce gave squeals of joy and flung themselves on them.

"Mother seems to be out, and we've come to tea."

"We didn't expect you this week," said Jenny. Her colour had risen. She looked very pretty indeed.

Mac smiled at her. He might do worse. He might do much worse. She could have been a plain lump, and here she was, very far from being plain. Very, very far indeed.

Alan had the two little girls one in each arm and was swinging them. Mac leaned a little closer to Jenny and dropped his voice.

"Have you missed me, Jen?" he said softly.

"A little—perhaps—"

"Perhaps a lot?"

And with that there was a good resounding crash. Alan had tripped over a chair and was down with a tangle of shrieking, excited little girls. Jenny sprang to her feet.

"Oh, my goodness! What are you up to, Alan?"

"I'm not up at all—I'm d-down," he said laughing and got up, his hair rumpled.

Jenny seized Meg with one hand and Joyce with the other.

"Shocking children! Now behave, or I'll send the boys away."

"Oh, you wouldn't do that!" said Meg.

"Oh, Jenny *darling!*" said Joyce.

Mac and Alan struck an attitude and repeated her words, "Oh, Jenny *darling!*" and the whole group dissolved into laughter.

Looking back on it afterwards, Jenny thought that was her last happy time with them—her very last, though she didn't know it. She only felt happy, and as if the old bad times had gone away and would never come again.

It went on being happy. The little girls, protesting, were removed by Carter. They could go to tea with Nanny any time, they said.

"Just any time at all, Carter—you know we can! But we can't have Mac and Alan to tea with us—only once in a blue moon!" they protested.

Carter was very firm indeed.

"I don't know when I heard such nonsense," she said. "It's come out quite bright and clear, and the rain over as anyone can see. And Nanny's been making cakes for you all morning, I shouldn't wonder."

"Will she have made the sort that has chocolate icing on it?" said Joyce in a hopeful tone.

"I shouldn't wonder," said Carter more indulgently.

Their protests had grown feebler. They hadn't had much hope of being let off. They went away to be washed and dressed, and finally set out, the very picture of two good obedient little girls.

When Jenny got back to the schoolroom she found only Alan there. He said,

"Mac's gone to the Raxalls."

Jenny felt a quite sickening disappointment. He didn't care—he didn't care a bit. Oh well, if he didn't care, then she didn't either. Or did she? She couldn't answer that, but the question went on in her as she got tea for Alan and herself and talked to him about his plans for the future.

CHAPTER 7

"*I'm really very glad that* Mac has gone for Mother," said Alan. "I don't often get a chance t-to talk to you alone."

Jenny smiled in an absent way. She was wondering whether it was a party that Mac had gone to, and whether Anne Gillespie would be there. She had to give herself a little mental pull and to come all the way back from the Raxalls. You couldn't do that in a moment. She thought that Mac and Anne would make a splendid pair. They were both all fair and golden, with dark blue eyes and the darker lashes which showed up the blue. She came to herself with a jerk.

"What did you say, Alan? I was thinking of something else."

Alan looked hurt. When he was hurt he stammered more than usual. He said with an angry rush of syllables,

"You w-weren't l-listening! You n-never do l-listen when it's m-me!"

Jenny was conscious of guilt. The consciousness put colour into her cheeks and a soft light into her eyes.

"Oh, Alan—I'm so sorry. I—I was just thinking of something else." Her colour burned brighter as she remembered what she had been thinking of.

That raised colour went to Alan's head. He took it for what it certainly was not, an interest in him. He reached out across the tea-table and caught at the hand which was offering him cake.

"Jenny, you've got to listen to me. I can't s-stand back and l-let things happen—I can't really. No one could expect me t-to. I don't so often get an opportunity that I can afford to l-lose one when it comes. You c-can't expect me to."

Jenny put the plate down. She hoped that Alan would take the hint and let go of her hand, but he only held on to it harder than ever.

"Alan, don't be ridiculous! You're hurting me!"

"I don't want to hurt you. Oh, my God, Jen—I'd do anything to stop you being hurt. It's because of that—oh, you m-must know—you m-must see!"

Jenny was shaking. She took hold of herself as firmly as she could. He was just a boy—a silly boy. She said as calmly as she could,

"Alan, what is it?"

He released her hand as suddenly as he had taken it. He got up, spilling his cup of tea, and went over to the mantelpiece, where he stood looking down into the little black fire.

"D-don't you know that I l-love you?" he said in a muffled voice.

"Oh, Alan, you can't—you don't really!"

"Because I'm not M-Mac," he said.

"Oh, Alan—"

"Why shouldn't I l-love you? Will you t-tell me that? I'm no one of c-course—no one to anyone."

"Alan—"

He swung suddenly round and faced her.

"N-no, you listen to me! I've got things to say to you; and this is a good time to say them."

He had stopped stammering, and he was very like his father. She had only seen Colonel Forbes angry once. It was a long time ago when she was quite a little girl. There was a man who had frightened a woman. The whole scene flashed back into Jenny's mind. It had frightened her very much then, but she wasn't frightened now. All her colour had gone. She lifted her eyes and looked at Alan.

"What do you want to say?" she said.

"This. I love you. I've loved you for a long time. I can't afford to marry yet—I know that. But if you'll be engaged, it—it would be a protection for you. We'll get married in about three years' time if—if you didn't mind starting in a small way. I didn't mean to say anything, but Mac's no use to you—he isn't really. And if you were engaged to me, he'd leave you alone—he—he'd have to."

Jenny had got paler and paler. This was one thing she had never thought of. Alan was just Alan, like a brother. She had never thought of him like this. If she had been older she would have reflected that a boy of his age must be in love with someone, but she hadn't enough experience to know that, and what she didn't know she couldn't say. She just sat there at the table and thought, "Oh, poor Alan! What shall I say—what shall I do?" She hardly knew what he was saying. She looked at him as if she didn't understand.

"Oh, Alan, *please*—"

He came across to her.

"It's no good saying 'Oh, Alan—' It's not a bit of use. You're mine—you're not Mac's—I won't let him. Oh, J-Jenny!" He went down on his knees beside her and caught her about the waist.

She felt suddenly sure of herself. She wasn't frightened of him, because he was just Alan whom she had known always, who had been like a brother. That was it. That was why she felt it was all wrong. When she spoke, her voice shook a little, but she felt an inner calmness.

"Alan, you mustn't—you mustn't really. And it's no use—it's no use at all."

He looked up at her wildly.

"Why is it no use? Why should you say that? I'd work for you—I'd do anything. Listen—I've got an idea. There's a friend of mine—his name's Manning. He's an awfully good chap. Strong as a bull, and he wants to go in for farming. His father's got a lot of money, and he was very disappointed because Bertie didn't want to go into the business. It's steel or something, and Bertie said he simply couldn't bear the thought of it. He says he doesn't want to be rich, he just wants to have enough, and he wants his father to put his younger brother in his place, and to let him have just enough to run a farm on. Reggie is quite different. He'd like to be the elder son, and he'd like to be in the business. He thinks Bertie is a fool, and as Bertie says, if he is it's his own look out, and it's all to Reggie's good. So you see—"

At this point Jenny made a determined effort and freed herself. She pushed back her chair and walked over to the fireplace. Alan followed. He stumbled as he got up, and upset Jenny's cup, but he was much too busy with his argument to notice it. He came to the other side of the mantelpiece and stood there frowning.

"Where was I? I was telling you about Bertie Manning. I don't know why you wanted to get up. Well, I w-wasn't going to say anything, but I c-couldn't help it. If I g-go in with Bertie, we ought to be over the first expenses in three years, and if we w-were engaged—"

"But you were going into the Civil Service, weren't you?"

"It t-takes too long," he said frowning. "I haven't said anything about th-this except to you. I've been w-waiting for an opportunity, but if you'll be engaged to m-me—"

"I can't," said Jenny.

He took a step towards her with his hands out.

"J-Jenny—"

"It's no good. It's no good, Alan—it really isn't. I

don't think of you like that. You'd be just like a brother. I couldn't—couldn't—"

He had turned very pale as she spoke. It was like seeing the blood drain away out of something. It was horrible.

When he spoke again his voice choked.

"Is it Mac?" he said. And then, quick and hot, "He doesn't love you—he d-doesn't. If you'd heard him as I have you'd know I was telling the truth. He doesn't love you at all. But he wants to m-marry you—I d-don't know why."

Jenny's heart gave a jump. Mac wanted to marry her. He wanted to marry her, Jenny Hill, with no name except her mother's, with nothing at all—nothing at all. Her head went round. She turned giddy and held tightly to the mantelpiece. She bent her head down and blinked away the tears which filled her eyes. They sparkled and fell, and she could see again. She heard herself say, "He doesn't."

"He does. I tell you he does. I don't know why he wants to but he d-does. Th-that is why he's gone over to get hold of m-my mother. Th-that's why I had to speak to you. I'd n-never get a chance otherwise."

Jenny's head had cleared. There were no more tears. She said,

"Why do you say he wants to marry me?"

"I don't know. He d-does want to."

"Why?"

"I t-tell you I d-don't know."

Thoughts knocked at Jenny's brain. She wouldn't let them in. She wouldn't let them in, but they were like the wind trying to get through the door, through the window, down the chimney. If she were Jenny Forbes, if she were the lawful daughter of Richard Alington Forbes and Jennifer Hill—if she were their lawful daughter instead of a come-by-chance, then

Mac would have a reason for marrying her, a real solid reason. The thoughts clamoured so loudly that she could hear them through all her shuttered windows, and closed doors. She wouldn't listen—she couldn't, she—mustn't. She stamped her foot and said,

"Stop it, Alan! Do you hear—stop it!"

He came forward a step. Jenny listened.

"I know Mac," he said. "You only see him. Well, that's all right. I wouldn't say a word, only it's your whole life. He doesn't care for you—not like I do. No, I didn't mean to say that. I'm not talking for myself now, I'm talking for you. You don't know Mac—I do. He's my brother, but I'm going to tell you the truth about him. There's only one person he cares anything for, and that's himself. He's got everything—looks, strength, brains. And he's the eldest son. Do you think he's going to let that be taken away from him by anyone? By anyone at all? I tell you he isn't going to. He—he'd wade through blood—" He stopped himself, half horrified by the sound of his own words. The stammer came on him again. "It's t-true," he said on an altered note. His voice trembled and died away. There was silence between them.

After some time Jenny moved. She said in a low voice, "It's not—your business," and found him looking at her.

"I th-think it is," he said. "I th-think it's the b-business of anyone who loves you. I do l-love you, Jenny."

The tone of his voice got through her anger. She said, "I know you do. I don't want you to—not like that."

He gave a groan and put his head down on the mantelshelf. After a moment he said,

"It d-doesn't matter about m-me. I don't want you to g-get hurt—th-that's all."

Jenny stood irresolute. She didn't know what to say or what to do. And then Alan stood up.

"You'll th-think of what I've said. It's all t-true, you know."

The tears were running down his face, but he didn't seem to be thinking about that. He said, "Oh, Jenny—" and went out of the room.

CHAPTER 8

Jenny washed up the tea things and put away the cakes. Her hands moved mechanically over the china. She felt dazed, and she wanted to stay like that. She had had an anaesthetic once when she had fallen out of a tree and dislocated her shoulder. The doctor wasn't quite sure if there was further damage and she had had a whiff of anaesthetic. She remembered coming out of it, and how she hadn't had any feeling, and how gradually the pain had come in again and the dreamy feeling had thinned out and gone away. She thought this was the same. It was going to hurt. It was going to hurt very much like her shoulder had done, only worse, because the things that happened in your body were never as bad as the things that happened in your mind.

When she had quite finished washing up and putting the things away she went up to the schoolroom. She didn't know where Alan was. She thought he had gone out, and that meant that she was quite alone, because Mrs. Bolton, who went out on Wednesdays, might as well not be there, for she never came upstairs at all and had her bedroom in what had been the housekeeper's room. It gave her a lonely feeling in one way, but it was rather nice in another. Only tonight the house felt very echoey and lonely. She wished she had gone with the little girls, she wished she had done anything different from what she had done.

And then she heard the car. It came rolling to a stop at the front door, and she went to the window to look. Mrs. Forbes and Mac got out. Jenny's heart gave a jerk. At the sight of Mac's tall figure her heart had begun to ache quite dreadfully. It was just like that time with her shoulder—the pain got worse and worse, until suddenly it was too much for her. She pulled the curtain across the embrasure and sank down upon the window seat behind it in a flood of silent tears. Everything swept over her at once—Garsty—and the loss of her home—and what Alan had said about Mac. She fought against that. It wasn't true. It wasn't—it wasn't true. But out of the depths of her there came a little clear voice that said, "It's true, and you know it."

She had forgotten everything but the bitterness which had swept over her, when she heard footsteps on the stairs outside. Mac—she would have known his step anywhere. She shrank down behind the curtains. She couldn't meet him—not like this.

And then there was another step, and a voice—Mrs. Forbes' voice.

"Isn't she there?"

The door opened and Mac came in. The light went on. Jenny shrank back behind the curtains. He said,

"No, she isn't. She and Alan must have gone down to get the children."

Mrs. Forbes came across from her bedroom. The faint scent she used came in with her. It was very faint indeed, like the last reflection in water before the light goes. The thought went through Jenny's mind like a background to what she was feeling. She didn't mean to listen. She didn't know that there was going to be anything to listen to. She heard the click of the closing door, and she thought that she was alone. And then she knew that she wasn't, because the light was still on, and Mrs. Forbes was so terribly particular about lights being turned off. She sat there frozen with something like terror. Why didn't they go away? Why should they stay here?

Mrs. Forbes spoke from the far side of the room.

"Well, what did you want to say to me, Mac?" The tone was the indulgent one which no one else heard from her.

Mac didn't answer at once. Jenny couldn't see him, but she knew how he would look—frowning, his brows drawn together over the dark blue eyes.

Mrs. Forbes turned towards him and said,

"Mac, what is it?"

"All right, you can have it. I've only known for a week. I went away and thought it out. I didn't know how much you knew—or guessed."

Behind the curtain Jenny's heart beat to suffocation. She didn't know what was coming. Or did she? Did she? The pulses sounded in her ears, in her throat, in her breast. And then she heard Mac say,

"It's Jenny. He married her."

Mrs. Forbes was holding her foot to the fire. She turned now and looked at her son.

"What do you mean?"

"I'm talking about Jenny. What we all knew was that she was the daughter of Richard Forbes and Jennifer Hill."

Mrs. Forbes said in a hard voice,

"Well, isn't she?"

"Of course she is. There wasn't ever any doubt about that. The only thing there *was* a doubt about was the fact of their marriage."

Mrs. Forbes had turned to face her son. She looked him up and down with a cold piercing look and said,

"You're talking nonsense! There was no marriage!"

Jenny heard the anger in her voice. Mac didn't sound angry. He sounded like a person who had lived with something and got used to it, and for whom there are no surprises any more. He said,

"Oh, my dear Mother, be your age! And we haven't all day. They'll be back in a moment, all the lot of them, and we've got to get this settled. There was a marriage, and I'm not asking you to take my word for it. I've seen the certificate."

"You've *what?*"

"I've seen the certificate."

"You can't have!"

"I have. Will you get that firmly into your head! I'm not making this up—why should I? Now listen, because we may not have much time, and it's urgent—very urgent. I had my suspicions. Garsty gave the show away rather. She said something, and then stumbled and picked herself up."

"Do you mean that she fell?"

Jenny knew that voice. It was Mrs. Forbes fighting. She would fight to her last drop of blood for Mac. She heard it in her voice, and she heard the recognition of it in Mac's laugh as he said,

"I don't mean anything of the sort, as you know perfectly well. And don't talk! Listen to what I've got to say! The Thursday before she died Garsty and Jenny went to Camingford. I knew they were going, and I came down. I let myself into the cottage."

Mrs. Forbes said,

"How?"

Mac laughed.

"Never you mind! I did, and I went over the whole place till I found what I was looking for."

Mrs. Forbes' voice had changed—Jenny knew that. It was still steady, but it wasn't the same. There was something strained about it, something unnatural. She said,

"What did you find?"

"I found a letter from Richard Forbes to Jennifer Hill. It must have been the last letter he wrote her. He called her his wife."

Mrs. Forbes came in quickly.

"There's nothing in that."

"My dear Mother, I'm not a child, but there was enough to make me, shall we say, a little anxious. Anyhow I went up to Somerset House and—well, you can guess."

"I'm not guessing. If you've got anything to say, say it!"

"I've got this to say." His tone was still a smiling one.

Jenny knew just how he looked—the fair hair, the blue eyes, the height, the strength, the everything. A little giddiness came over her. No, no, not now—not when she *had* to hear. She had to. She pressed the nails of her left hand into the palm of her right, and the pain got through the faintness. She heard what Mac said. She heard it quite distinctly and past any possibility of a mistake. He said,

"They were married in January 1940 five months before he was killed."

"I don't believe it!"

He shrugged his shoulders.

"I tell you I've seen the certificate."

"Then why didn't she say?"

Mac shrugged again.

"You've forgotten. She was knocked on the head in an air raid the same night that he was killed. A splinter from a shell got her. Garsty told me all about it once. She must have told you, too."

"Yes, she did."

"Well, there you are. They thought she'd get her senses back when Jenny was born, but she didn't—she just died." There was a long pause.

Jenny's head cleared. What were they going to do about it? She hoped very much that she knew. She was afraid that she didn't know. If Alington was hers she would give it to them, oh, so gladly. If Alington was hers . . . She didn't know what she felt. She didn't know. She heard Mrs. Forbes say suddenly, quite loud and clear,

"This is all nonsense!"

And Mac laughed and said,

"It's going to be very dangerous nonsense for us unless we do something about it."

"What can we do?"

"Oh, it's quite simple. I can marry her."

"No—no—"

"Don't be silly, Mother. It's the one perfect way out."

"I won't have it!"

"I said don't be silly. You don't suppose I want to marry the girl, do you?"

"I don't know."

He laughed.

"Oh, come! I shouldn't have thought of it if it hadn't been for this! But you must see that it's the perfect way out."

"I don't see anything of the sort!"

"Oh, come, you're not stupid. And you needn't pretend with me. We're two of a kind, and you know it. I'm not Alan. And you don't have to pretend—not with me. I quite agree with having a little, shall we say, camouflage in the ordinary way. But just now, as things are, just between ourselves and for this once, let's be straight about it."

Mrs. Forbes said,

"What do you want to say?"

"This. I've had time to think about it, and you haven't. There's only one way out—that's the way I said. I marry her, and we hold our tongues. If she ever finds out, well it's just too bad, but there's nothing to be done about it. We didn't know, and she didn't know. And once we're married it doesn't really matter. I shall be the noble cousin who married her when she was an illegitimate poor relation."

Mrs. Forbes said, "Don't!" and Mac laughed and said, "Why not?"

Jenny couldn't see them, but they saw each other, and for the moment what Mrs. Forbes saw shocked her. It was one thing to suspect and to put the suspicion from your mind, and another to see the plain truth naked before you. The thought of her husband came to her and she put it away with a sort of terror. She knew very well what his judgment would have been on her for her hesitation, and on Mac for his certainty. She had her moment of choice. She looked at the alternative— Jenny in her place, herself a widow with a limited income, Mac with his way to make—She got no farther than that. There was a rush of everything in her to protect herself, to protect Mac. She said in a lowered tone but very firmly,

"No—no. I can't do it."

Mac smiled.

"You won't find it so difficult."

"No—no, I don't mean that. You're right—you must marry her."

"Of course I'm right! I always am. And why? Because I'm a clear thinker. I don't let my doings get diverted by morality. That's the mistake always. You have to decide what's best to do and leave the morality out of it."

Mrs. Forbes stared at him.

"I wish you wouldn't talk like that," she said. "You'll marry the girl and that will be doing well by her. And the best thing we can do is to forget this stupid story about a marriage which I don't believe in and never shall."

Mac laughed. Jenny wondered as she heard him. It was such a gay laugh—gay and infectious.

"Have it your own way," he said.

And with that there came the sound of children's voices and Alan speaking to them. The hall door opened and shut again. Mac took his mother by the arm.

"Come along, we'll go and meet them. We don't want to be found here like conspirators, do we?"

"Certainly not. Those children should be in bed. I never meant them to stay so late. That'll be Jenny's fault. She makes a game of everything."

They went out. Mrs. Forbes said, "Put out the light." The door shut. Jenny heard their footsteps go away. The room was dark. She was alone.

CHAPTER 9

Jenny moved cautiously. She had to get out of the room before Carter came and the children. Where was she to go? Where could she hide? The answer came bleak and plain. She mustn't hide. She must be just as usual. She must be where she would be expected to be. In her own room? No. Because Mrs. Forbes might have opened the door and looked in on her way to the schoolroom. Where, then? The bathroom. You could lock yourself in. She could wash her face and tidy her hair, and be ready for supper with the children.

She felt better with the bathroom door securely locked, but when she looked in the glass her reflection shocked her. There was no colour in it, no colour at all. And she looked older. She sponged vigorously, and didn't let herself think, and when she looked again she looked more as she usually did. Then as she stood there looking into the glass the colour faded and she was pale again.

She came out of the bathroom, and met Carter and the children.

"Oh, do you know, Jenny, Nurse has got a new kitten!" said Joyce.

"It's sweet!" said Meg. "It really is! Its name is Patrick! Its fur is as long as this!" She showed the length with her fingers. "And it purred at me! It didn't purr at Joyce! She didn't hold it comfortably, and she kissed it! Kittens don't like being kissed!"

"They do!" said Joyce. "They like it awfully!"

"Then why didn't Patrick purr for you? Oh, Jenny, I want a kitten so badly! Do you think Mother would let me have one?"

Carter broke in.

"Now Meg and Joyce, you come along and get your things off quick. The mistress isn't best pleased with us being so late as it is. And it's not the time to ask about cats and such-like, I can tell you that."

She swept them into their bedroom and went on talking.

"They won't want anything. Such teas as they ate I never saw! Anyone would think they'd been starved all the week! I'll take my own things off if you'll see them to bed. And hurry, you two, or your mother will be coming up."

She vanished, and Jenny was left with the children, who under pressure from the last threat whisked themselves out of their clothes and into the bathroom and out again like mice running away from a particularly active cat. They were ready for bed, washed pink and spotless, by the time Mrs. Forbes came up the stairs. Jenny thought she looked a little disappointed, and she thought she knew why. She had had to swallow a bitter pill, and it would have been a relief to find a legitimate reason for anger. There was no reason at all. There were two little girls, miraculously clean and neat, kneeling one on either side of Jenny as she sat on the bed to hear their prayers.

"Please God, bless Mother, and Mac, and Alan, and make me a good girl."

Joyce on the other side of Jenny repeated the same words,

"And make me a good girl."

"And bless Nanny and Carter and everybody. And bless Jenny and Joyce. Amen."

And Joyce repeating it.

"And bless Nanny and Carter and everybody. And bless Jenny and Meg. Amen."

Jenny felt as if her heart was breaking. She had her back to the door, and when it opened she did not see who came. She thought it must be Carter. It was a shock to hear Mrs. Forbes' voice, and to turn round and see her standing in the doorway waiting for the prayers to be over. She spoke with her usual briskness.

"Into bed with you both! Good-night, Meg—good-night, Joyce. Now, Jenny, you had better dine with us tonight. It will be company for the boys."

Jenny didn't know what she felt like. She couldn't do it—she couldn't. That was her first thought as Mrs. Forbes kissed the two little girls and left the room, putting out the light as she went.

Jenny stood for a moment in the darkened room. Then she kissed Meg and kissed Joyce and went out into the lighted passage, her mind full of the one thought. She couldn't do it.

Mrs. Forbes had not waited for her. She had gone into her own room across the passage and shut the door.

Jenny went to her room. She couldn't do it. But she must. She had got to get away. If they knew, they would stop her. She had got to get away. She couldn't stay here and meet Mac—she simply couldn't do it.

She had got to do it—just this once more. And then she would get away from them all and never see them again. The thought of the little girls tugged at her heart. They would forget her. She thought of the people she had known when she was their age. Not Garsty, because Garsty went on. Garsty would never become a shadow in a distant place. Garsty was for now and for always. She thought about old Mrs. Pennystone who had died when Jenny was Meg's age. She remembered her as a very kind old lady, very fat. She had pressed peppermints on her when they met, and she had given her a wonderful doll for Christmas the year before she died. What was the good of thinking about Mrs. Pennystone, or about any of the other people she had known in the village, and who had died or gone away? They weren't her own people, and the Forbeses were. That was the plain truth that you couldn't get away from. Your family was your family. Mac and Alan were her cousins, and the little girls, too. She didn't know of any other relations. If she went away she would have no one at all. She stopped and looked at that. It was better to have no one than to have people you couldn't trust.

She wanted to get right away, and she wanted to get away at once, and to do that she must go down and play a part. Something in her said, "I can't. I can't—I can't do it." And something else said, "I must." She listened to that voice.

When she came into the drawing-room Mac was there. He was reading the paper, but he looked up, smiled his charming smile, and said,

"Well, what have you been doing with yourself, Jenny my love?"

The colour whipped into Jenny's face. She came up the long room to the hearth and stood there. She had put on a black lace dress which she had made for Christmas last year. It was too old for her, but when you have only one evening dress it is better to have a black one, and if it is lace you can do all sorts of things with it, so that it will go on for a long time. You have to think of those things when you are young and poor.

Jenny didn't know it, but the black dress did something to her. It made her look older, and it was very, very becoming. She stooped forward over the fire and turned her head away from Mac. She couldn't look at him.

She said, "Oh nothing," in as careless a tone as she could manage. To her horror, she felt the colour run up to her face. It burned there and then slowly, slowly retreated.

Mac put down his paper and got up and came over to her.

"Why, Jenny," he said in a laughing, teasing tone, "what was all the colour about? It was very becoming. I'm not complaining about it, but I do want to know why the flags."

Jenny stood her ground. She laughed a little and said,

"What an imagination you have!"

"Have I?"

He laughed, too, and came to stand by the fireplace on the opposite side. He was so near that he could have touched her if he had stretched out his hand.

The feeling that he was so close came upon Jenny with an intolerable force. She had been so near, so near to loving him, and it was gone—it was all gone away for ever. How was she to endure having him so near?

She must, she must endure it. Just for this once. Until she could get away. For this one evening she must play her part. And then—oh, then she would be done with them all.

He was speaking now, looking down at her with the smile she had thought a loving one.

"You're very fine tonight."

"Am I? I don't often dine with you, do I? This is the only evening dress I've got."

"And very nice, too. A little old for you perhaps, but you're young enough to take that as a compliment. It's quite a sincere one." He bent nearer. "Jenny, will you come for a walk with me tomorrow afternoon?"

She lifted her eyes to his face and said gravely,

"I don't know."

"I want you to. Just you and me. *Please,* Jenny."

And with that the door opened and Mrs. Forbes came in. She was talking over her shoulder to Alan, who was behind her. When she straightened up and saw Mac and Jenny she came forward with a determined smile.

"Oh, there you are, you two! Well, Jenny, that's a very pretty dress. Have I seen it before?"

"I had it last Christmas," said Jenny. "Garsty had the stuff, and I made it up."

"You made it very nicely."

Mrs. Forbes was gracious with a deliberate graciousness that was hard to put up with. Jenny thought, "If I didn't know that she hated me, and why she was putting up with me, should I have seen that?" And she knew that she wouldn't. It would have been just Mrs. Forbes with her grand manner. She wouldn't have thought anything about it.

They went in to dinner. It was a long evening, and

for Jenny it went with intolerable slowness. Alan's wretched look went to her heart. He was suffering, and so was she. And so was Mrs. Forbes. Jenny knew that. She could even admire in a sort of way the manner in which Mrs. Forbes was carrying the whole thing off. There was a part to be played, and she was playing it very well. She was playing it very well indeed. And Mac? She knew now that he didn't love her. She even knew that he didn't love anyone but himself. She wondered whether it would have been easier if she had found that he did love someone else. It was dreadful to know that he didn't love anyone at all, that he was wholly set on his own advantage. She felt as if there was nothing left to love. She had not quite loved him, but she had come very near it. She had once had a dream in which she had been running lightly over a wide heathery space, and suddenly, quite suddenly, she had checked herself, and only just in time. Because the cliff ended. It ended right there before her feet. If she had taken one more step she would have been over the edge.

> *Down among the dead men,*
> *Down among the dead men,*
> *Down among the dead men*
> *Let him lie.*

Only it would have been, "Let her lie." If she hadn't slipped behind the curtain in the schoolroom she would have been over the edge. As it was, she had saved herself. No, she hadn't planned to do it. She had been saved, and she wasn't going down over the edge. She was going to escape.

CHAPTER 10

She said good-night when the time came. It was the last good-night that she would ever say to these people in this room. If they were ever to meet again it would be different for them all. Perhaps they would never meet again. She didn't know, and there was no one to tell her. She went slowly up to her room and shut her door. She thought about locking it. And then she thought, "I mustn't do anything different—not tonight. I mustn't do anything to make them say, 'Why did she do it?'" So she left the door unlocked. It wouldn't have made any difference, because nobody tried it to see whether it was locked or not.

After she had waited for a little she took off her dress and hung it up in the great gloomy cupboard which ran across all one side of the room. It looked very lonely there. Such a big cupboard and only that one little lace dress, her everyday skirt, and the dark grey coat and skirt which she wore on Sundays. There was room in it for a hundred dresses. She had pleased herself sometimes by imagining that they were hanging there—dresses for every possible occasion, grave and gay. But not tonight. Because tonight her mind was full of other things.

She hung up her black lace dress and considered. She would take the grey coat and skirt. It was new, and it would be useful. And she would wear a white silk shirt and take the other one with her. She set her mind to what she would take. Brush and comb. Toothbrush and toothpaste. Facecloth. Soap and nailbrush. She had a little case which she had used for week-ends when she was at school. It would hold these things, and the silk shirt and her pyjamas and two pairs of stockings. It wouldn't hold anything more. It wouldn't hold a change of underclothes—it was no good trying. She could tuck half-a-dozen handkerchiefs round the edge, and that was all.

As she turned from the packed case she saw her mother's little Bible on the pedestal by the bed. She couldn't part with that. It was a small book, and it slipped in beneath the pyjamas and was hidden there. She shut the bag and laid it on the chair by the window.

Then she put on her black laced shoes. She would have to leave her other two pairs behind, the spare pair of outdoor shoes and the indoor ones. No, she must have an indoor pair. A vision of getting sopping wet and having nothing to change into rose uncomfortably in her mind. She made a parcel of both pairs, and felt somehow safer. But even at that moment she had a horrid feeling about leaving the little black satin pair she had worn that evening. There was no sense in taking them—not the least atom of sense—and she wasn't going to take them, and that was that. But they were the nicest shoes she had ever had, and she didn't know whether she would ever see them again. She had got them from Heather Peterson, who had got them from a cousin in a fit of hopefulness and because they were so pretty, and then found that they were too small and unless she wanted to take the chance of being disabled by cramp she couldn't wear them.

Jenny held the shoes in her hand and looked at them. They were so pretty, and they must have cost a lot. Heather Peterson's cousin was rich, and she had bought these shoes in Paris. They were very cleverly cut, and they had a single brilliant very cunningly placed to make your foot look small. Jenny knew she was being foolish, and she was stern with herself. When you are running away you can't afford to be sentimental about a pair of shoes, no matter how pretty they are, or how much you feel that you will never have anything like them again. She put them inside the big dark cupboard and shut the door on them resolutely.

Time passed slowly. She was all ready to go. She didn't know where. She only knew that she must go, and she must get as long a start as possible. She waited until twelve o'clock. All the sounds in all the rooms came to an end. The house was still. The house was very still. It was an old house—early seventeenth century. Jenny's thoughts went back to its beginnings—the handsome young man who had built the house and his lovely wife.

He was Richard Forbes, and she was Jane. Jenny always wondered if they had called her that, or if it had been, like her own name, turned into Jenny. She liked to fancy that it was. Only of course her name wasn't from Jane, but from Jennifer. Still it did make a kind of link, and they were her own ancestors—her own lawful ancestors. Their portraits hung in a place of honour in the hall. Their son and his wife, painted half a century later, looked old after their radiant youth. There were portraits of them all, some by famous painters. Jenny's heart leapt up as she realized that she wasn't a foundling, an illegitimate child, but the real inheritor of all these other Forbeses. She would go, but something in her said, "I shall come again." In that moment she knew that the inner voice spoke truly. She would come again.

She put out the light and sat down in the dark to wait. She must have fallen asleep, for she woke with a start and the air was colder. She put on the light and looked at her watch, the watch she didn't wear openly because it was a family one given by her father to her mother, or so Garsty had said, though how she knew was more than Jenny could say. It had lain there among

Garsty's treasures until she died, and then Jenny had taken it. The astonishing thing was that after all these years of not being used it kept very good time. There was a long slender gold chain with it.

Jenny opened the bottom drawer and took out the things that she had put ready—gloves, a little black hat, the parcel with her two pairs of shoes. She put on the hat and put the gloves into the pocket of a dark prune coat which she took out of the cupboard. She was going to be too hot in it, and it was heavy, but at this time of year you didn't know what the weather might be going to do. And it was a good coat, new last winter. She remembered getting it in the January sales with Garsty. It had cost more than she had planned for, but Garsty had said, "It will go on for years, and you will always look nice in it, my dear."

She took her bag and considered the other things. There was the case which she had put under the counterpane on the chair by the window. Oh, she couldn't leave the room like that—untidy! She must put the bedspread back. Then she took up her things, the parcel with the shoes slipped over the handle of the little case, and her left hand free for the handbag. She stood with the open door of the room in her hand and looked round. Everything was quite tidy. Now she must go.

She lifted the hand with the bag in it and switched off the light. With the door shut, no one would come near her until half past seven. She had seven and a half hours' start of any search that might be made. She felt her way to the head of the stairs and began to go down.

It was like going down into deep waters. Deep, dark waters. The darkness wasn't frightening. It felt very safe. And behind the darkness there were all the people of her blood and her name who had lived in this house since it was built. That made her feel very safe indeed. She didn't know where she was going or what she was going to do, but she knew who she was. She wasn't any longer a nameless come-by-chance brought up by charity. She was Jenny Forbes, and the house and the pictures were her own.

She was half way down the stairs, when the moon came from behind a cloud. The house faced south-east, and the moon was full. The moonlight shone in through the windows above the door and to either side of it. It was so bright that it made the portraits on which it fell look as if they were alive. Jenny thought, "They are saying good-bye to me. But I shall come again." She stood still on the half-landing and looked at the pictures. Some of them hardly showed at all, some were just shadows. Then as she turned this way and that the brightness of the moon shone down the hall to the portrait which she liked best of all, Lady Georgina Forbes, painted by a famous artist in the year of the Crimean War. A hundred years ago and she was still beautiful without a mark of age or sorrow on her, painted in her wedding-dress with flowers in her hair, smiling. Jenny said under her breath, "Good-bye, great, great-grandmother. I'll come back some day."

CHAPTER 11

The young man in the car was enjoying himself. It was a fine night very heartening to behold. The moon was out now, quite clear of the clouds. He would have liked to switch off his lights and drive through all this country by moonlight. He shook his head a little mournfully. There were so many things he would like to do, and he couldn't do them. Not because they were difficult or impossible, but simply because you had been brought up hedged in by laws and by-laws until they had got you down. He laughed a little and considered what a modern world would be like with everyone doing as he pleased. Come to think of it, no one was ever free. Different times had their own restraints, personal, political, what have you. You were brought up in a certain code, and you kept to it. If you kicked over the traces you came to a sticky end. Each generation made its own rules, and the next one altered them. What was quite unacceptable in one generation was the fashion in the next, and so you went on.

He liked driving alone, and he liked driving by night. If you kept off the beaten track you didn't meet anyone much after twelve o'clock. His plan was to drive within a strategic distance of Alington House and sleep out the night in the back seat of his car. Then in the morning, when a country inn would be open, he would have breakfast and from there on follow the reasonable inspiration of the moment. He wanted to see the house and the portraits. He wanted it very much. After all, if they were in any way decent people they couldn't object to him. It wasn't as if he was claiming anything, or wanting to claim anything. He was simply a distant connection of the family who had come into possession of some papers about the house and the people to whom it had belonged. It was natural enough that he should want to come down and see the place for himself.

He had turned rather an abrupt corner just out of a sleeping village, and a long flat stretch of road lay before him. Quite suddenly there was someone in the road. It stretched flat and open at one minute, and the next there was something there. Something? No, someone. He braked and brought the car to a standstill.

The someone was a girl. She had a case in one hand, and with the other she had signalled him to stop. He leaned out, frowning.

"You shouldn't do that, you know."

"But I wanted you to stop."

"Why?" He was terse because for a moment he hadn't been sure that he could stop in time and the road was narrow.

The girl moved from the front of the car and came round to the door on his side. In the moment that she stepped across the lighted patch of road in front of the car he saw her, and he saw that she was young and pale—or perhaps that was just the lights of the car. She came up to the window on his side and said,

"Will you please give me a lift?"

The anger had gone out of him. He said,

"Where do you want to go?"

"It doesn't matter. I mean, just anywhere will do."

"Are you running away?"

It was quite obvious that she was. What does one do with a stray girl who asks one to help her? He said,

"You're running away, aren't you? Why?" It wasn't in the least what he had meant to say.

The moonlight shone on her face. It looked sad and rather tired. There were dark marks like smudges under her eyes. She said very earnestly,

"I've got to—I really have."

It was the sort of thing that any girl would say if she had had a row with her people or with her school.

He said, "Why?" and she came nearer and dropped her voice.

"I can't tell you. You wouldn't believe me."

"You might try."

Jenny considered. All this time he was in the shadow—she couldn't see his face. She must see him. You can't tell whether you can trust a person whom you can't see. She said quickly and a little breathlessly,

"Will you get out for a moment? I want to see you."

"Why do you want to do that?"

He had a nice voice, but she must see him. She said,
"I want to know whether I can trust you."

"Do you think you would know?"

"Oh, yes, I should know if I could see you." There
was a confident ring in her voice.

Without a word he pushed open the door and got
out. He shut the door behind him, leaned against it, and
said,

"Well, here I am. Take a good look and make up
your mind."

She said,

"It's you who have to make up your mind, isn't it?"

They stood looking at one another in the bright,
clear moonlight. He heard her draw in her breath.

"Who—who are you?" she said.

"My name is Richard Forbes."

She echoed him in a faint whisper, "Richard
Forbes—"

"That is my name."

Jenny stood still. It was unbelievable, but it had happened. Unbelievable things did happen. This one had
happened. He stood there with the moonlight across his
face, and she saw feature for feature the Richard Forbes
who had built Alington House. The Richard Forbes in
the picture had had long curling hair, and he had worn
fine clothes, not a raincoat and slacks. But it was the
same face, it was the same expression—the laughing
look in the eyes, the humorous quirk of the mouth. And
then the humour faded. He had the air of being very
much in earnest, and he said,

"Why do you look at me like that?"

Jenny said, "Because I've seen you before."

"Where? When?" He had never seen her before, he
was prepared to swear to that.

"All my life. You're the portrait in the hall—the picture of Richard Alington Forbes."

He caught his breath and said,

"But that's my name."

He saw her colour rise, not as colour, but as a shadow, because they were all black and white in the moonlight. He could only just catch the tremor in her voice when she said,

"Is it?"

"Yes. What's yours?"

"I'm Jenny Forbes. I'm from Alington House."

It was the first time she had given her name as Jenny Forbes—the very first time. She had been Jenny Hill all her life, but she wasn't Jenny Hill any more. She was Jennifer Hill's daughter, but she was Richard Forbes' daughter too—Richard Alington Forbes. She was their lawful daughter. She held her head up and looked Richard Forbes in the face and said his name.

Something in that straight look of hers got through. He said in a puzzled voice,

"I don't understand. I thought the sons were grown up, but the daughters—they're little girls, aren't they?"

"Yes. I don't belong to that family. I'm the daughter of Richard Forbes, the one who was killed at the beginning of the war. They said he wasn't married to my mother. She was ill. There was an air raid—it was the day my father was killed. Her head was hurt—she didn't talk. She came down here to Garsty." She went on looking at him straight. He had never seen such truthful eyes. "Garsty had been her governess. She came to her because that was her home—she hadn't any other. That's how she met my father. But no one knew they were married. I only found out last night."

"What did you find out?"

She had put down her case on the ground. She put out her hands with the little shabby bag in them and said,

"Don't you believe me? I'm telling you the truth because you're Richard Forbes. I wouldn't tell about this to anyone else—I wouldn't really. But you are different."

That struck home in a most curious way. He felt it with every nerve of his body. And he felt it because it was true. There was a deep relationship between them—kinship, and something more than kinship. They were two of a kind. That was the difference which she spoke of.

She was speaking again.

"I'll tell you—because you're Richard Forbes. I was upstairs in the schoolroom, and Mac came in and his mother."

"That's the eldest son?"

"Yes. I was behind the window curtains. The room was dark. I'd been crying because of something that had happened, and I didn't want to see anyone, or anyone to see me. . . . Where was I?"

He said gravely, "Mac had just come into the schoolroom."

She nodded.

"Yes. I thought he'd come to see me. I didn't want to see him, so I stayed quiet. And then Mrs. Forbes came in, and she shut the door and they began to talk. She said, 'What did you want to say to me, Mac?' and when he didn't answer she said, 'Mac, what is it?' And he said, 'All right, you can have it.' He said he had only known for a week. And then he went on, 'It's Jenny.' And then he said, 'She's legitimate. He *married* Jennifer Hill.' Mrs. Forbes said, 'What do you mean?' and he said, 'I'm talking about Jenny.' And she was angry—she was very angry. She said, 'You're talking nonsense! There was no marriage!' And he said, 'There was a marriage. And I'm not asking you to take my word for it. I've seen the certificate at Somerset House.' "

"What!"

Now that it was said, Jenny felt better. It was like a calm after the storm. She said,

"They went on talking. There was a letter from my father. Garsty talked about it when she was dying. She said it was in a little chest. She said my father called my mother his wife. She said she didn't read any more but she kept it for me. Poor Garsty—she loved me so much—she was so good to me. She wasn't sure about the marriage, and she didn't like to make sure because she was afraid that I should be taken away from her. That was how it was. You didn't know Garsty. Nobody who didn't know her could tell how good she was. She died ten days ago, and I went up to Alington House to look after the little girls. That was how I came to be there in the schoolroom. So I waited till they would all be asleep and came away."

There was a long, long pause. She stood there waiting. Waiting for him to make up his mind. If he helped her, it wouldn't end with his giving her a lift to wherever she wanted to go. He was quite sure about that. This wasn't a lighthearted adventure, it was deadly serious. His brows drew together in a frown.

"Where do you want to go?"

She answered without any hesitation.

"I don't mind. I want to get away."

"Have you any money?"

"Oh, yes, I've got nearly ten pounds. I thought they'd take me in at a cottage, and I could look for something to do—something with children. I like children."

He said reluctantly—he was surprised to find how reluctantly,

"Look here, don't you think you had better go back and do things properly? If you are really Richard Forbes' daughter, they can't make any bones about it. They're bound to acknowledge you, and it will save a lot of talk."

She shrank back, and then checked herself. She said, "I can't do that."

"Why can't you?"

Jenny caught her breath.

"I can't." The colour rose in her cheeks.

He said a little impatiently,

"It's the sensible thing to do."

"I can't do it. Oh, you don't understand."

"I can't understand if you don't tell me."

"It's because of what he said—Mac. He said—he could marry me. He said it just like that. When his mother said, 'No—no,' he laughed, and he said, 'You don't suppose I want to marry the girl, do you?' And he went on to say worse things. He said he would marry me, and they would hold their tongues. If it ever came out it would be just too bad, but there would be nothing to be done about it. They didn't know, and I didn't know. Once we were married it didn't really matter. That's what Mac said. He said, 'I shall be the noble cousin who married her when she was the illegitimate poor relation.' "

Jenny had said her say. She had said it quietly. If it had come out, as it might have done, in a storm of sobs, it would not have been nearly so convincing. As it was, he was convinced. And something more. He was swept by such an insensate fury against Mac that it took him all he knew to fight it down. He said shortly,

"All right, get in. We'd better be on our way."

CHAPTER 12

They drove along without speaking. He had to swallow his anger, and that wasn't easy. It was in fact quite surprisingly difficult. Surprisingly? Yes, that was it. Why should he have flashed into that sudden state of anger with Mac? He had a hot temper, but it very seldom got away with him like this—not since he had learned to control it. Jenny sat beside him quite quiet. He was glad she didn't chatter. Instantly, indignantly, the thought came pushing up—she wouldn't. He stopped being angry in his surprise. What did he know about her to be sure what she would or wouldn't do? He had a quick answer to that, a factual answer. He did know. He knew her as she had known him. There was kinship between them, and something more than kinship. He drove on in silence, thinking.

Jenny did not say a word. It all seemed quite natural, as things feel in a dream. She had put her case in at the back. It was a comfortable car. She was very lucky to have found a cousin. She felt as if she knew him quite well—as if she had known him always. It was very strange, but in a way there was nothing strange about it. It had just happened.

When they had gone three or four miles, he turned a little and said,

"What were you going to do?"

She said,

"I was going to go as far as I could. Because they'll look for me, you know—they're bound to. And then I was going to get a cottage to take me in, and try and get some work to do."

He was appalled. She had said it before. He remembered that now. He said,

"No one would take you in like that."

"Wouldn't they?"

"Not respectable people—not the sort of people you ought to be with."

She said, "Oh—" and then, "Are you sure?"

"I'm quite sure."

There was a little pause. She said,

"Then what am I to do?"

He said, "I'm going to stay with an aunt. She's a very nice person. She's not a Forbes. She's from the other side of the family. My father and mother were killed in an air raid—she looked after me. You'll like her. Everyone does. Her name is Caroline Danesworth."

Jenny said, "Won't she think it rather odd your turning up with me?"

"She won't when she sees you." He felt so sure of this that it wasn't until afterwards that he thought it was rather a strange thing to say.

Jenny looked at him earnestly.

"Are you quite sure?"

He was quite, quite sure. He said so in a matter-of-fact way that carried conviction.

Jenny gave a little sigh. She had begun to feel dreadfully tired. She wondered how much farther she could have walked. She leaned back and felt at peace. He was Richard Alington Forbes. He had her father's name. She could trust him—he would look after her—she hadn't got to bother about anything more. . . . She fell asleep.

Richard drove on through the night. He had taken on an obligation, and he knew it for what it was. It was a very serious obligation. She wasn't really his business—that was what anyone would say. She wasn't really a relation. A hundred years had gone by since Lady Georgina had been painted in her wedding-dress. That picture he knew only from a photograph of it in his father's album. It was a good photograph. He wanted very much to see the original. And now he was driving away from Alington House and from the portraits.

Jenny—he thought about Jenny. He had never seen her before, and he had the familiarity which only comes with years. Lady Georgina had had two sons, just the two, and they were George and Stephen. Jenny descended from George, and he descended from Stephen. The two sons had fought bitterly about this and that, and finally about a girl. She was engaged to George, and she ran away with Stephen. There had been the father and mother of a row and a complete separation of the brothers. Stephen and the girl, whose name was Susanna Cruickshank, lived long and happily on the estate which they inherited from his mother. George married a sickly heiress with whom he was neither happy nor unhappy. She was a nonentity with a large fortune, and when you had said that you had said everything that was known of her. The brothers never met, and the quarrel was never made up. There was no communication at all between the elder and the younger branch. What turn of fancy had made his father go back to the beginnings of the family for his name, he wondered. Richard Alington Forbes had been the son of an earlier Richard who married the only daughter of John Alington, Esq., by which marriage came wealth and an extraordinary tradition of happiness. There was no picture of him. The pictures began with his son Richard Alington Forbes who had built the house. That was the family history so far as he knew it. Odd that he himself should be a throwback to the first Richard Alington Forbes whose name he bore. He drove on mile after mile, thinking.

After a while his thoughts turned to Jenny. He was taking her to his mother's sister, Caroline Danesworth, who had brought him up. It was a complete give-away of course, but he couldn't help that. Caroline would understand.

He looked down at Jenny sleeping like a baby beside him, and he was surprised at his rush of feeling. He supposed it was because one was used to seeing girls in every possible mode of activity, but one was not accustomed to seeing them asleep. Jenny slept deeply. Her hands were on her bag. Her face, against the side of the car, looked shadowy. He had the feeling that she wasn't all there, that she was really somewhere else and he didn't know where. He would like to know where she was, and what she was dreaming.

She smiled suddenly in her sleep. Her eyes half opened, looked at something he did not see, and closed again. Her lips moved. They said his name—"Richard Alington Forbes." But was it his name that they said? Her father had borne it too, and the first Richard Alington Forbes who had married Jane and built Alington House.

Jenny went on dreaming. She dreamed that she was flying and she was not alone. There was someone with her, caring for her, someone with a strong arm which held her. If he let her go, she would fall down, down to the ground. But he would not let her go. She felt perfectly safe, and she felt perfectly happy. She could not see who was holding her. She knew who it was. It was Richard Alington Forbes. She was quite safe, because she was with him and he was helping her. She half opened her eyes and said his name. Then the dream closed round her again and she slept. The time went on.

CHAPTER 13

It was a very curious experience driving through the night with the sleeping girl. He had a sense of familiarity which there was nothing in the facts to justify. It was one of those experiences which you can't talk about. If he was to talk of it, it would be gone. A line of poetry came into his mind:

Thinned into common air
like the rainbow breath of a stream.

He didn't know where that came from, but it was what would happen to this feeling if he ever spoke of it. He knew that if he kept it secret it would remain inviolate.

He drove steadily on. Mile after mile, mile after mile. An hour—two hours—three. He was going to get there too soon. He couldn't wake Caroline up before dawn and say baldly, "I've brought you a girl." Not tactful— not even with Caroline. He turned off the road on to Hazeldon Heath. It was getting on for four o'clock. He thought he would sleep till seven and then be on his way to Caroline's cottage. He was not conscious of feeling sleepy until he stopped driving, when it came over him in a rush. One moment he was running off the road on to the broad grassy border and switching off the engine, and the next he was asleep. The interval in which he turned and got into a position suitable for sleeping didn't seem to exist. He slept, and wasn't conscious of anything at all until suddenly he was awake again and it was hours later. He came to himself, blinked a little, and looked round him. There was something missing. No, not something—someone—Jenny.

It took him a moment to get straight. She had been there when he went to sleep, he was quite sure of that. Well, then, where was she now? He opened the door on his side and got out. As he did so he saw her bag, the one she had put down in the road when she talked to him in the night. It was on the back seat where he had put it. His heart gave a jump.

And then he saw her. She was coming across the patch of heath to his left. She had a singularly radiant air, as if there wasn't such a thing as trouble in the world. Her head was bare. When she saw him she waved and called out,

"There's a lovely place down there just behind those trees! Did you think I'd run away?"

It was exactly what he had thought, but he wasn't going to say so. She laughed and said,

"I suppose you did!"

Then she came up to the car and got in.

"I had such a lovely sleep," she said. "Thank you so much."

He didn't know exactly what she was thanking him for. He said so.

"What for?"

"Oh, everything. Are we near your aunt's now?"

"Yes, quite near. If you don't mind, I'll go in first and explain you."

"Will she mind?"

"Not when I've explained. You leave it to me."

They drove in silence for a time. There was a long hill. Then they turned and ran into a village street which looked as if it were asleep.

"Half past six," he said. "And very nice, too."

"Is this it?"

He nodded.

"Third house on the left. She's got a wonderful garden—wait till I get my key."

He pulled up at a wicket gate. There was a cottage garden in front with all the late-blooming things in it. There were Michaelmas daisies, and sunflowers, and phloxes, and marigolds—lots and lots of different sorts of them. Jenny gazed entranced at the garden.

"She's got a green thumb—everything grows for her," said Richard. He came round and opened her door. "Be quick and I'll get you in before Mrs. Merridew sees you."

Jenny stopped with her foot on the step.

"Why?"

"Because she makes a mountain out of a mole hill," he said, but he laughed as he said it.

He took Jenny's hand as he spoke, and they ran together up to the little porch which was covered with purple clematis. He bent to put the key in the door, and suddenly he had the feeling that he was bringing her home.

Jenny had a feeling too. It wasn't the same as his. She felt frightened in spite of all those welcoming flowers. Suppose Richard's aunt didn't like her. "Oh, she must, she *must*. Why should she?" She had a sudden dreadful feeling of what it would be like to be rejected by Richard's aunt. She was young and inexperienced, but she did know that the arrival at half past six in the morning of a nephew whom you loved very much with a girl whom you didn't love at all because you didn't know her was not the thing you could expect an aunt to be pleased about.

The door opened, and they came into a passage which seemed dark, Richard leading the way as if it was his house. She supposed in a way it was—it was his home. There was a narrow passage and the stairs going up. He opened a door, and there was a dark room with the curtains drawn against the light that was so bright outside.

"Can you see?" he said, and took her hand.

Jenny found herself holding it tight. She was afraid. She was horribly afraid. Richard felt the hand which he held quiver in his. The quivering did something to him. He heard himself say, "You'll be all right here, darling." Jenny gripped his hand as if she would never let it go. He said "Jenny—" on a moved note, and Jenny looked up at him. Her eyes were full of tears.

"Will she—will she like me?" she said in a whispering voice.

Richard took a hold on himself. What he wanted to do was to take his hand from hers and put both arms round her and hold her close so that she would never be frightened or tremble again. It was madness, he knew that. He had only known her a few hours. He said,

"Jenny, there's nothing to be afraid of. Caroline's a lamb—she really is. I'll go up and tell her about you. You just sit down here and wait. This is a nice chair."

It was dreadful to have to wait. Jenny let go of his hand and sat down. She heard him go up the stairs, and then she heard two people talking. It took her all she knew to sit there in the dark room and wait. It was the hardest thing she had ever done.

And then there were steps, and behind them others not so quick and light. With her heart beating to suffocation Jenny stood up. There came in a tall woman with a rush of words.

"My dear child—oh gracious, how dark it is in here! Wait a minute and I'll let in the light! Richard is a fool! Fancy his leaving you in the dark like this! Now just a minute—" She went to the far end of the room and drew back what the light showed to be brightly patterned chintz curtains with an apple-green lining. The garden side of the house came into view very reassuringly. There were apple trees well set with fruit, and there was a herbaceous border full of flowers. There were a blue sky and sunshine.

The tall figure whisked round and came back. She was half a head taller than Jenny and she had grey hair. Those were the first two things that Jenny saw about her. The grey hair curled vigorously and was tossed into untidy waves. Jenny saw that, and there was something very reassuring about it. Even at half past six in the morning no one had ever seen Mrs. Forbes' hair untidy. Caroline Danesworth had obviously jumped straight out of bed and only waited to put on a dressing-gown. The dressing-gown was a cheerful shade of blue, and her eyes matched it.

Richard at the open door strayed in and said with an air of pride,

"Jenny, this is Caroline."

"Who else would it be?" said Caroline. "If you want to be useful, Richard, you go and put on a kettle for tea. And there are biscuits on the shelf in the blue biscuit-tin. Now shoo—get along! We don't want you here."

When he was out of the room, she shut the door and turned back to Jenny, who stood waiting. She had a sense of belonging to no one and being most utterly alone. And then in a moment it was all gone. Caroline's eyes smiled at her and Caroline's hands took her cold ones. "My dear child, what is it?" she said, and Jenny began to cry. Caroline being what she was, she could have done nothing more endearing. As the tears ran down her face she felt Caroline's arms round her.

"My dear! Now don't try and stop it. It's much better to cry it all away. You're quite, quite safe here. I'll look after you, and so will Richard. There's nothing to cry about—nothing at all. But you just cry all you want to and get rid of it."

It is really very difficult to go on crying when you are urged to go on. Jenny stopped half way through a sob.

"I'm all right now," she said in a shaky voice.

"Well, come and sit down. I expect you want something to eat. We'll all have some tea, and then we shall feel better. Richard is quite good at making tea."

They sat on a green sofa and Jenny looked out at the garden. It looked happy and peaceful with the early morning sun upon it. She said,

"It is *very* good of you to be so nice to me. I don't know what Richard has told you."

Caroline considered. Her face was soft and kind. Her eyes were very blue and very soft.

"He said he hadn't been to Alington House. He has always wanted to go there to see it, and the pictures and everything. But of course he wasn't stupid enough to think he could go there in the middle of the night, though really when you come to think of it men are quite inexplicable. But anyhow he said he meant to get near the place and sleep in his car until the nearest pub would be open and he could get some breakfast. And then, I suppose, he thought he'd be welcome! On a Sunday morning!"

It was Sunday. It seemed such a long, long time since Saturday afternoon.

Caroline went on talking.

"Then, he says, you started up out of nowhere and stood in the middle of the road with your arms out to stop the car."

Jenny felt that she had to explain.

"I felt desperate. The bag wasn't heavy to start with, but it seemed to be getting heavier and heavier. I knew that if I didn't get a lift I shouldn't be able to get far enough not to be caught. I knew they would try to catch me. Has he told you who I am?"

"He told me your name—that you were Jenny Forbes."

Jenny repeated the words.

"Yes, I'm Jenny Forbes. But I didn't know it till yesterday afternoon. I knew that Richard Forbes was my father and Jennifer Hill was my mother, but I didn't know that they were married. They kept it a secret. It was the war, you know, and my father was killed, and my mother was struck on the head in an air raid—she never spoke again. They sent her to Garsty."

"Who is Garsty?"

"She had been my mother's governess. She took her in. Her house was just opposite the gates of Alington House. When the Forbeses came there—Colonel Forbes inherited, you know—Mrs. Forbes came to see Garsty. She wanted her to move right away, and to take me with her, but Garsty wouldn't." It all came pouring out—Garsty's accident, and how she had said that the letter from her father to her mother was in the little chest of drawers, and how she had looked for it after Garsty was gone, and how she couldn't find it, and how Mac had taken it. "I heard him say so. I wouldn't have believed it from anyone else. You just can't believe that sort of thing about the people you know, can you?" The truthful eyes looked into Caroline's. "You just can't. But I heard him say it. I was behind the curtain, and they didn't know I was there, and he said it. He took my father's letter, the one in which he called her his wife."

Caroline looked back. Was the child really as unworldly as she seemed? It didn't seem possible, not at this time of day. She said,

"He called her his wife? But—" she hesitated—"it may only have been that that was how he thought of her. That wouldn't make a marriage."

"No—I know it wouldn't. I'd known about the letter when Garsty died. She told me about it, and I thought, like you said, it was just that he thought of her like that. But Mac said when I was behind the window curtain and he was talking to his mother and they thought they were alone—Mac said he'd been to Somerset House and he had seen the certificate. They had been married five months when my father was killed."

"Oh, my dear child!"

Jenny went on looking at her.

"It's a sad story isn't it? My mother died the night after I was born. I've thought about it a lot, and it seems as if it was sad for me and for Garsty, but not really sad for them—for my father and mother. I think they loved one another very much, and they would be together again. So it wasn't sad for them, was it? Do you think that Mac burned that letter?"

"I don't know, my dear. I think he would do what was safest for himself."

"Yes, I thought so too." She gave a deep sigh and said, "It doesn't really matter, does it? He wrote to her and she saw it, and that is all that really matters."

There was a little stir at the door and Richard came in with a tray. There were large cups on it, and a big teapot, and a gold and white milk-jug. On a plate there were slices of plain cake and piled-up biscuits.

"I'm frightfully hungry," he said.

Jenny suddenly felt hungry too. Her spirits rose. Everything was all right. She was quite, quite safe.

CHAPTER 14

They were just finishing the plate of biscuits and the cake, and Richard was drinking his third cup of tea, when there came a tapping at the door.

"Oh, *no!*" said Richard. He finished his tea in a hurry and put down his cup. "Not at this hour! It's not decent! Shall I tell her so?"

Caroline laughed. "It's no use," she said. Then she turned to Jenny. "It will be my next-door neighbour, Mrs. Merridew. I wonder what she'll have thought up this time. I'd better go and see."

The tapping continued—three taps and a pause— three more taps and another pause. It suggested what Caroline knew only too well was behind it, inquisitiveness and pertinacity. She opened the door, and was aware as she did so that it was being noted that this was not the first time it had been opened that day. Oh dear, no—Mr. Richard had been in and a girl. Now why a girl so early in the morning? The words, unspoken, floated almost visibly on the air.

Mrs. Merridew stood there with a jug in her hand. She was dressed. She had tidied her hair, and she had put on a hat. She was a small woman with little grey eyes which were sharply aware of everything in range and suspicious of everything beyond it. She held out the jug and began at once on what was obviously a prepared speech.

"Oh, my dear Miss Danesworth, do forgive me, but I am short of milk for my early morning tea, and you've always been so kind about obliging me. The fact is that Timmy has been a very naughty cat. You know, I told you how clever he was at knocking off the top of the milk-bottle when he wanted a drink—"

"Yes, you did."

"He's too clever about it—he really is. But this morning he knocked a little too hard, and the bottle fell down and all the milk was spilt. So if you could just let me have enough for his breakfast—and perhaps for my early tea—"

Caroline had not a suspicious nature, but the excuse had served before and she had her doubts—she had her very grave doubts about it.

Mrs. Merridew stepped over the threshold, jug in hand.

"Your nephew came back this morning? Very early, very early indeed?"

"Yes, he did. Come this way, Mrs. Merridew, if you will. I've got plenty of milk."

"Was he alone?" said Mrs. Merridew, cocking her head on one side.

"Oh, no. He brought Jenny Forbes to stay with me."

"Jenny Forbes? And who is she? It's not a very usual name in these parts—Scotch, I believe. But of course it's his name, too. How stupid of me! Really so very stupid! Is she a relation?"

Caroline said with a calm born of long practice, "I suppose you may call her that. She's a connection at any rate."

"Oh, that sounds quite exciting!"

They had reached the kitchen at the back of the house. Caroline said,

"I haven't been able to get excited about it, but then I haven't your imagination."

Mrs. Merridew took this remark as a compliment, a little to Caroline's relief. She didn't want to give offence. She wanted peace. She remembered with a slightly guilty feeling that Richard was wont to accuse her of preferring peace at any price. She went rather quickly into the larder and fetched out a big jug of milk.

"How much do you want? I've got heaps."

"Oh, you *have!* Did you know this girl was coming?"

"Jenny? Well, it was always possible."

This was as far as Caroline could go in the direction of concealment. She argued against her own sense of guilt. Well, it wasn't quite true, but it was very nearly true, Richard being what he was. Anything was possible.

And then Mrs. Merridew was saying, "They must have made a very early start—very early indeed. Why, you're not dressed!"

She had been aware of that from the first moment when Caroline had opened the door. She herself *was* dressed. She had flung on her clothes in record time, and she had combed through her neat grey curls, so different from Caroline's large untidy ones, and she had put on her shoes and stockings, and thought of the story about Timmy, and taken the milkjug, all in less than a quarter of an hour. She had been very clever, she had been very clever indeed.

"No," said Caroline. "I must have overslept. I'm not dressed, and I must get dressed."

"Oh, yes, of course you must. I'm just going."

But Mrs. Merridew didn't go. She didn't even pick up the jug of milk which she had borrowed. She came a step nearer, and she said in a confidential undertone,

"It's a very early hour. They're not—not engaged—"

There were two courses open to Caroline, she could laugh, or she could lose her temper. She chose to laugh.

"I haven't the least idea," she said, "and I shouldn't dream of asking."

Mrs. Merridew picked up the milk-jug, and then set it down again.

"Oh, no—no. Of course not. I didn't mean—it's just—so very early in the morning—I couldn't help wondering—"

"I don't think there is anything to wonder about. We can go in and ask them why they started so early if you'd really like to know."

Mrs. Merridew picked up the jug again in a hurry.

"Oh, no—no, of course not. It's so very good of you to oblige me with the milk. Timmy will be *most* grateful. I won't keep you. So thoughtless of me—and you must be wanting to dress."

Caroline saw her to the door and shut it after her. Then she came back to the sitting-room.

The two young people were standing at the window which looked out on the apple trees and the flowery border. They turned as she came in.

"That was Mrs. Merridew."

"It would be!" Richard's tone was exasperated.

"Yes, I know. She is very inquisitive, and I'd love to snub her, but it's no use. If you live next door to someone you've just got to get on with them, and I don't think she knows how inquisitive she is. Now I've got to go up and dress. I shan't be long. Would Jenny like to come up with me? And you can put the car away, Richard."

CHAPTER 15

Meg was the first of the children to wake at Alington House. It was only half past six, and she wasn't supposed to wake Joyce until a quarter past seven. She wasn't really supposed to wake her up then, especially when they had been out to tea the day before. Joyce was not really supposed to be waked up before half past seven. A quarter past was as far as Meg would go, and if she was awake earlier— well, there were ways. You couldn't say she was waking Joyce up if she got out of bed and pulled out a drawer and then shut it again with a good vigorous push. She tried this twice, and Joyce just lay there and slept. It was *too* aggravating.

Suddenly she thought about Jenny. She would open her own door very softly and creep across to Jenny's door and open that, and there she would stay. She would get into Jenny's bed, lovely and warm. And it would serve Joyce right if she woke up and found she was alone. She wouldn't like that.

She got out and went tiptoe to the door and across the passage. She wouldn't feel safe until she was inside Jenny's room with the door shut. And she must go slowly, slowly. It was all she could do to restrain herself, especially when she got near the door into Jenny's room, but she managed it.

She was well inside the room with the door shut behind her before she saw that Jenny wasn't there. She stood just a yard inside the door. She had stopped to turn round and fasten the door very carefully. She had been so intent on what she was doing that she hadn't noticed the bed. And it was empty. There was no Jenny. It was empty, and the bed was made. It was quite made. The eiderdown was on and a chintz coverlet over it. Meg came slowly forward and put her hand on the blue roses of the coverlet. They were quite, quite cold. There was no warmth left in the bed. Jenny must have been up a long, long time.

Meg was frightened, and she didn't know why. If she had known why, it wouldn't have been so frightening. She didn't know she was frightened, but she *was* frightened. She stood quite still and thought. It was Sunday morning. Perhaps Jenny had gone to church. Then she remembered that she had asked Jenny if she was going to church early, and Jenny had said no. Perhaps she had changed her mind. Perhaps she had gone to church after all.

She hadn't. She hadn't gone to church. Meg knew it. And then her eyes fell on the clock which stood on the mantelpiece. It was an old-fashioned clock in a brown leather case, and it said half past six. The early morning service wasn't till eight o'clock. She had waked up early, and Jenny had been earlier still. Where had she gone to? Where had Jenny gone?

Meg was shivering. She went to the dressing-table. Jenny's comb and brush were gone. They had been her mother's and the brush had a little J.H. on the back. The comb had a silver ridge, but no initials. Meg looked in the drawers. She looked desperately, but she did not find anything. Jenny had gone. Her washing things were gone too—her toothbrush, her nailbrush, her nailscissors. And her shoes.

It was no use looking any more. Jenny had gone

away. She hadn't said she was going, and she hadn't said good-bye. She had just gone.

Meg crept back to her room.

Things you can't understand are always the hardest to bear. To know why is the first step to consolation. Meg didn't know anything at all except that Jenny had gone. It seemed like the end of the world. She lay and cried until she couldn't cry any more.

The house woke slowly. Carter brought Mrs. Forbes her tea at half past seven. As she passed the little girls' door on her way back she saw Meg standing there barefoot and trembling.

"What is it? Meg, what is it? What's the matter? Is Joyce ill?"

Meg shook her head. The tears came rushing from her eyes again.

"No, not Joyce. She's still asleep. How she *can!* It's Jenny—she's gone."

It was a shock. Carter's temper flared.

"What nonsense are you talking, Meg? And Jenny had better be more punctual in the mornings, or she'll have your mother after her!"

Meg dissolved into helpless weeping.

"She's gone! Oh, Carter, she's gone! Oh, *Carter!*"

Carter ran across the landing and opened Jenny's door. Its neatness, its silence, its emptiness, seemed to paralyse her. It looked as it had done before Jenny came there to live. It just wasn't Jenny's room any more.

As they stood there together, Mrs. Forbes opened the door of her room. She wore an expensive dressing-gown, and her hair was as neat as if she had spent the preceding hours at a ball. She frowned, told Meg to go to her room, and asked Carter what she was looking for. Meg, with her door opened a chink, listened, ready to run and get into bed if her mother's attention should turn her way. At the moment it was all taken up with Carter.

"Where's Jenny?" she asked sharply.

"I don't know."

"What nonsense is this? Isn't she with the children? She ought to be!"

Carter shook her head dumbly.

"She's—she's gone," she said.

A cold fear sharpened Mrs. Forbes' voice. She said quickly,

"What do you mean?"

"Her brush and comb's gone, and her washing things. Oh, ma'am, I think she's gone!"

"Nonsense!"

At the tone of her mother's voice Meg trembled and ran for safety to her bed. Out on the landing Mrs. Forbes pushed past Carter, who was too dumbfounded to get out of her way, and herself made a quick and thorough search of the room. When she had finished she knew very well that Jenny was gone, and she knew what she had taken with her. That meant a case. Jenny had brought up a case with some of her things in it. It had been in the cupboard. It was not there now. Without a word she turned and went along the passage to Mac's room.

He was awake, lying on his back with his hands behind his head. Mrs. Forbes shut the door and came to the foot of the bed.

"She's gone!"

When she spoke the anger came up in her so strongly that she could have killed Jenny. For a moment she knew it and exulted in it. The next she commanded herself. She was even a little shocked. She must take care. Yes, she must take care.

Mac did not move. He said in a voice which he kept lazy with an effort,

"What did you say?"

"I said Jenny had gone."

"What makes you think so?"

"I don't think anything. It's the plain fact."

"I asked you what made you think that she had gone."

His eyes were on her. He was the stronger of the two. She threw out her hands in a gesture and said,

"I don't think anything about it. I know she has gone. She has taken the small case that she brought here with her night things in it. Her brush and comb have gone, and her washing things. Her bed has not been slept in, but the dress she wore last night is hanging in the cupboard. Her coat is gone. She has gone."

There was a pause. Then he said,

"Why?"

Mrs. Forbes stared.

"How should I know?"

"Are you sure?"

"Of course I'm sure."

"You didn't come into her room last night and say anything?"

"Of course I didn't!"

Their eyes met. She sustained his look and was inwardly thankful that she had nothing to hide. Mac took his hands from behind his head and got up.

"I'd better get dressed," he said. "She can't have gone very far. What money has she got?"

"I don't know. Not very much."

"You don't know how much?"

"No, I don't."

"All right, I'll get dressed, and then we can decide what to do. We shall have to be careful. If she's Jenny Hill, we have no control at all. But if she's Jenny Forbes—"

Mrs. Forbes said, "Hush! Are you mad?"

He laughed.

"No, I'm not mad. It just wants thinking about, that's all. Now go along and let me get dressed."

She turned and went out of the room. There were things she wanted to say, but she did not say them. She was a strong high-handed woman, but there were times when her eldest son frightened her. This was one of those times. She turned and went.

CHAPTER 16

All that was on Sunday morning, and no one heard anything until Tuesday. Mac and Alan went back to London on the Sunday evening. It was a relief, though Mrs. Forbes would not have admitted it. It was not what Mac said, for he said very little, and it was not what he did, for there was nothing remarkable about that. She could have borne it better if he had been upset. He was not, so far as she could see, the least upset. And that frightened her. She didn't know why, but it did.

And then on Tuesday morning she went into the village. She had been uncertain as to whether she would go, and then it came over her that it was important she should show herself—let people see her—see that she wasn't upset—that Jenny's going had made no difference to her. And why should it make a difference— could anyone tell her that?

She put on a new tweed coat and skirt. It was oatmeal-coloured, and it set off her golden hair and the smooth tints of her complexion. No one but herself knew just how much assistance the complexion and the hair required. No one ever saw her until that assistance had been applied. She put on a golden brown felt hat and a scarf and gloves that matched it and set out for the village.

It was no more than half a mile, but as she walked, the feeling of dread which had been upon her lifted. Mac had been sensible about it, and she hadn't been sensible at all. There was no need to suppose that Jenny had found out about anything. How could she have? If she had run away, it was probably for some ridiculous schoolgirl reason of her own. There had been some love affair, some quarrel, perhaps a row with Mary the house-parlour maid, and she had lost her head and run away. This last theory relieved her mind very much. It set Jenny where she belonged, on a level with Mary. She hoped very heartily that they had seen the last of her. Her spirits rose, and she turned into the main street of the village with a lighter heart than she had had for two days.

She went first to the general shop, where you could buy everything from bootlaces, the strictly utilitarian kind, to sweets. She came into the shop and was aware from outside of lively conversation that died away as she opened the door and went in. A tall woman in a shabby draggled raincoat was the only one left talking. She had her back to the door and did not see Mrs. Forbes. She said in a high dogmatic voice, "And as I say, there's no smoke without fire—" And there she stopped, firmly checked by Mrs. Boddles, a large comfortable woman with a spreading bosom and an imperturbable calm.

"Good-morning, Mrs. Forbes," she said, "and what can I have the pleasure of doing for you?"

The tall woman swung round with her mouth open. The other people in the shop stood still and listened with all their ears. Mrs. Forbes didn't hurry herself. She came up to the counter and said with a beaming smile,

"Good-morning, Miss Crampton. Don't let me interrupt you."

Miss Crampton rallied.

"Oh, Mrs. Forbes," she said in her jerky way, "I didn't see you."

"No?"

"No, I didn't. I had my back to the door."

"Yes?"

Miss Crampton was recovering. She remembered what she had said. There was nothing that anyone could take hold of—nothing at all. She said,

"How are you, Mrs. Forbes? Well, I hope?"

"Yes, thank you." Mrs. Forbes turned back to Mrs. Boddles.

Miss Crampton was angry. No way to behave—no way at all! Mrs. Forbes should remember that she was the late Vicar's daughter! She wasn't to be treated with this cool impertinence in front of a shopful of villagers! She would show her that she wasn't to be treated like that! She turned, an ugly woman with harsh features not improved by a crushed black felt hat on the back of her head and the drab-coloured raincoat which accentuated her height and her thinness. She turned, and she said in her loud strident voice,

"I thought you might be glad to have news of Jenny."

Mrs. Forbes said,

"Of Jenny?"

"She's at Hazeldon, isn't she? I had a letter from my cousin there this morning, and she mentioned having seen her."

Mrs. Forbes said, "Oh. It was Jenny?"

"Yes, I suppose so. But she's calling herself Jenny Forbes. She shouldn't really do that, you know."

A scorching anger shook Mrs. Forbes. She dared! Here—in the shop—with three pairs of listening ears attentive! She commanded herself with an effort and said coldly,

"It was certainly very foolish. These things make talk."

Miss Crampton was delighted. For once she had got in under that icy guard, that air of being so much better than other people. As if she was—as if she could be! Dear Papa . . . She said,

"Of course, if it hadn't been for my cousin living next door to his aunt and being on such very friendly terms with her—"

"Whose aunt are you talking about?"

"Oh, didn't you know?"

"I didn't say that. You must excuse me, but I have my shopping to do. We are keeping everyone waiting."

"I've finished mine," said Miss Crampton. She smiled. It wasn't a very pleasant smile. "I'll wait for you."

Mrs. Forbes turned back to the counter.

"In a real temper she was, too," as Mrs. Boddles explained to her family afterwards.

Her son Jim said, "Well, I wouldn't work for her, not if she was to pay me a guinea an hour. How old Jackson stands it I don't know."

Mrs. Boddles gave a little crow of laughter.

"Mr. Jackson just takes his own way. He says, 'Yes, ma'am' and 'No, ma'am,' and then he just does as he chooses. A very opinionated man is Mr. Jackson. But he knows his work, and Mrs. Forbes she don't know a thing about gardening. It was her husband that had it all at his fingers' ends."

"Ah—he was a gentleman, the old Colonel was," said Jim.

At the time Mrs. Forbes continued her shopping. She bought what she had to buy, queried a price which was a penny dearer than the Stores in London, and finally withdrew, only to find Miss Crampton waiting for her outside the shop.

"So difficult to talk with your shopping on your mind and those women listening to every word," she said. "They are such a gossipy lot. My father always said that gossip was the prime sin of the English village."

There was an easy retort to this, and Mrs. Forbes was sorely tempted to avail herself of it, but she resisted. If she let fly, Miss Crampton would take offence, and that might quite easily result in the sudden closing of the conversation. And she had to find out more. She said, "That's very true," and waited.

Miss Crampton nodded.

"Oh, yes, he was wonderful at sizing people up. I've often thought that it was quite a pity I did not take more notice when he said things like that. They would have been so valuable written down and—and *preserved*."

Mrs. Forbes came to the point.

"Could you let me have Jenny's address?"

Miss Crampton stared.

"Do you mean to say you haven't got it!"

Mrs. Forbes assumed her best manner. It cost her a considerable effort, because what she really wanted to do was to box Miss Crampton's ear for her—now in the middle of the street for everyone to see. She said,

"Well, girls are so careless. It seems she went off without leaving it. I thought she had given it to Carter, but it seems that she forgot."

Miss Crampton stared.

"How very extraordinary! Even in these days I should have thought—but of course it's not my business."

"No," said Mrs. Forbes. "And as the silly child has left half her things behind, I shall be grateful for her address."

"Well, I don't know the name of Miss Danesworth's house, but my cousin is Mrs. Merridew and she lives next door—Mrs. Merridew, Ambleworth, Hazeldon. I'm sure she'd be only too pleased to be of any use. She'll see that Jenny gets the parcel, I'm sure."

Mrs. Forbes made herself give a civil answer. She was about to turn away, when Miss Crampton said,

"Of course you know this Richard Forbes?"

Mrs. Forbes was too taken aback to be altogether wise. She said, "What Richard Forbes?" and she said it more sharply than she should have done.

Miss Crampton was delighted. Her smile bordered on the genial as she said,

"Why, don't you know him? How very extraordinary! He is Miss Danesworth's nephew. She has the house next to my cousin Mrs. Merridew, and Jenny is staying with her. You surely knew that!"

Mrs. Forbes said firmly, "Oh, yes. Yes, of course. You confused me. Oh—so Jenny is with Miss Danesworth—and the nephew is staying there, too—"

Miss Crampton didn't know when she had felt so pleased and excited.

"My dear Mrs. Forbes, they arrived together! He and Jenny arrived together at seven o'clock in the morning! What do you think of that?"

Mrs. Forbes was brought to a standstill. Her tongue burned with the things which she must on no account say to Miss Crampton. How she restrained herself, she did not know. She stood quite still and gathered herself together.

"A most inconvenient time to arrive anywhere," she said. "The young man is a cousin of ours of course, but a very distant one. I've never met him myself, but I believe that Jenny has. I forget where. It may have been with those friends she made at school, but I really forget."

Miss Crampton was enjoying herself. She said, "Oh, really?" and Mrs. Forbes said, "Yes," in her most decided voice. And then,

"Well, I'll be getting home. Good-morning, Miss Crampton."

Miss Crampton went home and sat down and wrote a letter to her cousin Mrs. Merridew.

My dear Laura,

Your letter has interested me very much indeed. I met Mrs. Forbes in the village shop this morning, and I don't think there is the *slightest* reason to suppose that she knew *where* Jenny had gone. It is really the most extraordinary thing, and I can only imagine that the girl had run away. You know, you didn't *meet* her when you were here with me two years ago, because she was still at school then. And you didn't meet Mrs. Forbes either. But I spoke to you about the girl, and you *seemed* quite interested. Only you seem to have forgotten that her name is *not* Forbes *at all.* She is the *illegitimate* child of the Richard Forbes to whom Alington then belonged. He was killed in the war. And Jenny's mother came back to her old governess Miss Garstone, right at the gates of Alington House. I must say Miss Garstone behaved in a *very* peculiar way about the girl. *No one* was allowed to see her. Miss Garstone said she was ill. And I did hear that she never spoke. Not from Dr. Horton, who was most aggravating about the whole thing. He was attending my dear Father at the time—it was during his last illness—and you would have thought he would have spoken freely to *me.* But no! Not at all! He simply said, 'Ah, Miss Crampton, sad things do happen during a war.' And he went on to say that the only thing to do was to leave the girl alone. *Alone!* She wanted rousing—I said so all along. And I was perfectly right, because she died when the baby was born. Which *shows!* But to return to this girl Jenny. From what you say, it looks to me as if she was pretending to Miss Danesworth and to this Mr. Forbes that she was legitimate. That is to say, if you are right about her calling herself Jenny Forbes. It doesn't do to make a mistake about that sort of thing. Please write again *without delay* and let me know on this point. If Jenny is really passing herself off as a Forbes, Miss Danesworth should be informed and the fraud exposed.

> Your affectionate cousin,
> *Melita Crampton*

Mrs. Forbes walked home. At first indignation lent her a certain force. She moved quickly and with a very determined tread. And then, as she got out of the village, her step slackened and she began to walk slowly and yet more slowly. She had felt as if the time taken to walk up to Alington House was too long. She couldn't wait to get on the phone to Mac, and to tell him what she had just been told.

And then, as her first fury died down and her step slackened, a change came over her mood. The girl in the telephone exchange—she would be listening. Mrs. Forbes didn't see her missing a call at this juncture. She would know all about Jenny going off, and she would listen her very hardest to any call from Mrs. Forbes to Mac. She came slowly up the drive and into the house. She must write—that was what she must do. She mustn't do anything to show alarm. She must write to Mac.

It was unlucky for Meg that she chose this moment to intrude.

"Mother—"

Mrs. Forbes turned.

"What are you doing here?"

Joyce would have run away, but Meg stood her ground.

"I only wanted to know—about Nanna's kitten. It's the dearest little thing—black with greeny blue eyes—and it will be ready to come away from its mother in a fortnight. But Nanna wanted to know, because her niece would have it if we don't."

Mrs. Forbes turned a quite uncomprehending look upon her little daughter. She simply didn't know what the child was talking about. Her temper had begun to rise.

"What is it—what is it?"

Meg began again. Grown-up people were very stupid. She had put it quite plainly.

"It's Nanna's black kitten—the one she was keeping for us—for Joyce and me. It's got a white star on its chest, and it's the dearest little thing—it really is. *Please*, Mother, do let us have it."

Mrs. Forbes turned on her.

"I thought I told you to go up to the schoolroom! Don't you know enough not to disobey me?"

Meg knew danger when she saw it. She saw it now. It was not the time to continue the conversation about the kitten. She scuffled away, and Mrs. Forbes turned and went into the writing-room. She wrote:

Dear Mac,

I have just had a very unpleasant experience. I was down in the village at Mrs. Boddles', and that Miss Crampton was there. She is a most impertinent woman, and I have never had more to do with her than I could help, but on this occasion there was no avoiding her. She informed not only me but Mrs. Boddles and everyone else in the shop that Jenny was staying next door to her cousin Mrs. Merridew at a place called Hazeldon in the next county. It seems that she arrived at seven o'clock on Sunday morning with a young man. Goodness knows how or where she picked him up. His name, if you please, is Richard Forbes. He is probably no connection, but on the other hand I do seem to recollect your father saying something about a cousin—quite a distant one—who was killed in an air raid with his wife. They left a boy. I remember your father saying something ridiculous about seeing him through his schooling, and then later on saying it wouldn't be necessary, as there was quite a lot of money and his mother's sister was willing and anxious to look after the boy. That would be this Miss Danesworth whom Miss Crampton mentioned. She said that Jenny arrived next door to her cousin with this man at seven o'clock in the morning! And she said further that Jenny was calling herself Jenny Forbes! If this is a fact, it can only mean one thing—*Jenny knows!* How she can, I can't imagine. I think you should come down for the week-end.

Your loving Mother

When she had finished the letter she went up to the schoolroom, collected Carter and the little girls, and sent them out to the post. Mac would get the letter next morning.

Mac got it. It was lying on his table when he came out of his room whistling. He stopped when he saw the letter, picked it up, and opened it. He read it through twice. Then he lit a match and set fire to it. It burned away to a black ash. He opened the window and crumbled up all that was left of it. Afterwards when he had shut the window again he stood by it for a long time thinking and planning. It wasn't as nice weather as it had been in the country. The thought went through his mind and was gone again. How many people knew that she had written to him? He must be careful—he must be very careful. He wouldn't go down—no, certainly he wouldn't go down. He frowned at his hands. Some of the black ash from the burned paper had smudged them. He went into his room again and washed off the smudges. It was easy enough to have clean hands if you took a little thought.

CHAPTER 17

Mrs. Merridew had not been idle. By the same post that she had written to Miss Crampton she had also written to another cousin, a Mrs. Richardson who had a long family and a short purse.

My dear Grace,

I shall be so glad if you will spare one of your girls on a visit. I think perhaps Miriam if she is free. I think you said that she had left Mrs. Nettleby. It's a great pity she changes so often. A girl is apt to get a bad name. I hope that entanglement you spoke of is *quite* over. It doesn't do when a girl has her way to make, as I told you in the summer when you spoke to me about it. Miss Danesworth has a girl staying with her—you remember

she is next door—and her nephew who is in the
Army is staying there too. So I thought it would be
a pleasant change for Miriam. . . .

She went on to meticulous enquiries about the whole
family.

Mrs. Richardson put down the letter with rather a
helpless gesture. She was a large, fair, untidy woman
with the vague air of one who is doing her best, but who
really can't see why she should have to do it. She had
lost her husband, and though of course she was very
sorry, she did find life just a little easier without him. He
had been accustomed to so much and had had so little.
Every year that they were married he had less, and
prices went up and up, and the family grew and grew.
Grace Richardson didn't wish him dead—the idea
would have shocked her very much—but she told herself after the funeral that it would be easier to manage
now that there wasn't a man in the house. One of her
four girls was adopted by a cousin, and that left three to
be provided with clothes, and food, and jobs. Miriam
was the eldest. She was also the best-looking. She had
curly dark hair, a pair of bold rather staring eyes of a
bright blue in colour, and she had a most unfortunate
habit of getting into scrapes. She was in a scrape just
now. How bad a scrape, she wasn't quite sure. At almost any other time she would have kicked at going to
stay with Cousin Laura, but in the present circumstances it might be just as well.

Mrs. Richardson sighed and looked up from her letter.

"I suppose you wouldn't care about paying Cousin
Laura a visit?" she said.

Miriam looked undecided.

"What does she say?"

Mrs. Richardson told her.

"There's a girl staying next door—she thinks you might be company for her. Oh, and Miss Danesworth has her nephew there too. I think you met him when you were there in the spring."

"When does she want me to come?"

"Oh, yes—she says at once."

Miriam's heart gave a leap. Yes, she'd go. And she'd tell Jimmy where she was, and say she *must* see him. He'd come all right. She could deal with him there—or if she couldn't . . . She said not too graciously,

"Well, I shouldn't mind."

Eleanor and Lilian, the other two girls, breathed again. They were seventeen and eighteen years of age, and they were definitely concerned with *not* going to stay with Cousin Laura. They avoided looking at each other until they were out of the room. They were a devoted pair, but they did not love their sister Miriam very much. It was unfortunate that at this juncture Jimmy Mottingley should have come to the same conclusion.

Mrs. Merridew heard from Mrs. Richardson on the Wednesday.

My dear Laura,

It is indeed good of you to ask Miriam to pay you a visit. As it happens, she is at a loose end just now and very pleased to accept your kind offer. Her last employer was *most* unkind, and the child's feelings were *deeply* hurt. I would really be glad of this change for her. . . .

There was a lot more, but Mrs. Merridew barely took the trouble to read it. Miriam was coming. That was really all she wanted to know. As for Grace's supremely dull catalogue of events, they would keep. It would not be the first letter of hers which she had consigned to the waste-paper basket half read. She pursued Mrs. Richardson's letter far enough to discover that she might expect Miriam on Friday, and abandoned the rest of it to go in next door and impart her news.

There was no sign of Richard or of Jenny. She had a good look round, but she could not see them anywhere. Miss Danesworth wondered why she had come, but she was not left to wonder for long. Mrs. Merridew, after her customary survey of anything and everything, pounced firmly on a handkerchief.

"That's not yours!"

Miss Danesworth smiled.

"No, it's Jenny's—careless child."

Mrs. Merridew sniffed.

"Is she still with you?"

"Oh, yes. I hope she will stay with me for some time."

Mrs. Merridew resumed.

"I asked because I have a cousin's daughter coming to stay. Such a nice girl."

Miriam would have been astonished, and with reason. She had never had any occasion to observe that her cousin Laura thought her a nice girl.

Miss Danesworth said everything she could. She had met Miriam, and she did not like her very much. She was conscious of a certain pressure from Mrs. Merridew. She did not know of any particular reason for this pressure, but it made her uneasy. She thought she would not encourage too much intimacy. And she felt that in Mrs. Merridew she had an opponent.

Jenny and Richard were up on Hazeldon Heath. It was the sort of day that is not an everyday. There was a lark singing. It went up and up, and its song came floating down. The air was cool with the wind which always blows over the heath, and it was warm in the sun. Richard looked at Jenny, and Jenny looked away to the May trees which stood in a thick clump over against them. She said,

"I wish I had seen them in flower. Are they all white?"

"There's a pink one right in the middle."

Jenny looked where he pointed.

"I didn't know there were ever pink ones except in gardens."

He laughed.

"I expect it escaped! Or perhaps someone planted it."

"Things are interesting, aren't they?" said Jenny with a sigh of contentment.

Richard looked at her. He went on looking until he thought he had better say something. What he said was not what he had meant to say. He said it because he couldn't help himself.

"Do you know that when you look that way it makes me want to kiss you?"

Jenny gave a comfortable little laugh.

"You mustn't say things like that, you know, or I shall have to go home."

"Did you mind?"

"Oh, no. You didn't mean anything."

"Didn't I?"

She was watching a little green and white spider that kept on climbing to the top of a stalk, and when it got there it seemed to have forgotten why it had come and it ran all the way down again. She said,

"Of course you didn't. And I don't want to go home a bit."

"Then why go?"

"I won't. Unless you go on talking nonsense."

"Suppose it wasn't nonsense—" he said.

"It couldn't be anything else, could it? Not when we've only known each other for two or three days."

He said slowly, "I suppose not." Then with a sudden sense of having said something which he didn't mean, which he never could mean, he broke in,

"Jenny—does time mean all that to you? It doesn't to me."

She gave him a hasty look over her shoulder. He was in earnest. A sense of standing on the brink of something she didn't quite know what came upon her. She was afraid—not of him, or of herself. She didn't know why she was afraid. She looked at him with startled eyes, and he saw that he had spoken too soon. She wasn't ready.

"Jenny, don't look like that. I didn't mean to startle you."

Jenny sat up straight. She said in a voice which she tried to keep quite steady,

"It's nothing." She looked at her watch. "I—I think we ought to go home now—I really do."

"No! I won't do it again, I promise. Look, you can see the spire of Chiselton Church. There. No, a little more to the left—straight in line with the thorn trees. You can only see it when the weather is going to be very fine, and then only in the middle of the day."

Jenny said, "Oh, why?" She didn't really want to go home. She was quite ready to talk about a distant church spire. It seemed a very safe subject.

"Because—" said Richard, "because there's a spell on it. If you see it with someone in the middle of the day and the sun is shining and you don't tell anyone, it makes a spell."

"Richard!" She looked at him between laughter and disbelief.

"It does. If you don't believe it you must wait and see."

Jenny turned back to her spider.

"I don't believe a word of it," she said.

CHAPTER 18

Miriam Richardson sat in the train and thought. She didn't really want to go to Hazeldon. She didn't want to stay at home either. She had told Jimmy she was going, and he hadn't exactly said that he would come down and see her, but she thought she could count on it. She could make things very unpleasant for him if he failed her. Oh, yes, they might be unpleasant for her too, but she could certainly guarantee that they wouldn't be pleasant for him. Mr. and Mrs. Mottingley were very strict. They belonged to the local church, and Jimmy had been brought up to belong to it, too. Miriam's lip curled a little as she thought of what the Mottingley family would say if they knew. Well, they were going to know, unless Jimmy came to heel.

She thought about that. They would have to get married at once. Yes, that would be best—a register office, and then break it to the parents on both sides. If they wanted a church wedding they could have one. *She* didn't mind. What she wanted was to tie Jimmy up so that he couldn't get out of it, and whether it was church or register office that did it was nothing to her. All she wanted was to make things safe.

Underneath this smooth flow of efficient planning there were terrifying currents. She hardly knew what they were, but she felt the drag of them every now and then—the drag and the pitiless horror that it brought.

She made a great effort, and was aware that every time she fought the realization of what would happen if Jimmy let her down—every time the effort was greater, and the realization of it was clearer. She turned away from it with a determined effort and thought about a plan of campaign.

Mrs. Merridew met her at the station. Unusually gracious, she kissed the air in the neighbourhood of Miriam's cheek, summoned a porter with a peremptory wave of her parasol, and accompanied Miriam to the luggage van to pick out and claim her shabby little box. Miriam stood by with an impatience thinly disguised.

"Is that your box? Atkins, it's that one! Dear me, Miriam, hadn't your mother a better box to send you with than this? That strap is quite dangerous, I declare. It looks as if it might come off at any moment."

Miriam hated her fiercely. She knew very well that her luggage was fairly shabby. If you looked as if it didn't really belong to you you could carry that sort of thing off with a high hand, but Cousin Laura had no sense at all. She hated her, and if it hadn't been for Jimmy she wouldn't have come.

Chattering all the time, Mrs. Merridew superintended the collection of the box, repeating all she had said before about its shabbiness, and interspersing her remarks with a perfunctory enquiry about Mrs. Richardson's health and well-being and a passing query as to what Eleanor and Lilian were doing now that, she supposed, they had left school.

"They haven't left," said Miriam shortly.

"Dear me!"

Mrs. Merridew got into the taxi and made room for Miriam beside her.

"No, Atkins, the box can come in here perfectly well! What were you saying, Miriam?"

"I said that neither Eleanor nor Lilian had left

school," said Miriam in a bored tone of voice. She was thinking that Cousin Laura was the absolute end.

As they drove away from the station Mrs. Merridew said brightly,

"Now, I want you to make a special effort to be friendly with the girl whom Miss Danesworth has got staying with her just now. I have a particular reason for wanting you to be friends."

She began to explain the particular reason, but until she mentioned Richard Forbes, Miriam's attention was of a very haphazard nature.

"He actually turned up with her at half past six on Sunday morning!"

Miriam came out of her thoughts.

"Who did?"

"My dear, you weren't listening! I was *telling* you! Why, Richard Forbes, to be sure. You remember he was here when you were before, and I thought—"

Miriam's shoulder gave a twitch of exasperation. She could have done very well with Richard Forbes, but she knew that he had no use for her. She didn't put it quite as badly as this, but that was what it had amounted to. All the same, she might be able to use him. If Jimmy could be made jealous . . . She gratified Mrs. Merridew by paying a good deal more attention.

They got back to Hazeldon in good time for tea, and as soon as they had finished Mrs. Merridew led the way next door. Miss Danesworth discovered them without pleasure. Then her heart smote her and she went out of her way to be kind.

Richard heard the change in her voice and groaned inwardly. There was nothing to be done about it either, for the front door gave directly into the passage which divided the house. Left to himself, he could have escaped through the back window, but he was not quite mean enough to abandon Jenny. Or was he? The mo-

ment of indecision was fatal, but he might have known
that it would be. Miss Danesworth turned, preceded
her guests down the passage, and stood aside for them
to enter the sitting-room. Miriam saw Jenny, and Jenny
saw Miriam. Both disliked the impression they received. Mrs. Merridew's voice, which had not been silent for more than a moment, took up its tale again.

"Well, here we are. Richard, you remember Miriam?
But of course you do. You met her here in the spring.
You saw a good deal of each other, I remember. And
Jenny—you haven't met Miriam before, have you? This
is my cousin's daughter, Miriam Richardson. I hope
you will be great friends. This is not a place where there
is a great deal going on, but I always say that if young
people can't amuse one another, well, what is the world
coming to? I'm sure I don't know."

Jenny did not like Miriam, but that was no reason
for not being polite. She did what she could without
much help from Miriam herself. Miriam was bored. She
hadn't come here to talk to Jenny. She showed her bore-
dom so visibly that conversation became very difficult.
But when Richard joined in, impelled by a pleading
look from Jenny, Miriam's manner changed. She
flashed into a spirited and not unamusing account of
her journey.

"There were two dreadful children," she announced.
"The sticky sort—they positively oozed peppermint
drops. I do think there's something sickening about
children who eat in trains, and these were thoroughly
nasty little toads."

"You don't like children?" said Jenny.

"I like properly brought up children. But these were
horrid little brats—the sort you would like to drop out
of the window and leave behind on the railway track."

Richard had an amiable smile for that.

"You weren't tempted to oblige?"

"Well, I was. But of course it wouldn't have done. Their mother obviously didn't mind, and she'd have been peeved with me."

Jenny faded out of the conversation.

"How you *could!*" she said to Richard when their visitors had gone away.

"How I could what?"

"You played up to her—you know you did. I think she's a horrid girl."

"Now I wonder why?" said Richard innocently.

"Richard, you *can't* like her!"

He said, "Can't I?" in rather an odd tone of voice.

They were tidying up the drawing-room. Jenny stood with a cushion in her hand and looked at him.

"Richard—*do* you?"

"Frantically!" he said, laughing.

Jenny threw the cushion. The minute she had done it she was afraid. But she wasn't sorry. He dodged the cushion and caught her by the wrists. There was a tense moment. And then he kissed her. He couldn't help it. And yet the moment he had done it, and whilst he was still wanting to do it again, he was afraid, because Jenny didn't blush, or tremble, or laugh. She just went white and still with his hands on her. And he was afraid of what he had done. He let go of her.

"Jenny—"

"It's all right."

"Jenny—"

She stamped her foot.

"I said it was all right!" And with that she turned and ran out of the room.

Miriam and Mrs. Merridew let themselves in to the house next door.

"I thought you got on very well with Richard," said Mrs. Merridew. "Where's that cat? Here, Timmy—

Timmy! . . . Yes, very well indeed. He must be dread-fully bored with that little cousin they've got staying there."

"Oh, she's a cousin, is she?"

"Some sort of. Of course, you know, her name isn't really Forbes at all. I know all about her because my cousin Miss Crampton lives in the village this girl comes from. Her father—Miss Crampton's father, that is—was the Vicar there—my old Uncle Thomas—and this girl is the illegitimate daughter of the last Forbes, the one who was killed in the war. Her mother died when she was born, and she stayed on with her mother's old governess who lived just at the gates of the Forbeses' house. *Most* awkward. I believe Mrs. Forbes did try very hard to get the governess to move away, but she wouldn't budge. That will show you the sort of bring-ing up the girl had. And now that the governess is dead she's had some sort of a row with Mrs. Forbes, and she turns up here with Richard at seven o'clock in the morning, if you please!"

"What a joke!" said Miriam.

"Well, I call it disgraceful—Oh, there you are, pussy! Now come along and see what I've got for you!" As she left the room she turned round to say, "A girl like that just doesn't understand that Richard would never think seriously of her for a moment. I don't know what she was doing gadding about with him as she was, but I wouldn't put up with it if I were Miss Danesworth and Richard was *my* nephew."

Jenny was very quiet all the evening—very quiet and very still. She didn't come down again until just before supper. Then she excused herself and went to bed as soon afterwards as she could.

As soon as the door was shut on her Miss Danes-worth turned on her nephew and said,

"What have you been doing?"

"I?" Richard's tone was one of conscious innocence.

"Yes, you. And it's no good your being like that about it. If you don't want to tell me about it you needn't. But don't pretend that there is nothing to tell."

Richard was standing by the fireplace. He had his back turned to Caroline. He was very fond of her. She was absolutely to be trusted. It was too soon to say anything. And then suddenly he was saying it.

"It's Jenny," he said.

"Yes?"

There was something in the tone of her voice that made it easier. He said,

"I've gone right overboard for her. I expect you know that."

"Yes."

There was a long pause. Then he said,

"I've rushed things, I'm afraid."

"Yes?"

"I—I'm afraid I kissed her."

"Well, that's not the end of the world."

"It might be."

"What do you mean?"

"Well, it was all very light-hearted, and then suddenly she threw a cushion and I kissed her and it wasn't light-hearted anymore. She turned as white as a sheet and ran out of the room. I suppose now she thinks I kiss every girl I meet."

"Probably." After a pause she went on. "You are really serious about this?"

"Of course I am."

"Well then, I should leave it all tonight. She's had a shock. I think you've got to be careful what you say and do."

"I think I have."

"Well then, I shouldn't do anything tonight. In the morning you can apologize for kissing her. See how she takes it. Don't rush things. I think she's had a fright. You want her to trust you."

CHAPTER 19

In the morning—it was Saturday morning—Jenny seemed more normal. She was rather pale and rather quiet, and she did rather cling to Miss Danesworth, or so it seemed to Richard. After suggesting two plans for the day and having them both turned down he acquiesced in Miss Danesworth's suggestion that he should go over and see his friend Tommy Risdall.

"He'll be wondering where you are, you know." Then she turned to Jenny. "Tommy's a pet—I'm most awfully fond of him. And he's Richard's oldest friend. He's in the Navy. It's such a chance his being on leave just now when Richard is. I don't think he ought to miss the opportunity of seeing him—do you?"

Jenny said, "Oh, no," without raising her eyes.

A call having established the fact that Tommy was at home, that he was bored stiff—"Well, you know how it is. The parents are both as busy as can be, and you'll be a life-saver, I give you my word."

Richard turned from the telephone to find Jenny in the room.

"I've been thinking," she said.

"What have you been thinking about, Jenny?"

"About my being here."

"Yes—"

"Well, I didn't mean to stay—like this. I—I must think of something—to do—"

He made himself stay steady where he was by the telephone, but it wasn't easy.

"Is that because of yesterday?"

Her colour rose.

"No—no—of course not. It's just—" She stopped there because she couldn't go on. It was dreadful. It was the most dreadful thing that had ever happened to her, but she couldn't help it. And she couldn't go on. She just stood there with her eyes wide and they looked at one another.

Richard couldn't bear it. It was all very well for Caroline to say, "Give her time. Don't rush her," but there were things you couldn't bear. He had started across the room to her, and she had lifted her eyes and looked at him, when there were steps in the passage and Miriam's voice called out.

"Are you there, Richard? I'm coming in."

Richard said "Damn!" under his breath and pulled up short. And with that Miriam came in.

"I've a message from Cousin Laura," she said. "She wants you to come to lunch today, only it's so fine that I suggested our making a picnic of it. There's quite a nice place up on Hazeldon Heath. I don't know if you know it."

"I'm afraid," said Richard, "that I can't say yes. I've arranged to go over and spend the day with a friend at Tillingdon."

"Oh—perhaps he'd like to come too."

"Well, I'm afraid he won't be able to do that."

"Oh, dear—what a pity! What about tomorrow?"

"It's Sunday," said Richard.

Miriam smiled what she considered to be her most attractive smile.

"Does that matter?"

"Yes, I think so. This is a village, you know. A very

fierce light beats upon villages. The only excuse for not going to church is the bed of sickness."

"Well, Monday then—"

Jenny did not seem to be in on this conversation at all. Was she, or was she not, being invited? She didn't know. She felt very, very angry, and she felt as if she was ten years older, and ten years younger. If she was really ten years older she would know what to do, and if she was ten years younger it wouldn't matter so much. It mattered dreadfully. But at least she didn't want to cry any more. Being angry dried up your tears. All this time she had not moved, but she moved now. She said, "I think Miss Danesworth wants me," and she went out of the room.

"What an odd girl she is—isn't she?" said Miriam. She laughed as she spoke—a derogatory sort of laugh which was intended to put Jenny in her place.

Richard did not reply. He was too angry. The derogatory tone in which Miriam referred to Jenny, and the fact that she relied on him to second her, gave him so hotly partisan a feeling that it was all he could do to restrain himself from a candour of free speech which would not have gone down at all well.

Miriam stared at him. She was quite enjoying herself. If Richard disagreed with her he could say so, couldn't he? She was not troubled with any delicacy of feeling herself. She laughed and said, "Oh well, if she doesn't want to come, I suppose we can do without her," and left it at that.

Richard let her out of the front door and returned. In reply to Miriam's attempt to tie him down to the picnic-lunch on Monday he had said firmly that he would find out what Jenny was doing and let her know.

With an inward determination to avoid the occasion even if he had to be rude he found Jenny in the kitchen. She neither turned nor looked at him as he came in.

"Where's Caroline?" he said.

"She's gone into the garden for some flowers. Do you want her?"

She didn't look at him. Why didn't she? He came up close.

"If I see much of that girl I shall be rude to her," he said.

Jenny felt a lightening of the spirit. He didn't really like Miriam—he couldn't. She was a horrid girl. She went on washing china with most particular attention. She was rather pale.

He said, "Jenny—" and then Caroline Danesworth came in with a bunch of roses in her hand.

There was no more opportunity for private speech. Jenny clung to Caroline, and Caroline gave them no more opportunities. She was quite aware of Richard's desire to be alone with Jenny, and she had no intention of giving way to it, or of making things easy for him. Jenny wanted time, and Richard had no business to stampede her.

She was very pleased to find that Jenny revived as the day went on. They went down to the village and shopped, and then they came back and cooked their lunch, and afterwards when the things were all cleared away Jenny curled up in a big chair with a book and forgot that she was running away. She really forgot everything except that every now and then the thought of Richard stabbed in and took her breath. Where were they going? Was it the same way? Did he want her to go with him? He didn't really want her at all.

And then there came the thought of Mac. It was such a little time ago that he had filled her world. She hadn't been here for a week yet, and it was only that length of time since she had heard him talking with Mrs. Forbes on the other side of the schoolroom curtains. It was just as if their words had had a corrosive quality which had burned out her picture of Mac. It wasn't a true picture. She knew that now. It wasn't true, and it never had been true. She had taken all the things she liked, his height, his fair complexion, and the pleasant tones of his voice, and she had made them into a picture of what she thought he was. And then as she sat behind the curtain in the schoolroom the real Mac had come out from behind the picture she had made of him, and this real Mac was—horrible.

She shuddered away from the picture, but she couldn't forget it. Nearly a week had gone by, and she had had time to think. It hadn't been a conscious sort of thought, but for all that the processes of healing and adjustment had gone on. The Mac whom she had imagined and loved, or come very near to loving, had never existed at all. He was a romantic fancy. She said it to herself, and it did her good.

Her mind turned to Richard. It wasn't his fault that that odious girl Miriam was next door. As far as she could see, it would take them all their time ever to get a minute to themselves. Miriam was the most unabashed person she had ever come across in her life. Short of getting up very early in the morning and escaping for the day before Miriam was up, she could see no chance of their ever eluding her. It was nice to feel on the same side as Richard. What she hadn't been able to bear was the feeling that he and Miriam were on one side, with Jenny a long, long way off on the other and a great thick hedge all set with thorns between them.

Caroline had gone in to see a sick neighbour. When she returned they had tea. It was a day which Jenny was often to look back to in the days that were to come. There was no hint of those days now.

When tea was over and washed up Caroline and Jenny talked. Jenny told her about Garsty and about the little girls, but she didn't mention Mrs. Forbes or the two boys. Caroline was a very easy person to talk to. She didn't pounce on what you told her and try to make it mean more or less, like Mrs. Merridew did. She spoke very little, but you felt a flowing tide of sympathy and understanding. The time passed very quickly.

It was just as it was getting dark that Miriam came. They had been sitting in the dusk, but now Caroline got up and turned on the electric light. At once the half-seen dusk outside retreated and became vague and dark.

"Richard's not back?" said Miriam. "Cousin Laura's gone to some meeting or other. They do have them at inconvenient hours, don't they? I wanted to see Richard."

Jenny did not say anything. Miss Danesworth at the front windows looked over her shoulder to say,

"He's not back yet. I never do expect him until I see him."

"Oh—that's very inconvenient, isn't it? Well, I can wait for a little, but not for very long." She sat down in the most comfortable of the easy chairs and continued to talk in her rather loud voice. "It's not very complimentary to you, Jenny, his going off like that for the whole day, is it?" she said. "I mean, I shouldn't feel flattered if I was visiting in a house with a young man and he made off like that."

Caroline finished drawing the curtains and turned round.

"Oh, he didn't really want to go," she said in a laughing voice. "We fairly drove him, didn't we, Jenny?"

Jenny lifted her head. She felt defenceless. But Caroline was defending her. She couldn't defend herself. She wouldn't do it. Miriam could say anything she liked, Jenny wouldn't answer her. She had been mending a pair of stockings until the light got so bad. Now she picked them up again. The neat interwoven stitches were soothing to do. She would leave Miriam to do the talking.

And Miriam talked.

She talked about her sisters and her home, about the last place she had been in, and about how sorry they were when she made up her mind to leave.

"I suppose I shall have to think about getting something else," she said. "Such a nuisance! I think employers are simply the limit—don't you? And what they expect of one!"

She discoursed in this vein for some time. And then, suddenly looking at the clock, she said, "Is that right?"

"Yes, it keeps excellent time."

"Oh—then I must go. Tell Richard I want to see him, will you? Not tonight—I'm doing something else. But if he'd like to he can come round in the morning." She was already on her feet and out of the door as she finished speaking.

Jenny wondered a little. She thought that Miriam was a very odd girl, and she was very much relieved to see the last of her. If she had known that she was indeed seeing the last of her she would have had a more painful feeling.

CHAPTER 20

Miriam went out of the front door. Coming from the brightly lighted hall, she blinked at the sudden darkness. The door behind her shut, and she stood for a moment to get her bearings. The two houses were at the end of the road. There was nothing beyond Mrs. Merridew's, a fact upon which she was apt to be complacent: "Here I am, just on the edge of the common, and no one can build beyond me.

At the same time, with that nice quiet Miss Danesworth next door I have all the advantages of company."

There was a little line of thorn trees on the far side of Mrs. Merridew's garden, and then the heath dotted with thorns and carpeted with bracken.

Miriam walked past her own door and on up the road. Jimmy would be waiting for her. Half a mile up the road was what she had said. She had better fix things up with him. Really, Richard didn't mean anything. She couldn't flatter herself that he did. But Jimmy—well, she'd got a hold on him, hadn't she? Jimmy was a cert provided she played her cards right, and there was no reason why she shouldn't play them right. The best way would be to get Jimmy to marry her now, then there wasn't anything people could do about it except make the best of a job that was out of their hands. There would be a colossal row of course, but who cared about rows if you got what you wanted? As she meant to.

It was dark. The man who walked behind her could not be seen, or only as a shadow among the many black shadows that lay across the path. Miriam was too much taken up with her own thoughts and plans to hear the faint sound of his footfall. He was walking very carefully. Sometimes the impatience in him throbbed itself to a climax. When this happened he stood quite still for a moment until he had it in control again. And all the time his purpose looked plainer. He had been waiting for an hour. He had given her that length of time. If she did not come then, he would have to think of a plan. There was an arrogance in him that would not contemplate failure. If she did not come out, or if she did not come out alone, he would have to think of another way. You succeed if you will hard enough to succeed. You succeed if you do not contemplate failure. He had never contemplated failure, and he had never failed in what he had set his heart on.

He went over his plans. He did not know that the boy to whom he had given the note was renowned for his carelessness. He had put on his skilfully planned disguise, the moustache and the dark wig, and he had stopped his car half a mile on this side of the village. No one could possibly recognize him. If she didn't come . . . He pushed the thought away. She would come. He recalled the wording of his note—

> Jenny, *don't say anything to anyone,* but come out and meet me up on the heath as soon as it is quite dark.
>
> > *Mac*
> > Bring this with you.

Well, they were far enough now. He quickened his step and came up with her just where a high clump of gorse stood by the side of the road and darkened it. He called to her softly under his breath,

"Jenny—"

Miriam halted. It wasn't Jimmy. And he had called her Jenny. It wasn't Richard either. So Jenny was playing a deep game, was she? She thought she would learn a little more. He had taken her for Jenny. Well, she had come out of Miss Danesworth's. Let him go on thinking she was Jenny for a little. She might learn something more. She tingled with a sense of adventure. She wouldn't need to speak. She turned, and for a moment they were there in the black shadow with nothing stirring round them.

It was Miriam's last conscious moment, lighted by a flash of anticipation, a sense of triumph. And then the blow fell.

She slumped to the ground with no more than a deep

sigh. He picked her up, carried her round to the far side of the clump of gorse, and dumped her there. Then he bent to the inert body. He had to make sure.

He made sure. Then he walked away.

Ten minutes later he had come up with his car and was driving away up the country road with a sense of triumph in his heart. He had gone nearly ten miles before he remembered the note.

He had told her to bring it with her. Had she done what she was told? If she had, he must go back. Every instinct in him recoiled. The dead thing lying behind the clump of gorse, that was part of the past. You can't go back into the past and correct your mistakes. They say a murderer always makes one bad mistake. What a fool he had been—what a damned, damned fool. He turned the car and drove back.

But when he came to that stretch of road he knew that he was too late. He saw the light, a lantern swinging from a man's wrist, and the whole tall threatening clump of gorse standing up in front of it. There was only one thing to do, and he did it. As he went past it at about thirty-five, he could hear a vague clamour. Voices called to him. He heard them for a moment, and then they were away. He was away.

The boy to whom he had given the note was called Dicky Pratt. As it happened, he was probably the most unreliable boy who could have been chosen for the purpose. His mother often said so. "Give Dicky a message," she would say, "and the first thing will put it out of his head." But she was wrong in this. Dicky had a very strong sense of what suited himself. On this occasion he went on his way with the intention of delivering the note with which he had been charged. He was always a most obliging boy with a cheerful manner. He had fully intended to deliver the note, but then he fell in with Roger Barton and Stuffy Craddock and they had a marvellous scheme on. Mr. Fulbrook's apples would be ripe—well, ripe enough—and Roger had had a bright idea. There was a wheel off the old cart that was smashed up no more than a fortnight ago. It had gone into the pond, and they hadn't troubled to fetch it out yet.

"Now if we could have it out of the pond we could run it up against the wall, and the two of us could hold it and the third get over and get the apples, and no one would know."

The note which he had promised to deliver was for the moment wiped as clean from Dicky's brain as if it had never existed. To him, indeed, it ceased to exist. He said it was a smashing idea, and the three of them rushed off helter-skelter to put it into practice. It is pleasant to record that they never reached their objective, the wheel having stuck in the mud at the bottom of the pond. It refused all efforts to detach it. When at last they desisted they were soaked to the skin and regretfully decided to give up for the day.

The undelivered letter had miraculously survived. It lay crushed together with the mixed contents of Dicky's pocket. If his mother had been a tidy woman she would have thrown the whole lot out, but she was a weak-willed, complaining sort of creature. She hung up Dicky's trousers on the line over the stove and left the things in the pockets to dry as best they might.

The note survived. Also in Dicky's memory there was the number of the car. The man had been sitting in it. He had got out and come after Dicky. Dicky collected car numbers. He ran off towards the village, stopped when he had gone a little distance, and made his way back carefully. The man had got into the car again. He was a large man. He might object to Dicky getting the number. Besides it was more fun if you stalked the car. Dicky was a very expert stalker.

He reached the back of the car and discovered a very curious thing. The car lights were off. There was something hanging out of the boot, and it covered the number plate. Coo—that was a rum start that was! The man in that car didn't want to be recognized—that's what that meant! Very secretive and all that! Dicky reflected that it was a good thing he had got a box of matches in his pocket. Very useful things matches. He struck one now and read the number at the back of the car. There were the letters that meant the county, and then 505. Quite easy to remember. He let down the flap again and proceeded on his way towards the village and to his meeting with Roger Barton and Stuffy Craddock.

CHAPTER 21

Jimmy Mottingley was a very unhappy young man. He had done wrong, and he was going to have to pay for it. He was going to have to pay very heavily. When he thought of being married to Miriam, living with her, sleeping with her at night, and sitting down to meals with her every day, he felt that he simply couldn't do it. And he'd got to. There wasn't any way out. He couldn't face his father.

As he drove along in the car which his parents considered an extravagance and disapproved of, though he had got it a bargain from Chadwick who was always changing cars and had more money than he knew what to do with, he thought with a good deal of apprehension of the parental wrath. Whatever he did or he didn't do, he would have that to face, and at the thought of standing up before his father and confessing about Miriam he felt as if he simply couldn't do it. There wasn't any way out of it. Not that he could see. Unless Miriam could be persuaded not to drive him. She wouldn't be

any better off if he were to commit suicide. He didn't
really mean to do it of course. It made him feel most
awfully wicked even to think of offering it to Miriam as
an excuse, but if she were to believe it . . . Yes, that
would be a way out—if he could get her to see that she
wouldn't really be any better off if she pushed him too
far. Yes, something could be done on those lines. He
simply didn't dare to marry her and defy his parents.
And it wouldn't be any good either. Miriam didn't
know his father. He was a man of his word. If he said he
would do a thing, that thing was as good as done. He
was perfectly capable of cutting Jimmy off without a
penny, and that was that. Miriam couldn't possibly
want to marry him when he had made her understand.

He didn't dare to go against his father. Why, before
Miriam there had been Kathy Lingbourne. He looked
right back, and there had always been Kathy. And
Kathy was nice. She would never have treated him this
way. She would never have made him marry her. As the
thought of Kathy entered his mind it produced an ex-
traordinarily soothing effect. How could he have left
Kathy for Miriam? He didn't know. It was like being ill
and getting well again. It was like having an awful
dream and waking up from it. Kathy was good. Not
just going-to-church good but every-day good. Her
mother had died when she was seventeen, and she had
taken her place. Jimmy had always been welcome there.
He was a friend of her elder brother's. He had seen
Kathy day in, day out. He knew what she was like. And
then he had met Miriam. Miriam—He shuddered violently. It was no use thinking about Kathy. He wasn't fit
to lick her boots—he knew that. She would never look
at him again if she knew—if she knew.

He drove on towards Hazeldon. The thought of
Kathy had steadied him. He began gradually to see a
little hope. Miriam wouldn't want to get into a row any

more than he did. What had she to gain from it? And then suddenly he saw Miriam's face in his mind, the lips so firmly set that they reminded him unpleasantly of a trap, and the eyes a little too close together. As he saw them in his mind they had a fierce fixed look which made his blood run cold. When he thought of kissing her he had a shudder of disgust. The mood of apprehension closed down upon him again.

He drove through the village of Hazeldon and on up the road to the Heath.

He came to the clump of gorse and drove past it for a little way. She wasn't there. That was curious, because he had in his mind a picture of her there, waiting for him. Come to think of it, she always had been first at their meetings, and she had usually been angry and said that he was late. He hadn't always been late, though she had said so, but he knew that he was late today. Well, it wasn't his fault—she would know that if she would listen to him. It wasn't his fault that old Mrs. Marsden had come to call, and that his mother had caught hold of him and dragged him in to say how do you do. He had said that he had an appointment, and he had said that he would be late for it, but a lot his mother had cared. He could hear her now—"It's Mrs. Marsden, Jimmy. She was so kind when you were a little boy and had chicken pox. You had it quite badly, you know, though it is usually such a simple thing. And she was more than kind. Then she moved away, and she wouldn't be back now if it weren't for her cousin Mrs. Dyson dying and the family things all coming to her."

Well, I ask you, what could he do about that? He had to go in and sit there whilst his mother and Mrs. Marsden talked and talked. And every time he worked himself up to saying that he had an engagement and must be getting along, one or other of them would turn round and include him in the conversation. If Miriam would only listen. But she wouldn't, he knew that. He had a moment of clear-sighted apprehension. If he were to marry Miriam, that was what it was going to be like. Every time he went anywhere she would know just how long he ought to be, and if he were any longer he would have to account for the extra time. He saw what lay before him if he wasn't firm now, and he determined, no matter what she said, to hold his ground.

He ran on past the clump of gorse and stopped a couple of hundred feet beyond it. As he walked back his courage began to give way. By the time he reached the clump of gorse it was nearly non-existent. The darkness, the silence, were undermining, but his spirits rose a little. She wasn't here. She had told him to come, and he was quite half an hour late. Perhaps she hadn't waited for him. His spirits soared, but only to drop again. It wasn't like Miriam—it wasn't like her at all. If she wanted to see him, well then she wanted to see him, and that was that. He had never known her to change her mind about anything. That wasn't Miriam's way. And with that a deeper wave of depression swept over him and he realized that if Miriam wanted him for a husband he had no defence against her. If she wanted him she would get him. It was as simple as that.

He stood quite still, the realization that he was for it seeping in and depriving him of any chance of resistance. It was some minutes before he could rouse himself. Gradually it came to him that the silence was an ominous thing. Where was Miriam? He had been walking up and down on the road side of the gorse bushes. It came to him that she might be on the other side. Watching him, letting his anxiety mount, waiting for the moment to break in. The thought made him angry, and the anger did him good. He had a torch in his pocket. He took it out, switched it on, and went round the clumps of gorse. He saw a foot and stopped dead. The torch seemed frozen in his hand. He called her name, and the sound of his own trembling voice scared him.

"Miriam—"

But Miriam lay there and didn't move or speak. He moved the torch. It showed her bare hands, her coat. She was lying on her side, her head at an unnatural angle.

Fainting. Yes, that was what it must be—she was fainting. Why? He didn't know. He didn't know at all. His mind was confused. Things like that didn't happen to you. Things like what? He didn't know. He didn't know what to do. He took her by the shoulder and shook her.

"Miriam—Miriam—"

The head fell sideways on its broken neck.

Jimmy Mottingley sprang back. He didn't know much, but he did know that much. Your head didn't fall like that if you were alive. Your head didn't fall like that unless your neck was broken. He stood back shaking with terror. He must get help—a doctor. He must get someone. The dizzy thoughts clamoured in him. He didn't know what to do, or where to go.

He found himself back on the roadside without any clear idea of how he had got there. The torch in his hand shook. He must get help. An under voice in his mind said, "No good to get help. She's dead. Miriam is dead." He covered that voice up by lifting his own. He called out before he knew that he had seen the bicycle. Then he called again, because he had seen the light and knew it for what it was—a yellow bicycle lamp coming quickly down the slight slope towards the village.

Mr. Fulbrook, who had been out to see his daughter on the other side of the Heath, stopped, jumped off, and enquired in his loud hearty voice,

"What's up?"

He had no thought of being nervous. Man and boy he had lived in Hazeldon for forty-five years, and he had never been afraid of anything yet, nor had reason to be. He had a good farm, and a good wife, and good children. It was his eldest he had been out to see—Elizabeth married a year and abed with her first baby, a boy and likely to bring credit to the family if he was any judge of young stock, which he thought he was.

He turned to the wavering light of Jimmy Mottingley's torch. The nervous voice that came back to him in the darkness would have reassured him had he been in any need of reassurance.

Jimmy stammered out, "I think she's d-dead—"

"Who is dead? Have you had an accident?"

"N-no. I f-found her. I th-think she's dead."

"Where?"

"This way."

Jimmy led the way back. The ground was rough. He stumbled and nearly fell. Mr. Fulbrook put out an arm like a crowbar and pulled him up.

"Hi—steady!" he said. And then the wavering light of Jimmy's torch slid over the hillocks and the holes and touched the still shoulder and the unnatural turn of the head.

"Hi—give me that light!" said Mr. Fulbrook, and Jimmy handed it over.

Mr. Fulbrook stooped over the body. He knew at once that the girl was dead, and he knew how. She had had her neck broken. The question was, who had done it? He said,

"She's dead. Know who she was?"

Jimmy said, "Yes—she's Miriam Richardson. She's staying with Mrs. Merridew. I came down to see her." He spoke blankly. Miriam was dead. It was a deliverance, but he hadn't got as far as thinking of that. He hadn't got any farther than the fact that she was dead.

That one terrible fact killed everything else—Miriam was dead.

Mr. Fulbrook straightened himself and took Jimmy by the arm.

"You know her then?"

Jimmy answered him, still in that blind, bewildered way.

"Yes. I came here to meet her. But she was dead."

"And you are? . . ."

"I am Jimmy Mottingley."

It didn't seem real—not in any way. It was like questions and answers in a dream. The whole thing was like a dream.

Mr. Fulbrook said, "How did you get here? Is that your car up the road?"

"Yes, it is." For the first time the thought came to him. He could have got away. But it was too late now. He had had his chance and lost it.

Mr. Fulbrook took him by the arm.

"Well then, come along. I'll leave my bike here, and you can come with me to the police station."

Jimmy stared blankly.

"The police station?"

"That's what I said. They're the people to see into this, and you found her. Come along now!"

CHAPTER 22

*The news came to the cot-*tages at the edge of the Heath nearly three quarters of an hour later. Mrs. Merridew had been home nearly half an hour. She had been in to Miss Danesworth twice to say that Miriam wasn't in, and what did they think had happened to her. She was just prepared to go in for the third time, when there was a loud rat-tat on her front door, and when she opened it there was Mr. Dobbs the policeman with a very grave face, and he was telling her, only she simply couldn't believe it, that Miriam had been murdered up on the Heath. She didn't believe it, but hearing it made her feel queer. She held on to the back of the nearest chair and stammered,

"W-what's this? I d-don't believe a word of it. Y-you're making it up. M-Miriam—"

"It's a shock," said Dobbs in his slow voice. "Bound to be when you didn't expect it. But it's true."

Mrs. Merridew sat down on the sofa and burst out crying. It took Dobbs quite a while to get anything coherent out of her, but in the end she pulled herself together and went with him to the police station, where she identified the body and Jimmy Mottingley.

"Yes, he was a friend of hers. I didn't know that he was coming to see her. She never said a word about it. I suppose they had a quarrel—"

"No-no!" gasped Jimmy. "I never saw her. She was lying there dead!"

"Nonsense!" said Mrs. Merridew. "No one would hurt her here. And what was she doing up on the Heath—you tell me that, young man!"

"She'd gone there to meet me. But when I came to the place she was dead. I never touched her. She was lying there dead, I tell you. I had nothing to do with it!"

Mrs. Merridew laughed. The laugh shocked Mr. Dobbs extremely. He said in his most repressive tones, "Now, now, Mrs. Merridew—" but all he got by that was that she did it again louder and more scornfully.

"You had nothing to do with it? That's what you say! The girl goes to meet you and she's found murdered, and you have nothing to do with it? Of course not!"

Mr. Dobbs acted with decision. This wasn't no way

to go on—no way at all. He said so, and he got Mrs. Merridew out of the room and told her to go along home. Then he went back to his office, where he found Jimmy Mottingley crying like a schoolboy. When he saw Dobbs he turned round on him.

"That's what they'll all say, won't they? They'll say I did it! And I didn't—I didn't! I swear I never touched her!"

"That's not for me to say. I've rung up Headingley, and the Chief Constable will be over. You'd better just think what you're going to say for yourself."

Jimmy rolled his wet handkerchief between his fingers.

"There's nothing I can say," he said in a hopeless tone.

Mrs. Merridew went along the dark road. The anger which had supported her died slowly. She began to take note of every movement, every breath in the darkness. It wasn't quite dark either. She began to think it would have been better if it had been. She had only a very little way to go, but murder can be done in the least possible space. Dobbs had no business to fetch her down here and leave her to come home alone.

She came to the last house but one, and felt suddenly that she could not go any farther. She stopped at the wicket gate and went in. They were having supper. Richard had not been home very long. He had come back with an eager feeling. As he drove along the lane he was conscious of suppressed excitement. In half an hour—in twenty minutes—in ten minutes—*now*—he was going to see Jenny again! And when he came to the cottage and put the car away, it was now—now—now that he was going to see her.

But Jenny was cold. She didn't respond. He mustn't startle her. He must go slowly. He helped to carry soup from the kitchen. Caroline was a dab at soup. He told her so. And then as he was clearing away the plates, there came that exasperating tap on the door, followed immediately by the entrance of Mrs. Merridew, her eyes reddened and her hat on one side.

In a moment all was confusion. Mrs. Merridew subsided upon a chair. She wept, and all the time discoursed in a high shaken voice.

"I never liked him or—or trusted him. I said so to Miriam—but she wouldn't listen. Young people never do listen—until it's too late. And what's the good of it then, I ask you—what's the good of anything when you're dead?" She began to sob very loudly. "I said to Miriam, 'Be careful what you're doing,' and she only laughed and said, 'He's nothing but a boy.' And I told her then—three months ago when she was staying here I told her. She said he was only a boy, and no harm in him, and I told her, 'That's what *you* think,' I said."

Caroline Danesworth was appalled, but competent. She told Richard to get Jenny away, and when they had gone she ministered to Mrs. Merridew. It was some time before she discovered what had happened. She hadn't liked Miriam Richardson, but it was too shocking to think that it was from her house that she had gone to her death. It really didn't seem possible. She said so.

"But she was here! She came in to see Richard, but he was out and she couldn't wait. It was dark when she went. She said she couldn't stay."

Mrs. Merridew sat up and dabbed at her eyes.

"That was because she had an appointment with this murdering wretch."

"You knew of it?"

"Of course I didn't know of it! I shouldn't have allowed it to happen if I had known—the wicked murdering creature!"

In the next room Richard stood by the window and looked at Jenny. She was trembling a little. He didn't see how he could bear it. There were things you could bear, and things that you couldn't. He came across the room to her and knelt down. She was sitting on the sofa, looking down at her hands which were shaking a little. When Richard touched her she looked up. Her eyes were big with unshed tears. Her hands clasped each other tightly, as if she needed something to hold on to.

He said, "Jenny—" in a moved voice, and she spoke in a trembling way.

"She was here. She couldn't wait. She said so. She wanted to see you, and you weren't here."

"Jenny—darling—"

The tears overflowed and rolled down her cheeks. He couldn't stand it any longer. He put his arms right round her and held her close.

CHAPTER 23

Miss Maud Silver was writ-ing to her niece Ethel. She had just turned the page and sat with her hand poised while she considered how to introduce the subject of Ethel's younger sister Gladys Robinson. There had been so much trouble with her, and really Ethel had enough anxieties of her own. These recurrent troubles between husband and wife! To be quite candid about it, the marriage had always been an unsuitable one. Gladys was vain, light-minded, and unappreciative. She had been thoroughly spoilt as a child by a silly mother who had dwelt fondly on her looks and entirely neglected the correction of her faults. It was, however, too late to repine over that now. Some kind of peace must be kept between her and her justly exasperated husband. She decided that she would not say anything to Ethel at present. Later on if necessary, but not at this moment when Ethel was sufficiently burdened by the serious illness of her second boy. The dangerous turn of his illness had, thank God, not persisted and he was now doing well, but Ethel should not be subjected to any further anxiety.

She was about to pursue her letter, when the door opened and her faithful Hannah Meadows appeared.

"Will you see Mr. Mottingley, miss?"

Miss Silver did not know the name, and yet it had some fleeting familiarity. She said, "Yes, certainly," laid down her pen, and got up.

There came into the room one of the largest men she had ever entertained there. It was not only his height, but the width of him. He saw a little lady of an old-fashioned appearance with neatly netted hair and a manner which commanded his respect. He found himself explaining his arrival in a much more subdued manner than he had intended.

"You are Miss Maud Silver?"

"Yes." Miss Silver came out from behind her writing-table and shook hands. "What can I do for you, Mr. Mottingley? Will you not sit down?"

She indicated a chair with its back to the window. Mr. Mottingley was strongly reminded of his grandmother's house in Bristol. She had had a lot of furniture like that. You didn't see it much nowadays. It wasn't fashionable, and it wasn't quite old enough to be antique, but it made him feel better. There was something homely about it, as there was about nearly everything in the room. Not the desk though. That was a right-down practical piece of furniture, that was. He fixed his eyes upon Miss Silver and said,

"I can't make up my mind. I thought I would come

and see you and have a talk. I was told about you by Mr. Grimshaw. I have just had a matter of business with him, and he recommended you. Very highly."

Miss Silver had settled herself in her favourite chair on the other side of the hearth. She recalled the Grimshaw case, a simple affair but one which had necessitated very delicate handling. She smiled and said,

"I have very pleasant recollections of Mr. Grimshaw. I hope that he is well?"

Mr. Mottingley said, "Yes—yes—" with an air of not thinking what he was saying. And then he came to the point. He leaned forward, crushed his great hands together, and said,

"My wife and I, we've got a boy—the only one that lived. We lost three, but this one lived. He is twenty-three now—old enough to be putting away childish things and getting down to the business of living. But he's been a disappointment."

Miss Silver had taken her knitting-bag from the table beside her and had extracted a baby's vest of a delicate pink shade. She paused for a moment now and said,

"In what way, Mr. Mottingley?"

"He doesn't take things seriously. I am a religious man, Miss Silver. Jimmy was brought up to be religious, but that's one way he's been a disappointment. And I wouldn't have you think that he was spoiled. We realize our duty in that respect. Many's the time we've been tempted to pass over a fault because he was the only one we had, but we've hardened ourselves for his good—" He came to a stop because he couldn't go on.

Miss Silver spoke gently.

"And what is the trouble now, Mr. Mottingley?"

"He's been accused of something he never did. Look, Miss Silver, I'm not one to cover up any faults my son may have. God knows he's got enough to answer for— I'm not saying he hasn't. He carried on with this girl, that's bad enough. But if you ask me to believe that he went down to Hazeldon Heath and murdered her, I say that I don't believe it. And if you knew Jimmy you wouldn't believe it either."

A light broke on Miss Silver. She had placed the name of Mottingley, and the whole story sprang to her mind. If she had not been so taken up with Gladys's affair she would have got there sooner. Jimmy Mottingley—that was the name of the young man in the Hazeldon Heath murder case, and this was his father. Her expression became even graver than before.

"One minute, Miss Silver. Will you read this letter before you say anything? It will tell you why I have come to you."

He handed her over a letter in a thick square envelope. As she took it, a memory stirred in her. She unfolded the letter which it contained, and the memory which it conveyed became clearer and stronger. It was a long time since she had seen Miss Twisledon's writing, but as she read the letter she was back across the years which had elapsed since she had last seen her. She looked up and inclined her head.

"I remember Miss Twisledon," she said. "She was a most dependable woman."

The rather unusual phrase struck Mr. Mottingley as appropriate. He said,

"Yes, she is that," and continued, "Would you be so good as to read what she says?"

Miss Silver turned back to the letter in her hand—

My dear Mr. & Mrs. Mottingley,

I am writing without any delay at all to say that I don't believe a word of it—about Jimmy, I mean of course. That is to say, I can believe that he got into trouble with the girl. I remember her of course, and a determined, bold-faced piece she was. I never liked her, and I see no reason to pretend that I did, just because she has got herself murdered. What I am *quite sure* of is that Jimmy didn't do it. As you know, he was one of my boys in Sunday School, and what I didn't know about them all wasn't worth knowing. Jimmy's faults were plain enough—I don't need to tell you about them. But that he would strike a young woman down and strangle her is a thing that I find quite impossible to believe. And impossible things don't happen. Now, will you be guided by me? I urge you very strongly to get into touch with Miss Silver, 15 Montague Mansions, S.W. You will remember the horrible affair of the Poisoned Caterpillars and my connection with it. It was Miss Silver who exposed the whole plot and saved an innocent family from a most distressing accusation. I can never say enough for the support and comfort she afforded me during a time of the deepest anxiety. Do get in touch with her. Show her this letter if you want to. I think she will remember me. She sent me a very kind message a little while ago by the Ridleys, whom you will remember. They met her in the Midlands, where she was staying with a niece.

Yours very sincerely,
Kate Twisledon

Miss Silver finished the letter and handed it back to Mr. Mottingley.

"I remember Miss Twisledon perfectly," she said. "I think I should trust her judgment, unless she has changed very much."

"I have known her for twenty years, and she hasn't changed at all," said Mr. Mottingley. "A fair wonder with boys, that was what she was. She's gone to nurse an elderly relative, and she's very much missed in the church, I can tell you that. And now will you listen to me? About this affair—Jimmy went down to Hazeldon on Saturday. He was going to see this girl—he had an appointment with her. *But* he started late. He started late because my wife called out to him just as he was about to leave the house, and she did that because an old friend had come in—one that had known Jimmy as a boy. She had moved away, and she was back on a visit, and my wife wanted her to see him. Well, it was half past six before he got away, and that they can both swear to. His story is that he drove down to Hazeldon and up on to the Heath. He left his car and came back to some gorse bushes near the road, which was the place she had set for them to meet. Well, he walked up and down for a bit, and he wondered whether she had gone because he was late. And he thought that wouldn't be like her. And he was quite right, it wouldn't. A more determined young woman I never set eyes on, and that's the truth. I don't say it excuses Jimmy for what he did, but I do say that she asked for it, and got nothing but what she asked for."

Miss Silver's eyes were upon his face. They had a very keen look.

"Mr. Mottingley," she said, "are you justifying murder?"

"*I!* Miss Silver, what do you mean? I'm telling you the sort of girl she was!"

She watched him closely. There was no doubt that he was badly shocked.

He said, "No—no. I don't know what I said to give you any such impression. Jimmy has been sinful enough, God knows, but he wouldn't do murder. Look here, Miss Silver, there are some that could do it if they were wrought up. And there are others that couldn't.

Now Jimmy's one of them. I swear it, and I'm not one to swear lightly."

Miss Silver said, "I see that I misunderstood you. If you will go over what has passed, you will, I think, agree that there were grounds for my mistake."

He said very earnestly, "Miss Silver, if I believed that Jimmy had killed that girl I shouldn't be here now asking you to get him free. I should be telling him that he'd got to face the consequences of his own act." A scarlet flush passed over his face. "It would be hard to do, but I'd be doing it. Thank God I haven't got to. He's a sinner, and he'll suffer for his sin. But he's not liable to the law. That I say, and that I'll stick to. Will you help me to prove it?"

Miss Silver looked at the massive face with its scarlet flush. She looked at the great hands clenched until the knuckles showed as white as bone. She said,

"Yes, Mr. Mottingley."

CHAPTER 24

Miss Silver was on her way to Hazeldon. She had to see the prisoner, and she wished also to see the place where the tragedy had happened, and to make such local enquiries as seemed good to her. As far as the first of these objects went, she had, paradoxically, deferred it to the end, since she wished to examine the scene of the crime and acquaint herself with all local details first, and Jimmy had been removed to the prison of the county town. She left the train and was looking about her for a cab, when a familiar voice hailed her.

"Miss Silver! And what might you be doing here?"

She turned with a smile to greet a very old friend, Detective Inspector Frank Abbott.

"I imagine that I am on the same business as you are," she said.

Frank Abbott contemplated her with something approaching dismay.

"My dear ma'am, you don't mean to tell me that you are in on this murder case!"

Miss Silver's head rose a little.

"If by 'this murder case' you mean the charge against young Mr. Mottingley, I certainly mean it."

Frank groaned in spirit.

"He did it, you know. Went too far, and when she threatened him with exposure he struck out."

Miss Silver moved towards the entrance to the station.

"That is your opinion?" she said.

He nodded briefly.

"Oh, yes. And it will be yours, too, when you have seen the evidence. It's all as plain as a pikestaff. I'm sorry you've let yourself in for it. But if you're on your way to Hazeldon Heath, let me give you a lift. I'm going there, too."

Miss Silver accepted the lift. It was a great advantage to have a foot in the other camp. She did not put it in quite this way, but that is what it amounted to. As they drove towards the Heath, she received a picture of the case against Jimmy Mottingley. It looked black enough, she could not deny that. She seized on the one point in Jimmy's favour.

"No one knew that they were meeting," she said. "Then why, if he had killed the girl, did he not make off? His car was just up the road. He could have been at a considerable distance from the spot, but instead he waits about and positively invites the attention of a passing cyclist."

"Oh, my dear ma'am, this is a boy! He has killed the girl in a moment of madness and he loses his head. He is distraught—doesn't know what he is doing. It's common enough." He shrugged. "Boy makes a fool of himself and takes the quickest way out. When it's done he's sorry—bitterly sorry and ashamed. The girl seems to have been a hard piece. I daresay she taunted him."

"Nevertheless," said Miss Silver gravely, "he stepped out into the road and hailed the farmer. His story is that he found the girl dead."

Frank Abbott shrugged his shoulders.

"He had an appointment with her—he admits that. She is there first. He was late. He admits to that—says his mother had a visitor and kept him to see her. Well, there's the makings of a row. He comes late and she has been waiting there for nearly an hour. Do you suppose she was in a very sweet temper?"

She said gravely, "I suppose not."

"From what we have collected about the girl, I should say that she wasn't. They have a row, and he knocks her down and then strangles her."

Miss Silver turned to him with a look of attention.

"Say that again, Frank."

"He knocks her out with a blow on the temple and then strangles her."

"That is what happened?"

"That is what happened."

"I did not know that. Do you not see that it makes all the difference? A young man not given to violence might conceivably strike an initial blow, but I find it quite impossible to believe that he would follow up that first blow with such determination that death would be inflicted. I have only had the elder Mr. Mottingley's account of what happened, and he was so much distressed that I left the details for the moment. I knew that I should get them, and probably with less bias, when I came down here. If there was a first blow, I find it impossible to believe that Jimmy Mottingley was the murderer."

Frank Abbott turned his head for a moment. He knew his Miss Silver very well. If she said she found it impossible to believe a thing, he might not share her view but he respected it.

"Well then, we know where we are," he said. "I'm sorry we're not on the same side, but what have you?"

Miss Silver's expression deepened from gravity to reproof.

"My dear Frank," she said, "antagonism between those who are seeking the truth is an impossibility. I am not for Jimmy Mottingley, neither are you against him. We are both, I hope, earnestly determined to seek for the truth of the matter, lay blame where it should be laid, and keep that open mind which alone can discern the truth."

Frank, feeling quite unable to reply to this formidable peroration, was thankful to have come in sight of the two houses half way up the hill.

"Here we are," he said. "The first house is Miss Danesworth's. The next one is Mrs. Merridew's. The murdered girl was her cousin, and was staying with her. I don't mind telling you that Mrs. Merridew is a tough proposition."

"Miss Caroline Danesworth?" enquired Miss Silver turning an interested face upon Frank.

"I believe so. Don't tell me you know her!"

"I had the pleasure of meeting her last year. She was a friend of Mrs. Lucius Bellingdon's. You will remember her as Mrs. Scott."*

He nodded.

"A very charming person. Well, well, do we see her first? Or do you wish to make your enquiries privately?

*The Listening Eye

In which case I have an errand to Mrs. Merridew."

"That I think will be better." Miss Silver smiled graciously and got out. "I do not know at all how long I shall be. Perhaps we should say good-bye."

"No, I don't think so. I'll give you a little time, and then I'll come in. Mrs. Merridew is an acidulated person. I have an errand to her, but it won't take me very long."

As Miss Silver stood knocking at the door of Miss Danesworth's house, her thoughts recurred to the strange case of the Listening Eye. She had met Lucius Bellingdon and his wife occasionally since the time when the whole house-party had been shaken by the strange events which led up to the tragedy on Emberley Hill and the deaths of Clay Masterson and Moira Herne. Sally Foster, too, now Mrs. David Moray. She had seen her and her young husband at her friends', the Charles Morays. It really was a very small world, and it was pleasant to meet again, and in happier circumstances, those with whom one had lived and worked during cloudy and storm-threatening days.

She knocked for the second time, and the door was opened to her by a young girl of a most charming appearance. This would have been Miss Silver's own description of her. She had dark curling hair and very clear brown eyes.

Miss Silver said, "I wonder if I can see Miss Danesworth. My name is Silver—Miss Maud Silver."

CHAPTER 25

Jenny led the way to the sitting-room. Under her bright look of welcome there was something disturbed. Miss Silver wondered whether she had known the dead girl well. Two girls of very much the same age, living next door to one another—no, the dead girl was three or four years older, but that was no great matter. It would be natural enough for them to be friends. In any case the shock of this sudden and tragic death would be bound to affect a sensitive girl.

Miss Silver had remained standing. She turned as the door opened and Miss Danesworth came in.

"My dear Miss Silver, I am so pleased to see you!" she said.

Miss Silver smiled and responded,

"But I must tell you that I am here on business."

"This Mottingley case—it's dreadful, isn't it? I met the boy in the summer. I can't believe that he would commit a brutal murder. He always seemed such a quiet lad—gentle and rather repressed. But do sit down, won't you?"

Miss Silver seated herself. She said,

"You interest me very much. I should make it clear at once that I am here on behalf of the Mottingleys. They have engaged me to go over the case, and to see what can be said for the young man who is accused."

Miss Danesworth was silent for a moment. Then she said,

"I don't know that you ought to ask me about it, for if ever I disliked a girl in my life it was that unfortunate girl who was murdered."

Miss Silver looked at her gravely.

"Miss Danesworth, will you give your own account of what happened as far as the circumstances are known to you? I am not asking you for a weighed and balanced account. I want simply to know how the whole thing seemed to you. I am not asking you to be fair, or to weigh your words. I want to know just how the affair struck you at the time. Will you do that for me?"

Miss Danesworth met Miss Silver's eyes, and experienced what so many people had experienced in similar circumstances. She felt a great many things that she could not have put into words. The truth—that was what mattered, and it was the only thing that did matter. The conventions did not matter. The only thing that mattered was the truth. She said,

"Yes, I'll tell you the truth as far as I know it. But I don't know very much—" She paused for a moment and then went on. "I have a nephew staying with me. His name is Richard Forbes. He is in love with the girl who let you in. She is Jenny Forbes, and she is a very distant cousin of his. They are not engaged, and there is nothing given out. I know that you will be very discreet—they have only known each other for ten days. I don't ask any questions, but I can see how things are with them. But that's another story. This girl who was murdered came down to stay on Friday—last Friday. She came in with Mrs. Merridew—that is her mother's cousin who lives next door—and she talked to Richard all the time, not to Jenny. She was that sort of girl. I remember she talked about the children in the carriage coming down. They ate peppermints, and she said there was something sickening about children who ate in trains. Oh, I don't know—I didn't like the way she talked—that's all. She was just trying to make up to Richard. And he did rather lead her on, I suppose. You know the way men do when they don't really like a girl. Jenny was angry about it—I could see that. I think they quarrelled afterwards—but you won't be interested in that."

"I am interested in everything," said Miss Silver. "Pray go on."

Caroline was silent for a moment or two. Then she said,

"You want to know everything, so I'll tell you. Jenny

went to bed early, and Richard talked to me. He said he was in earnest about Jenny, and that he had rushed things. Apparently he had kissed her, and she had turned as white as a sheet and gone out of the room. Well, in the morning they were just beginning to talk, when Miriam came in. She said she had come with a message from Mrs. Merridew to ask them to lunch. And Richard said he couldn't come because he was going over to see his friend Tommy Risdall. Tommy is in the Navy, and his people live at Tillingdon, which is about five miles away. Well, Miriam asked if Tommy wouldn't come too, and when Richard said he was afraid that was out of the question she said, 'What about tomorrow?' And when Richard said that would be Sunday, she said did that matter? And he said yes, it did, and that the only excuse for not going to church was a bed of sickness. I wasn't there, you know, but I've heard about it since. So then she said, 'What about Monday?' and he said, 'All right,' and she went away. Nothing more happened until the evening. Richard was away. I left Jenny here with a book and went to see a neighbour who isn't well. When I got back we had tea and just sat on talking until it got dark. Then Miriam came. She said her cousin had gone to a meeting. She said wasn't Richard back—she wanted to see him. And I said he wasn't back yet, and that I never expected him until I saw him. And she said, 'That's not very convenient, is it?' Then she said to Jenny that it wasn't very complimentary to her his going off for the day like that. She said she wouldn't feel flattered if she was visiting in a house and the young man made off. Oh, I suppose I oughtn't to say it now that she's dead in that dreadful way, but she really was a most odious girl. Well, then she sat there talking about the last place she had been in, and how sorry they were to lose her. And then suddenly she looked at the clock and asked if it was right.

When I said that it was, she jumped up and said she must go. She said to tell Richard that she wanted to see him, 'Not tonight—I'm doing something else. But if he likes he can come round in the morning.' And she was out of the door whilst she was speaking. And gone."

Miss Silver was silent for a moment. Then she said,

"When did your nephew come home?"

"About half an hour later."

"Which way did he come?"

"The opposite way—through the village. Miss Silver—"

"Yes, Miss Danesworth?"

"You're not thinking—you can't think . . . Oh—"

Miss Silver looked at her gravely.

"What have I said to disturb you, Miss Danesworth?"

The door opened and Richard came in. Miss Silver saw a good-looking young man. He was tall and straight, and just now he was very grave.

Miss Danesworth said with a noticeable effort, "My nephew Richard Forbes—Miss Silver."

Miss Silver bowed. Richard came forward. Miss Danesworth went on speaking. She had command of her voice now. She said,

"Miss Silver has come down here to get as much information as possible about Miriam's death. She is a private investigator. Forgive me, Miss Silver, but it is better for me to be plain."

Miss Silver smiled.

"There is nothing to forgive, Miss Danesworth. I have no wish to pass for any other than I am."

Richard looked from one to the other. He had heard of Miss Silver, and now he saw her. He could hardly believe his eyes. She really was incredible. He took in the neat elderly clothes, the hat with its bows of watered silk ribbon, the neat but rather worn black coat, the black kid gloves by no means new, and the speculation just touched his mind as to how he would have described her. Not as a detective—that was certain. And then quite suddenly she was looking at him and he changed his mind. Her eyes went straight through him and out on the other side. Nonsense, of course, but the feeling that they were doing so was very strong and persistent. He felt as if she were reading his very soul. Whatever was there to see, she would see it. He was thankful with all his heart that, whatever there was, it wasn't murder. It had only lasted a minute, but he knew that he would never forget it. And now she was smiling at him. She said,

"You have come to help us, I hope. Miss Danesworth and I are old acquaintances. It is very pleasant to meet her again, but I wish, as she does, that the circumstances were of a less tragic nature."

Richard said, "Yes." And then, "My aunt has told you what we know?"

"I think so. You did not see Miriam Richardson at all that evening?"

Richard looked her straight in the eyes.

"No, I did not see her. I gather that she came here to see me and waited for some time. Then suddenly she looked at the clock and said she could not wait any longer. She said, 'Tell Richard I want to see him, will you? Not tonight—I'm doing something else. But if he'd like to he can come round in the morning.' That's right, isn't it?" He turned to Miss Danesworth.

"Yes, it was just like that, and she was out of the door before either of us could answer her. She gave me the impression that she was afraid of being late for an appointment."

"Miss Forbes was in the room?"

Miss Danesworth said, "Yes, Jenny was here."

"Then perhaps I might see her—"

"Oh, yes."

Miss Danesworth was quite calm again. Looking at her, it seemed impossible that a momentary turn of speech should have brought her to the verge of breaking down. Miss Silver discerned compassionately that it was Richard for whom she had feared—Richard who was the weak point in her armor. She remembered what she had heard from Mrs. Lucius Bellingdon—"She lost the man whom she was engaged to in the war, and then her sister and brother-in-law. They were killed in a car crash—or an air raid, I forget which. She took their boy and has brought him up splendidly. He is in the Army—a very nice fellow, about five-and-twenty."

Miss Danesworth had gone to the door. She opened it and called, "Jenny!"

Miss Silver understood. Jenny was not to be biased. She was to come and answer whatever Miss Silver cared to ask her.

Jenny came in.

"This is Miss Silver. She wants to ask you about Miriam's visit on Saturday."

Jenny stood there. She didn't understand. She looked at Richard, and then back at Miss Silver.

"Miriam? She came here to see Richard. How much do you want?"

"All of it, I think, my dear."

Jenny stood there. She repeated that last conversation with Miriam. She was rather pale, but she had herself well in hand. Richard watched her all the time. When she came to where Miriam looked at the clock, her tone altered. She said,

"She looked at the clock suddenly, and she said, 'Is that right?' Miss Danesworth said, 'It keeps excellent time,' and Miriam said, 'Oh—then I must go. Tell Richard I want to see him, will you? Not tonight—I'm doing something else. But if he'd like to he can come round in the morning.' And she was out of the door almost before she had finished speaking. That's all. We—we didn't see her again."

CHAPTER 26

Frank Abbott came in on that. He was very much on duty, and he took Miss Silver away as soon as possible. It wasn't until they were in the car that he relaxed.

"Well?" he said. "Did you have a satisfactory visit?"

"I think so, Frank. Are you taking me to see Jimmy Mottingley?"

"I will if you would like me to. It would probably make things easier for you."

Miss Silver gave him a warmly sympathetic look.

"That is indeed kind. I shall be most grateful."

"Well, how did it go? Or shouldn't I ask?"

"I think that you should not ask me, but I will tell you. The thing that struck me when I asked to see the young girl Jenny Forbes was that Miss Danesworth went to the door and called for her. She wished me, I think, to understand that she was not putting words into her mouth. Jenny Forbes gave me an account of the dead girl's visit which was practically identical with what Miss Danesworth had already told me. The important thing about both these accounts was that they represent Miriam Richardson as looking at the clock suddenly and asking if it was right. Miss Danesworth said yes, it was, and Miriam said, 'Then I must go. Tell Richard I want to see him, will you? Not tonight—I'm doing something else. But if he'd like to, he can come round in the morning.' In my opinion this definitely contradicts any idea that it was Richard Forbes whom she was expecting to meet."

Frank Abbott threw her a sharp look.

"That had occurred to you?"

"Yes."

"And you regard it as a wash-out?"

"My dear Frank!"

He laughed.

"Language to be expressive must be, shall we say, apt."

"You may, and do, say what you like as long as you do not attribute your slang expressions to me."

He laughed.

"Oh, that was it, was it? I retract and apologize."

They came into Colborough half an hour later. Miss Silver had been silent for the greater part of the way. A good deal would depend upon what she thought of Jimmy Mottingley. His father's trust in him might not be justified. She was very well aware of the turns and twists possible to a man's conscience. Mr. Mottingley appeared to be under no illusions with regard to his son—but there were reservations in all of us. He could admit the utmost culpability in one direction whilst strenuously denying it in another. She thought that she would know when she saw Jimmy whether she could take his case or not. To justify the guilty was a role she would not undertake. She remained abstracted during the drive, and Frank respected her silence.

When they had arrived at the prison she left the talking to Frank Abbott. He was an old friend of the Governor's, and the way was smoothed for her. She was shown into a light, bare room with a long table and a chair at either end of it. Presently a warder came in with Jimmy Mottingley, whom he escorted to the chair at the opposite end of the table, and when Jimmy had seated himself, the warder withdrew to the door, paused there for a moment to say, "I'll be just outside if you want me, madam," and withdrew. The upper portion of the door being of glass, they were still under observation, but they could not be overheard.

Miss Silver turned back to the table, and to Jimmy Mottingley at the other end of it. She saw a boyish looking young man, fair haired and blue eyed, the kind of youth who in any average family would be rather a spoiled child. She wondered whether Mr. Mottingley had been as firm with his son as he declared.

And then Jimmy Mottingley was looking at her with a kind of bravado and saying,

"Why have you come?"

Miss Silver did not answer him for a moment. She looked at him, and saw the signs of weakness, the signs of pain. That the boy was on the verge of a breakdown was obvious. She smiled reassuringly and said,

"I have come at your father's request to try and help you."

He laughed.

"At my father's request! Do you know what he thinks? He thinks I did it. He sat there and lectured me. He said he would pay for my defence, but I mustn't imagine that I would get off the punishment due to me. And he talked about God's law which couldn't be broken with impunity."

Miss Silver said with composure, "Mr. Mottingley, I do not think that you understood your father. . . . No, one minute, please. You must try to control yourself, or we shall be interrupted. The warder on the other side of that door will only remain where he is whilst you conform to the regulations. If he has any reason to suppose that you are becoming violent he will feel it his duty to come in, and you will be taken away to your cell again. I must beg of you to preserve calm."

Jimmy stared at her. He shuddered and said in a whisper,

"Calm—Oh, my God! Do you know what it is like to be suspected of the one thing on earth that you could never do? Do you know what it's like?"

"I can only know what you tell me. Would you like to go back to last Saturday, and to tell me just what happened?"

"Yes—yes—I'll tell you." He rummaged in his pocket and produced a handkerchief. He blew his nose and said, "You want what happened on Saturday? I had an appointment with Miriam—you know that. She—she wanted to see me. I didn't want to come. I knew what she wanted—oh, yes, I knew. But I never saw her. I mean, she was dead when I got there, because my mother had a visitor she wanted me to see and they kept me. When I did get there it was nearly an hour late, and I knew how angry she'd be. She had said to meet her on the Heath just up the hill from where she was staying. We had met there before. There's a clump of gorse close to the road—she said she'd meet me there. Well, I ran on past it and left the car, and then I came back. There wasn't any sign of her. I was nearly an hour late, and I wondered if she'd given me up and gone away, and I wondered what I'd better do. Now that I was there, it seemed as if I'd got to see her. You know how it is, you screw yourself up to something, and it doesn't seem as if you *could* go away and wait for a week and come back and do it all over again."

"Yes, I can understand that. Go on, Mr. Mottingley."

A shudder passed over Jimmy. He was getting to the point which pursued him into his dreams. His hand which gripped the handkerchief shook. He said in a failing voice,

"I thought perhaps she hadn't waited. I went behind

the bushes—and she was there—" The words trembled away. He sat looking down at his shaking hand and the handkerchief in it. But he didn't see them. He saw only what he had seen that night—the circle of light cast by his torch, and within it Miriam's face horribly distorted. He went on speaking in a dead tone without emphasis. "She was there. But she was dead. She had been strangled. I ran out on to the road. There was a bicycle coming. I waved and called out. It was Mr. Fulbrook. I didn't know his name. I called out, and he stopped. I told him that I had come there to meet Miriam and found her dead. He came round with me—round the bushes—and he saw her. She was quite dead. Then he asked a lot of questions. I don't remember what I said. It doesn't matter, does it? I can't remember anything about that. But we got into my car up the road, and he drove—my hands were shaking too much. And we went to the police station. And everyone took it for granted that I had done it. But I didn't. I didn't, I tell you. I *couldn't* have! Even to think about doing it makes me feel sick and shaky. I tell you I've thought and thought about it. I've thought of what I could have done, and of what I could never, never do, and it always comes to the same thing, I *couldn't* kill anyone. There are things you know you can do, and things you know you can't do. This is one of those things—I just couldn't do it."

He bent forward, his hands gripping the edge of the table, and said in a smothered voice, "Look here, I'll tell you something. I've never told anyone, but I'll tell you because it proves what I've been saying. I suppose I ought to be ashamed of it—but I don't know. I can't kill anything—it makes me sick even to think of it—it does really. And Miriam—she was so much alive—so sure about everything. I didn't really like her, you know." He lifted his head and looked at Miss Silver. It was a puzzled look and it touched her oddly. "That seems a queer thing to say, but I didn't, you know. When I was away from her I used to think how dreadful it would be to be married to her, to have to sit down to meals with her every day, to—to—sleep—" He stopped, reddening, and brushed his hands across his eyes. "I used to think of all those things. And then when I saw her again she—she seemed to—to have the upper hand. I think she had a very strong will. I haven't. I used to think of what I was going to say to her about—about breaking it off—and it went quite well as long as she wasn't there. But when she *was,* all the things I had thought of to say seemed to be gone. She made plans about our getting married. When I said that my father would never allow it she laughed—she just laughed, and she said that he wouldn't be asked. I did try to make her understand, but it was no use. She just went on talking. When I said that my father would never forgive us if we got married in a registry office like she said, she just laughed. It was no good. She had a picture in her mind of us doing just what we wanted to—or what she wanted to, and she just didn't listen. That's what my father didn't understand. I don't think he has ever met anyone like Miriam—I never had before. If she wanted a thing she got it—somehow." The handkerchief came up to his eyes, and behind that friendly screen he broke down completely.

Miss Silver sat and waited. This was not a story that would make a good impression in a court of law. What the judge and the jury would see in it was the case of the weak creature driven too far, the young man who couldn't kill a spider or any creeping thing suddenly maddened to the point of defending himself from the horrifying prospect of a lifetime to be spent with Miriam Richardson. He had said things which would support this point of view. Miriam had gone to the place where she had been found dead to keep an appointment with him. No one else knew of this appointment. There had been no robbery, no other violence. She had been hit on the temple and then strangled. Miss Silver did not believe that Jimmy Mottingley, however maddened, would have knocked a young woman out and then proceeded to strangle her. But would a jury in a murder trial take the same merciful view? She thought not. It would be a difficult case, but she could not refuse to take it. She spoke in a cheerful voice and with a greater certainty of manner than she could really feel.

"Mr. Mottingley, I will take your case. Now there are one or two questions I should like to ask you."

CHAPTER 27

Mac Forbes had spent four days of what he himself described as "plain hell." He had done murder, and as he had learned, he had done it to no purpose. The girl whom he had killed was not Jenny. By what extraordinary accident she had been where he had expected to find Jenny it was fruitless to enquire. What mattered was that she had come out of the house in which Jenny was staying, and she had gone slowly up the road and on to the Heath. It had never crossed his mind for an instant that there could have been any mistake. If he had seen Jenny with his own eyes in the brightly shining light of day he could not have felt more deeply convinced as he drove away from Hazeldon Heath that he had killed her. He was not sorry. The thing was necessary, and it had been done. But he should have got back his note—that was where he had gone wrong. Thinking back on it after the first blind instinct of flight had asserted itself and had been expended, the possibilities emerged and he dwelt upon them. Jenny might have disregarded the instructions and torn the note up, or she might have done as he said and brought it with her. He regarded the two possibilities soberly. The third possibility that she might never have got the note at all did not enter his mind. He still thought of the girl he had killed as Jenny. The one piece of evidence that would connect him with her death was a half sheet of paper folded into a note. He remembered what he had put in it:

> Jenny, *don't say anything to anyone,* but come out and meet me up on the heath as soon as it is quite dark.
>
> > *Mac*
> > Bring this with you.

What he didn't remember—what he couldn't remember—was whether he had dated the note. He had the habit of dating things. Had he dated this? If he hadn't, it could be any old note written days ago—written before she left Alington House. Surely he would have thought of that and left the date a blank. But he couldn't remember.

The drive back to town was, if not enough punishment, yet a considerable first instalment. Sunday followed—a long, slow day. There was nothing in the papers. He had hardly expected that there would be. His mother rang up to know whether he was coming down. He said no rather curtly and rang off. He never remembered a week-end that passed so slowly. Yet by Sunday evening he had worked himself into a much calmer frame of mind. He was still thinking that he had killed Jenny, and he had won his way to thinking that she had got no more than her deserts. If she had stayed at Alington House, if she had married him, there wouldn't have been any need for him to take the risk of killing her. What had happened was entirely her own fault. If she had not run away in the middle of the night it would not have been necessary to kill her. He was not to blame for her obstinacy and her lack of all proper feeling. She was dead and out of his way. Everything would be all right. Jenny was dead.

Then Monday morning, and the papers with the unbelievable news—MURDER ON HAZELDON HEATH. He was expecting that, and read on. The paper dropped from his grasp. He hadn't killed Jenny. Jenny was alive. He had killed a stranger.

After a minute or two he picked up the paper again. There was something in his having killed a girl he had never heard of. He read all about her. She was Miriam Richardson, and she was the cousin of Mrs. Merridew whom he knew by name because she had a relation in Alingford—Miss Crampton, the late Vicar's daughter, for whom he had a strong detestation. Mrs. Merridew stayed there occasionally. He hadn't known that she was living at Hazeldon. There were too many old women in the world—that was a fact.

He went on reading about Miriam Richardson. She had gone up on to Hazeldon Heath to meet a man, one Jimmy Mottingley. A sense of her folly rushed upon him. Mrs. Merridew lived next door. What had possessed Miriam Richardson to come in where Jenny was before he arrived, and to leave the house in the dark to go up to the lonely Heath? What had possessed her? Well, he had only to read on to see. He read on. . . .

So the girl had a lover. That was who Jimmy Mottingley was. And he had arrived late, and he had killed her—killed her. Well, it made quite a good story, and quite a likely one. A girl with a hot temper would be pretty wild if she had had to wait three quarters of an hour or so on a dark deserted heath. It was a black empty place for a girl to wait.

A sense of its blackness and emptiness swept over him as he read. He crushed it down. It had nothing to do with him. None of it had anything to do with him. Miriam Richardson was nothing to him. It was Jenny whom he had meant to kill, and it was Jenny who was most damnably alive.

A cold rage possessed him. He had made a fool of himself—had run into the utmost danger and had gained nothing. And somewhere in all this welter of mistakes—somewhere there was the note that he had written to Jenny. he crumpled the newspaper together and stood up. Such a rage possessed him that he could have done murder at its bidding without a thought but the dominating impulse to kill. The keener, colder side of himself was alarmed. Alerted, it sprang back and took command. The rage subsided and reason held sway.

What must he do? That was what mattered now. That was all that mattered. He began to pace the room. What mattered most was the note. If he could only remember whether he had dated it or not—it had simply never occurred to him when he was writing it to think that Jenny would not do as he told her. He had that inflated sense of his own importance which is a little present in every young man who is the head of his family, and who has been flattered by an adoring mother and by the consciousness of his own talents.

As he paced the room he was not conscious of any remorse about Miriam's death. He regarded her as negligible. He had meant to kill Jenny, both because she stood in his way and because she had turned from him to a stranger. No, if it had been a stranger he would have borne it better. It was because Richard Alington Forbes had the name and the blood—because he had not been turned down for someone outside the family. He jerked away from that. He wouldn't think of that.

What you did not think of did not exist for you. Jenny did not exist. Jenny was dead—

The revulsion came—a cold, deadly revulsion. Jenny wasn't dead. Jenny was alive, and he would have to let her stay alive. It wouldn't be safe to kill her now—not for a long time. No use dwelling on that.

The note—what happened to it? He saw no reason to suppose that it had never reached her.

And the note lay in Dicky Pratt's pocket screwed up in a welter of the things boys carry in their pockets. No one had read it except Mac himself. There was no one to tell him that it was quite neatly and legibly dated in the top left-hand corner.

CHAPTER 28

By Saturday Mac had made up his mind that no harm was going to come of his unfortunate note. Either it had not reached Jenny, or, having reached her, she had decided to take no notice of it. He inclined to the second of these theories, and though it roused his anger it was definitely the more likely of the two. He would get even with her some day, but not now. And there would be no more killing. The game was not worth the candle. The week that had just gone by had taught him that. There were other ways, ingenious ones, of venting a grudge. Jenny should be sorry enough for having flouted him! His mind toyed with this idea and that. There would be time enough for everything. Meanwhile he could relax, taste relief, and stretch himself in the consciousness of safety.

He went down to Alington House on Saturday. Mrs.

Forbes looked up as he came in. He kissed her carelessly and went to stand in front of the fire. The day was a cold one for September, and he had driven fast.

"Any more news of Jenny?" he said.

Mrs. Forbes had been writing letters. She rose now and came to the fire.

"Jenny?" she said. "Why, my dear boy, haven't you heard? She has managed to get herself involved in a murder case—that's all."

"A murder case? Good heavens!"

Mrs. Forbes bent down and put another log on the fire.

"I told you she was at Hazeldon—I'm sure I did. Well, a girl who was staying next door was murdered, and they say that Jenny will be a witness at the trial, because the girl went straight from Miss Danesworth's house to meet the young man who murdered her."

"My dear Mother, this sounds interesting. Jenny would be rather good in the witness-box, I should think. What has she got to say about it?"

"Oh, just that the girl had dropped in to see them— that is, Jenny and Caroline Danesworth. They didn't know she was going to be murdered of course. I suppose they'll be wanted at the trial."

He said carelessly, "I can't think why."

"Oh, just to fix the time she left the house, I should think. I got a whole dose of it this morning in the village."

"The village? This village?"

"Oh well, I'm sure I told you about Mrs. Merridew being a cousin of Miss Crampton's. You remember?"

"Yes, I remember. A little squit of a thing with poison under a honeyed tongue."

"Yes, that's her. But don't let anyone hear you say it. Miss Crampton is very much respected." She made an impatient gesture.

Mac stooped down and adjusted the log.

"I saw something about it in the papers. I didn't really connect it with Jenny. Come to think of it, it's better for her to be away for a bit if she's going to be called up in a murder trial, though I don't mind betting that Meg and Joyce will get on to it."

"Good heavens, I hope not!"

He laughed.

"It's a wise parent who knows what his children are thinking about! Do you suppose that you *really* knew anything at all about Alan and me when we were that age?"

Mrs. Forbes felt a cold touch of fear, she didn't know why. The words were nothing, and the tone in which they were said was light enough, but something swept over her like a dark shadow. It was gone again almost before she had recognized it. It was nothing—nothing at all. She couldn't think why for a moment there had been that frightening blackness. In a revulsion of her feeling she laughed.

"My dear boy, how ridiculous that sounds!"

"Does it? I don't mind betting that what fathers and mothers don't know about their children would fill more books than what they think they do know. I could tell you all sorts of things." He pushed the log with his foot and a sudden flame shot up. "But I don't think I will. It might keep you awake at night."

Mrs. Forbes smiled rather vaguely. The mood that had touched her was so completely gone that she couldn't even remember it. She was thinking about Jenny. It was a very good thing that she should be away, with a murder trial coming on. Only if she hadn't been away she wouldn't have been connected with the murder at all. If she had still been in Alington House, this young Mottingley might have murdered Miriam Richardson without its being more than a paragraph in the papers as far as they were concerned. She had no knowledge, no instinct, to tell her that if Jenny had not left this house which was her home, Miriam Richardson would be alive and well, going about her own ill-natured affairs, and Jimmy Mottingley would be in no worse prison than was provided by his guilty conscience.

The door opened and there came into the room Meg, full of purpose. Mac was rather pleased to see her. He didn't really want to discuss Jenny with his mother, nor did he wish to talk about the girl whom he had killed. He felt a strong cold resentment against her for having deceived him. For she had deceived him, and she had done it knowingly. He had spoken Jenny's name before he struck, and it was because she had accepted his "Jenny—" that she was dead. He felt no remorse at all. She had asked for what she had got. She had pretended to be Jenny. Let her take the consequences.

He turned from the fire at the sound of the opening door and said, "Hullo, Meg!"

Meg was very pleased to see him. If he was in a good mood he could help her very much. Joyce was a fraidy cat. If she pulled it off she would crow over her. She ran up to Mac and took his hand. She must get in quick before Mother sent her away.

"Oh, Mac," she said, "I'm so glad you've come! Mother, if Mac says we can have the kitten, we can, can't we?"

Mac put out a hand to her.

"What's all this about a kitten?"

"It's Nurse's. Her cat had three kittens. They're the dearest little things, and she's saved the best one for us. Mother said she'd think about it. Oh, we do want it *so* much!"

Mac laughed. He had Meg's hands and was swinging her to and fro. Mrs. Forbes, watching them, thought how handsome he was, and how much like her family. The height, the fairness, they were all from her side. She forgot to be angry with Meg for bursting in. Her heart swelled with pride and devotion.

"Well, what about it? Are you going to have it—or not? What about it, Mother?"

Meg pulled her hands away from his and clasped them under her chin. She didn't speak. Some instinct told her not to. If Mac asked for the kitten she would get it, but if she asked herself—A creeping fear came over her. If she stayed quite, quite still and left Mac to talk, perhaps Mother would let her have the kitten. Perhaps—oh, perhaps—

"Well, what about it?" said Mac.

Mrs. Forbes gave the laugh which she kept for him.

"Oh, well—" she said. "But I won't have it till it is housetrained. Well, Meg, you may thank your brother Mac for that. Now go along back to the schoolroom. And I don't want to see you again."

Meg controlled her feelings. She had won! How she would crow over Joyce! But for now she must remember her manners. She said, "Thank you, Mac—thank you, Mother," and gave an exhibition performance of a grateful child leaving the parental presence.

But the moment she was outside and the door safely shut the decorum vanished. She gave a little skipping dance of satisfaction, and then away up the stairs with her. Bursting breathlessly into the schoolroom where Joyce was sitting rather gloomily dressing her old doll Madeline in the new clothes which Jenny had made for her, she danced right round the table, snatching at Madeline and making her dance too.

"I've got him, I've got him!" she chanted. "He's my own furry purry one. He's not yours at all. Because you were a fraidy cat. You wouldn't go down and ask for him. But I did—I did. And who do you think was there?"

"I don't know," said Joyce. "I wish you would give Madeline back, Meg. She doesn't like being jumped about like that."

"She does! You do, don't you, Madeline? There— she said 'Yes!' I heard her! And she and Patrick will be great friends. I'm going to call him Patrick."

"You said you were all along. Madeline's tired. I wish you'd let her rest."

"All right, here you are. She's rather a stupid really. What has she got to be tired about?"

"She doesn't know," said Joyce in a mournful voice. "There doesn't have to be a reason for being tired. I'm tired often—I'm tired now."

Meg stopped dancing round the table.

"Oh, Joicey," she said, "are you really? You're not ill-tired, are you?"

Two big tears rolled down Joyce's cheeks.

"I d-don't th-think so," she said.

Meg went down on her knees beside the chair and hugged her.

"Oh, Joicey, don't be ill again! I don't want you to be ill. Patrick shall be yours and mine. Perhaps he'll be a little bit more mine than yours, because I did get him for us. Oh, Joyce, don't cry! And we'll think of all the things we can do with him. Shall we?"

Downstairs in the sitting-room Mrs. Forbes was saying,

"Have you seen Alan at all this week?"

"Alan? No, I haven't. He was staying with those friends of his, wasn't he?"

She said, "Yes." She was frowning. "He's gone off with the son. It's all very sudden, and I don't know what to think of it."

"How do you mean, he's gone off?"

"I mean just that." She went over to the writing-table and stood there turning over the papers on it. "No, I can't find his letter. I must have torn it up. Yes, I remember I did. I was so provoked. But now I've had time to think about it I'm not at all sure it isn't the best thing." She came back to the fire. "Mac, did you ever think Alan was in love with that girl?"

He laughed with genuine amusement.

"With Jenny? My dear Mother! Of course he was! Everyone in the house knew about it!"

"Not Jenny!" Her voice had a startled sound.

"I should think Jenny most of all. You needn't worry—she turned him down, you know."

"Are you sure? How do you know?"

He laughed again.

"I have my methods. Well, I mean it was fairly obvious. You must have been very taken up not to be on to it yourself."

His words struck home. She frowned. It was true—when he was there she had no eyes or thoughts for anyone else. For a moment she had a clear-cut vision of herself concentrated on the one image. She was not a stupid woman. She knew what she was doing. She knew very well that of the four children of her body only the eldest, only Mac, was the child of her heart. Alan, Meg and Joyce were physical accidents. In Alan's case, he had been so linked with Mac that the realization of this fact had been, as it were, veiled. Mac and Alan were linked. For Meg and Joyce she felt only a decent family feeling. She would bring them up, and she would marry them off, and that would be the end of it. Meg was going to be pretty. Joyce . . . Too early to tell.

She came back to Alan. Just as well for him to be out of the way for a bit if he really had this stupid feeling for

Jenny. She supposed she should have thought of the possibility before. She said so.

"I suppose I ought to have thought of it, but I didn't. I oughtn't to have had her here."

Mac laughed.

"Oh, there's no harm done. If he wasn't in love with her, it would have been someone else. Where's he going?"

"I don't know. He didn't really say—I don't think he cared. I think the other boy wanted to go to Italy. He said they'd write when they'd settled on a plan."

CHAPTER 29

Kathy Lingbourne had made up her mind. She was twenty-two, and she had taken her mother's place at seventeen. Her father was a hardworking solicitor with very little time to spare for his children. In the five years that had passed since Kathy had become mistress of the house all her endeavours had been to supply her dead mother's place, and to keep her father from being worried. She wasn't the eldest of the family. That was Len. Then came Kathy, and David, and Heather. They were all close together. Heather, the youngest, was just eighteen. Jimmy Mottingley had been Len's friend to start with, and she had taken to him at once because he was shy and had very nice manners—much nicer than Len's. That was the worst of not being the eldest at home. She could manage David and Heather, but when Len wanted to take his own way he took it, and if she said anything he would laugh and say he was two years older than she was, and what about it? Jimmy Mottingley wasn't like that. He was gentle and rather shy, and he was frightfully afraid of his father and of his mother. Of course they were *grim*—Kathy admitted that. But he was their only child, and you ought not to be afraid. In a muddled sort of way she thought that to be afraid like that was *wrong,* and she dimly saw that the more afraid you were, the more harm it did, not only to you, but to the people you were afraid of.

Latterly she hadn't seen quite so much of Jimmy, and she knew why. She had met Miriam with Jimmy, and Miriam had made her blood boil—she really had. She spoke to Jimmy exactly as if she owned him body and soul, and no one had the right to do that with anyone else. And Jimmy had changed, she saw that at once. And here Kathy blamed herself very much because she had thought about herself and not about Jimmy. She had let herself feel hurt, and she had shown it not only to Miriam but to Jimmy himself. She could still see his look as she turned away, and she could still hear what Miriam had said, not loud but in that dreadful kind of whisper which carries more than anything, "What a frightful girl!" It was after that that Jimmy stopped coming to the house. And it was after that that Kathy began to find out what Jimmy meant to her.

It was no use of course. Jimmy had gone. Miriam had got him. And it wouldn't have mattered if she had been a different kind of girl. Jimmy wanted someone who was kind and firm, and who didn't care for herself but only for him. And Miriam wasn't like that—she wasn't like that at all. She was hard and self-seeking. She would be very bad for Jimmy. Kathy went through a bitter time of unhappiness, but no one knew about it. And then just when she had got through the worst of it there came that dreadful Monday morning. Len was down first for a wonder. She had come into the room and found him frowning over the paper. She had only to shut her eyes and the scene sprang to life. She came in with the eggs and bacon, and Len turned sharply and said, "Oh, I say, Kathy, here's a dreadful thing— Jimmy's got taken up for murder! That beastly girl he used to go about with, she got herself bumped off, and they say Jimmy did it—*Jimmy!* Why, he couldn't kill a mouse!"

Kathy saw herself standing quite still. Looking back at it, she saw the whole scene just as if two other people were acting it on the stage. She saw herself putting down the eggs and bacon slowly, carefully, and then turning round to face what was coming to her. She didn't know what she said. Her memory stuck fast on that one dreadful minute when she knew what had happened, and that Jimmy was accused of murder. It was quite unbelievable, but it had happened.

In the time since then she had gone about her usual jobs. They were not the kind of things you can leave undone. And gradually she began to know what she would do. Jimmy was at Colborough. She would go there and she would try to see him. If they wouldn't let her, she would try and find out what she must do to get permission. She wasn't going to ask her father—not yet. When she found out what she must do she would think about whether she would tell him or not. Just at present that would be enough. Things were like that with her— she could see one thing to do and she could do it. When it was done she would think about the next thing, but not till then.

It was Mrs. Crowley's day for coming in, so she saw her and said that she would be out for the day.

"Mr. Len and my father will be out, but David and Heather will be home to lunch. Just tell them that I've gone out for the day, and I don't know when I shall be back."

Mrs. Crowley nodded and smiled.

"Do you good to have a day out. Too much sticking

to your job's a mistake, that's what I say. Do you good it will to get right away from all of it. You're only young once. You get on with it and enjoy yourself, that's what I say."

Mrs. Crowley left a little warmth in her mind. She was a kind woman.

She took the train to Colborough. It was Monday morning. She didn't remember when she had come away on a Monday morning before. She had come away, and she had left everything. She was very glad that there was no one she knew in the train. She just wanted to sit quiet and think about Jimmy.

It wasn't until she stood at the prison gates that she thought, "I don't know what to do." The idea of getting to the prison had been so fixed in her mind that she had never thought past it to what she would do when she got there. Now, as she surveyed the grim gateway and the high walls, a feeling of despair threatened her. At once she rose to combat it. She had thought that it was all going to be quite easy. That was nonsense. But you couldn't do anything at all if you let things threaten you. She lifted her head and looked at the prison gates. "I won't be frightened of them—I won't—I won't," she said to herself.

As she stood there, a little lady in old-fashioned clothes came round the corner. She was walking quite briskly, and ordinarily she might not have noticed the girl who stood looking at the prison gates, but since she intended to turn in at the gates herself she did notice her and, noticing, became sympathetically attentive.

"Can I help you? Forgive me—but you look ill."

Kathy brought her eyes back from the gates. She said, speaking slowly,

"I was thinking what a difference there was between this side of the gates and the other."

Miss Silver's interest was awakened. That the girl was in an abnormal state was plain. She said,

"Yes?"

Her voice full of kindness and sympathy did something to Kathy. She felt suddenly protected, as if she had come out of danger into safety. She didn't know what she felt. In the confusion of her mind she didn't know that she was speaking until she heard her own voice say,

"I don't know how to get in. I've come a long way, and I don't know—I don't know—" Her voice trailed away into silence.

She stood looking at Miss Silver, and Miss Silver looked back at her. She saw a girl of two or three and twenty. She had grey eyes with very thick lashes which made them look dark, and she had dark hair. There wasn't an atom of colour in her face. She wasn't pretty. When she was happy she would be pleasant and—yes, rather appealing, but just now there was a dead weight of misery and hopelessness about her. It was not in Miss Silver to pass on unregarding. She said,

"You are in trouble, my dear. What is it?"

Kathy answered not so much the words as the kindness of her tone.

"I don't know how to get in."

"There is someone there in whom you are interested?"

"Oh, yes—"

"Then, my dear, you will have to take the proper steps. It is not possible to see a prisoner—"

"Not possible? Oh—but you were going in—"

"Yes, I was going in. But I have an appointment."

The girl jerked into life.

"Could you find out what I have to do to see him? Will you? Oh, will you?"

"I will do what I can. Who is it you wish to see?"

"It's Jimmy—Jimmy Mottingley."

Miss Silver looked closely at the girl. She saw what she had seen already. She said gently,

"You are a friend of his?"

"Yes, I'm his friend. Do you know him?"

"Yes, my dear. I was on my way to see him."

"Then—then can you take me in with you?"

Miss Silver's manner became even kinder.

"I am afraid that would not be allowed. I have had to get special permission. But I will take a message from you if you would like to give me one."

A little colour came into the pale cheeks and the eyes brightened.

"Will you tell him from Kathy that I know he didn't do it. Please, what is your name?"

"I am Miss Maud Silver—a private investigator."

"Oh—did Jimmy ask for you?"

"No, it was his father who came to see me and asked for my help."

"Is his father being nice? He doesn't think much of Jimmy, and he is terribly strict."

Miss Silver smiled.

"Do not be in too much of a hurry to judge, my dear. Mr. Mottingley is in an agony about his son. He is doing all that can be done for him."

"He doesn't believe it then? Oh, Miss Silver, no one who knew Jimmy could really believe it—they couldn't! It just isn't in Jimmy to do a thing like that. He *couldn't!* He really couldn't! Jimmy is *kind,* and—and—Miss Silver, if I could make you understand—"

"I understand that he has a very good friend in you, my dear."

"No—no—it's not that way. I forgot you don't know me. I'll try and tell you, or you won't understand. I am Kathy Lingbourne. My father is a solicitor at Collingdon. My mother died when I was seventeen. That's five years ago, and I have run the house ever since. There are four of us. Len is older than I am, and the other two are younger. Len is in Mr. Mottingley's firm, and that is how Jimmy started coming to the house. Len got to know Jimmy and they got to be friends, and that is how it was. I know Jimmy very well indeed. He couldn't have killed that girl. He couldn't kill anything. The other boys teased him about it—you know how boys are. He tried very hard, but he simply couldn't do it. That is why I *know* that he didn't kill this girl. She was a horrid girl, but he didn't kill her. He *couldn't* have done it—not if he'd tried ever so! And look here, Miss Silver, they say that she was knocked down first and then—strangled. Was it like that?"

"Yes, my dear, it was."

"Then Jimmy *couldn't* have done it—he simply couldn't. I know him so well. Even supposing he hit her—and he wouldn't have, he *wouldn't*—the minute she fell down he'd have been on his knees beside her asking her if she was hurt and doing his best to reassure her. I tell you I *know* Jimmy."

Miss Silver was touched. And she found herself in agreement. She said,

"My dear, I must go in. But I shall not be long. Will you wait for me, and then I can give you an account of my visit. There's a nice shop across the road. They make most excellent tea there. I had some when I came down before. You can say that you are waiting for someone and they will not trouble you. The woman is a nice placid creature. And now I must go."

CHAPTER 30

Kathy sat down to wait.
The minute she saw the woman in the shop she knew that waiting would be restful. She seemed to have been keyed up for a very long time, and now quite suddenly it was all over. Meeting Miss Silver had begun it, and when she had seen her go through the gates into the prison, and had turned her back and gone over the road to the tea-shop, the process had gone on. The shop was called Mrs. Brown's Teahouse, and when she lifted the latch and walked inside there was a large rolling Mrs. Brown all smiles and affability.

"Well, me dear, come along in with you! And shut the door, for it's a nasty day outside."

Kathy gave her a blank piteous look and said, "Is it?" And with that Mrs. Brown came bustling out from behind her counter and had Kathy by the arm.

"Now just come along with me. You'll sit down here in the back shop by the fire. And you'll take your gloves off and get your hands warm, for it's an aching cold today, and if gloves keep the cold out, so they can keep it in too, that's what I always say." She said a good deal more, but most of it went past Kathy.

When she opened her eyes and became aware of things again, the large woman was saying, "And you'll be as right as rain—you see if you're not."

It felt like a promise. Things were going to be all right. She must just wait. She opened those deeply fringed eyes of hers and fixed them on Mrs. Brown with a trusting look which went to the lady's kind heart, and said,

"You are very good. Are you Mrs. Brown?"

The woman laughed cheerfully.

"That's me, though to tell you the truth there's never been a Mr. Brown. But when you come to the fifties, well, I say it sounds better to be Mrs. Brown. But Brown I was born, and Brown I'll die when me time comes. And now, me dear, I'll go and make you some tea, and that'll put fresh heart into you."

Kathy was on a little settee in the room behind the shop. There was a sort of gauze curtain between the two rooms. The settee on which she was sitting was lumpy, and yet it was comfortable. Her troubles seemed all to have dropped from her. She said in a dazed, exhausted voice,

"You are so very good. I think I had better wait a little. The lady whom I am with has gone to see someone"—she paused and caught her breath—"someone in the prison. She said they wouldn't let me see him, so I came in here to wait for her. Is that all right?"

"Yes, of course it is, my dear. It's not likely I'll have anyone else in. Not a great day for visitors, Monday isn't, and not at this time o'day either. But are you all right to wait—that's what I want to know. What did you have for lunch?"

"Lunch?" said Kathy as if she had never heard the word before and didn't know what it meant.

"That's what I said, l-u-n-c-h—lunch. And you needn't tell me, because I know by the look of you that you never give it a thought. Gels—" said Mrs. Brown with strong reprobation, "I know 'em! I never had none of me own, but believe you me, there's nothing about gels I don't know. Seventeen nieces I've got, the darters of my five brothers, and what you can't learn from a niece you'll never learn from a darter—that's what I say. Now what could you fancy? I don't run to lunches as a rule, but a negg to your tea?"

"It's not time for tea, is it?"

"Well, not formal like it's not. But you can have tea any time, that's what I always say. And I've got some lovely eggs. My brother Steve he brought them in yesterday afternoon—come over with his youngest, Doris. She's got a look of you, me dear, if you don't mind my saying so, and a real nice gel she is. Well then, I'll do you a negg, and I'll do it right away, because your friend she won't be wanting more than a cuppa, I should say. I've seen her before. Last week it was—Thursday or Friday—and she come in for a cuppa. So you have your egg, me dear, and she'll be only too pleased."

Kathy sat still. She didn't know afterwards whether she had dropped asleep or not. She might have done, but if she did, it was only for a minute or two. She had the curious feeling that time had stopped.

Miss Silver went into the prison. She was taken to the room that she had been in before, and presently Jimmy was brought there. He looked a little brighter than he had that first time, and he was certainly glad to see her. She transacted her business with him—a matter of the time he had left his mother and her friend, and the time it had taken him to drive to his meeting-place with Miriam. He gave clear answers, and Miss Silver would have been a good deal more comfortable about his movements if it had not been for a most trying discrepancy between the evidence of the two ladies concerned— Mrs. Marsden stating that she looked at her watch just after Jimmy had left and had found the time to be ten minutes past six, whereas Mrs. Mottingley had said that Jimmy left the house at six-thirty. Both ladies had been obstinate in sticking to the fidelity of their timepieces. Jimmy said frankly that he didn't remember, but he added that the drawing-room clock was always going wrong. He did not seem to take in the importance of the twenty minutes' difference, and the mere fact that he did not do so tended to make his evidence the more credible to Miss Silver, though she doubted if it would have that effect upon a jury. However, there was no more to be done with it, and after all both times were open to argument. So much depended upon the speed at which Jimmy had driven.

Miss Silver turned to the subject of Kathy.

"You had another visitor this afternoon, Mr. Mottingley."

"Another visitor?"

"Miss Kathy Lingbourne. She did not know that she would have to get special permission to see you, but I met her at the gates and told her that I would give you a message and take back one from you. You have a very firm friend there, Mr. Mottingley."

She saw his hands catch one another close. He said in a shaking voice,

"I didn't expect her to come. I—I haven't treated her right."

"She is not thinking of that, I can assure you."

"I—I don't mean that there was anything between us—there wasn't. She was just kind to me, as she is to everyone. I was a friend of her brother's. His name's Len—he's in my father's business. And Kathy was wonderful to me—to all of us. Kathy's *good*."

"Yes, I could see that."

"Anyone could see it with Kathy. Oh, that sounds rude! I don't mean to be rude. What I mean is—"

Miss Silver smiled.

"You need not trouble to explain, Mr. Mottingley. I know exactly what you mean. Miss Kathy, as you said, is good. I would trust her judgment, and she is very sure of your innocence."

Jimmy brushed a hand across his eyes. Then he looked straight at Miss Silver.

"If Kathy believes in me it's something to go on. You

can see that, can't you? I didn't think anyone would, but you say Kathy does."

"Yes, Miss Kathy does. You can rely on that."

When her interview was over Miss Silver crossed the road to the bun-shop.

Kathy had just eaten an egg and some bread and butter and was looking much better. She looked up at Miss Silver with pleading eyes, but she waited while Mrs. Brown took the order and bustled away. Then she said,

"Miss Silver, how is he?"

Miss Silver smiled very kindly.

"I think that he is better, and I think that your message and the fact that you had come over to see him did him a great deal of good. I think he has been feeling very much forsaken. His parents, though truly devoted, have built up a wall of separation between themselves and him. He was their fourth child, and they lost the other three. I think that they imposed an iron discipline upon him, not so much for his sake as for their own, and instead of strengthening his character they weakened it."

Kathy's eyes were very soft.

"Oh, you do understand. It has been just like that, only I didn't know that they cared."

"They care very deeply," said Miss Silver.

"I didn't know," said Kathy. "And he didn't know either. If—if they really do care, do you think you could tell him so? I think it would make a great difference to him. And—and if you get the opportunity, do you think that you could get them to see that he doesn't need scolding. Anyone can think of things to say to themselves which are far worse than what anyone else can say to them. Only—only they won't do it while they are defending themselves. I do know that because of my sister. She's only eighteen, and if she has done anything stupid—like girls do, you know—and you leave it to her, she will say what she's done and how stupid it was. But if I were to say it, she would make a quarrel of it and say it was just what anyone would do. Oh, I'm putting it very badly, but I'm sure you know what I mean."

"Yes, my dear, I do."

The tea came, and Miss Silver enjoyed it.

"It is so seldom that one gets tea really properly made like this is. Most people do not observe the golden rule of making sure that the kettle has boiled, and freshly boiled."

A highly gratified Mrs. Brown responded,

"Ah, there you have it! That's what I always say. I remember when I first went into service at the Manor House the cook there she didn't believe in having the water freshly boiled, and it was pain and grief to me with the training I'd had from my dear mother, to see the haphazard ways of her. Well, another ten years and I was cook meself, and I give you me word they thought the tea had been changed, it made all that of a difference."

When she had gone away, Kathy turned to Miss Silver.

"Will you tell me what I must do to see Jimmy?"

Miss Silver was silent for a moment. Then she said,

"My dear, I know you only want to do what is best for him."

Kathy looked at her with wide startled eyes.

"Oh, yes I do—I do."

"Then I think I must say to you that I think it would be very unwise—"

"For me to see him? Oh, Miss Silver, why?"

"Can you not see why? I think you must do so if you think of the circumstances. Mr. Jimmy went down to Hazeldon to see this unfortunate girl. If it comes to a trial, the prosecution will suggest that they quarrelled, and that in the course of this quarrel he killed her. I think that you ought to abstain very carefully from doing or saying anything which may tend to supply a reason for such a quarrel. His interest in another woman would be such a reason. I think it would be absolutely fatal both for your own sake and that of Jimmy Mottingley himself that there should be any hint of his possible interest in another woman. You have spoken of a brother and sisters. Have you no father, my dear?"

Kathy started.

"Oh, yes. My mother died when I was seventeen, and I came home to look after the younger children and to run the house. My father is a solicitor. He is a very busy man, and he is not very strong. I didn't want to trouble him."

Miss Silver smiled warmly.

"I am sure you will find that he is in agreement with me as to the necessity of your remaining quite detached from this business. I think it would be very dangerous for Jimmy Mottingley if you were to involve yourself in this case in *any way.*"

CHAPTER 31

Jenny was out in the vil- lage. She had undertaken to do the shopping, and she was very anxious to show that she could do it without making any mistakes. There were not a great many shops to go to. There was Mrs. Dean who kept a general shop, and Mrs. Maples who had bread and cakes, biscuits, and groceries. In the general shop you could buy vegetables in season, and boots and shoes of the stoutly wearing kind, together with an assortment of tins ranging from peaches to boot-polish.

"No—no apricots today, Miss," said Mrs. Dean. "Mrs. Pratt had the last, and what she wants with it dear knows, but I'll lay she don't! I've knowed her since she was a girl, and she was always the same—no head for anything. But there, it don't do to talk about people, does it? It gets round to them something shocking in a village. Funny, isn't it—I can remember ten or twelve years ago she was the prettiest girl in the village and all the men after her, and she married Albert Pratt, and he got killed a year later. Funny sort of affair it was. There was she laid up with her baby, and there was Albert coming home along the road to her when a car come by and run over him, and he never moved nor spoke after. Well, Mrs. Pratt, pore thing, she was neither to hold nor to bind—carried on dreadful she did, and everyone thought as how she'd marry again, but she didn't, more's the pity. Her Dicky, he's a bright boy but heedless. Wants a man's hand over him, that's what I say. Now if you'd like a nice tin of peaches instead of the apricots—"

"Yes, the peaches will do very well," said Jenny.

She had been wondering when she would be able to get a word in, but it was a fine morning and she wasn't in a hurry. It was quite nice to saunter down the village street and feel that everyone was friendly and would talk to her, and Caroline was making a cake. She was just going to leave the shop, when a boy with a happy-go-lucky grin on his face looked round the door. Mrs. Dean said severely,

"Now, what are you not in school for, Dicky?"

Dicky smiled still more broadly. Jenny had the feeling that really it wasn't possible for any boy to be as innocent as he looked.

"I had a headache and a stomach ache when I woke up this mornin', and my mum said I needn't go."

"You mind what you're up to," said Mrs. Dean, "or you'll be getting into trouble you will."

"I was mortal sick when I woke up, Mrs. Dean. 'Orrible sick I was."

"Too sick to eat a peppermint drop now, I'll lay."

"Oh, no. It's quite gone off, Mrs. Dean—it has reelly."

"You're a bad boy, Dicky, and that's the truth of it, and you won't get no peppermint drops from me."

"No, Mrs. Dean, I won't—I know that. I've just come in to see if I could carry the young lady's stuff."

Jenny was waiting to get out of the shop. She gathered that she was the young lady concerned, and she smiled and shook her head.

"No, thank you," she said. "I can manage what I've got quite nicely."

But when she got out of the shop, there was Dicky beside her.

"You staying with Miss Danesworth?" he said brightly.

"Yes, I am."

Jenny couldn't help smiling. He was the untidiest boy she had ever seen. His bright yellow curls were a welter. They did not look as if they had been brushed for months. His clothes were a disgrace. The pockets of his trousers were stuffed full, his shirt was torn. All his clothes were stained and dishevelled. But those very blue eyes of his twinkled, and she wanted to laugh when she looked at him. Dicky had that kind of effect on a good many people. If he had not had the mistaken idea of producing stomach ache as one of his indispositions, she felt tolerably certain that Mrs. Dean would have had a peppermint for him. She thought he was a boy who would get what he wanted.

He walked along beside her scuffing up the dust with his toes. He hadn't made up his mind yet. It didn't do to be in a hurry, and he would want to make out what he was going to say very carefully. It wouldn't do to make a mistake. As he went, he thought and kept on smiling. That was a very good dodge with the soap. His mother hadn't noticed anything at all, and she hadn't missed the tiddy little bits. He smiled benignly as he thought of how he had got up and chewed on those little bits. They had a funny kind of taste. He wouldn't like to take too much of them, but they made a rare old fuzzygug in your mouth. It had frightened Mum all right—frightened her almost too much, for she wanted to send for the doctor, and he wasn't having any of that. Well, here they were now. The trick with the soap had come off all right, and here was Miss Jenny.

What he hadn't been able to make out at the time was the address on the note he had been given—"Miss Jenny Hill." Well, this wasn't any Miss Jenny Hill. This was Miss Jenny Forbes. Then why did the gentleman in the car tell him to give the note to Miss Jenny Hill? There wasn't any Miss Jenny Hill that he could see— not in Hazeldon.

That's what he had thought at the time, but then afterwards—after that chatterin' old body that worked for Mrs. Merridew had had her say—he did see different about it. Only he didn't quite know what he'd got to think. Least said soonest mended. Jenny Hill—he said the name out loud, "Miss Hill—Miss Jenny Hill."

Jenny looked up startled.

"What did you say?"

He looked at her with that carefree innocent smile of his.

"Ow, nothing'—nothin'. It was just a name as took my fancy. Did you ever hear it before?"

Jenny said, "Yes, I did. It was my name."

"Ow? Why did you change it?"

Jenny bit her lip. Was that smiling look of his really innocent? She wasn't sure. She laughed and said,

"You want to know too much."

"It's interestin'—that's why I want to know." The blue eyes gazed limpidly into hers. She found herself explaining, which she hadn't meant to do.

"Well, sometimes you grow up with a name and you think it's really yours, and then you find out that it isn't."

"It isn't what?" said Dicky, deeply interested.

"It isn't yours at all," said Jenny. "You've got another name, and everyone doesn't know it—not at first."

When she came to think about it afterwards, she simply couldn't imagine what had made her say it. She didn't know that she was not the only one to say things which she regretted afterwards under Dicky's innocent gaze. Nor would she be the last.

"That's very interestin'," said Dicky. He removed the gaze and fell to thinking about the note. After a moment he said, "Then if there was a note with Miss Jenny Hill on it, would that be for you, or wouldn't it be?"

Jenny was startled. She said quickly,

"It would be for me. Why do you want to know?"

The blue gaze turned interestedly in her direction again.

"Ow, I was just wonderin'."

Jenny stood still. She couldn't think who in the world would be sending her a note addressed Miss Jenny Hill. She wasn't Jenny Hill here. She never had been Jenny Hill. How on earth had this boy got hold of the name, and who could possibly have written her a note addressed to Jenny Hill? The thought of Mac passed through her mind with a shudder. She had never been afraid of him whilst she had lived next door or when she had moved into Alington House. She had never been afraid then, but she was afraid now. It was nonsense. She was making a fool of herself. She said,

"Why were you wondering?"

The blue eyes never moved from her face. He scuffed with his feet in the dust.

"Ow, I just was."

She said, "Dicky, I want an answer, and a true one. How did you know that I had been called Jenny Hill?"

"Everyone knows. It isn't only me—honest it isn't. That there Mrs. Warrington as works for Mrs. Merridew, she's the one that got hold of it. Proper nosey parker she is, and what she knows everyone knows. Come to think of it, there's somethin' excitin' about havin' two names. I mean, everyone knows as you have one before you're married an' one after, but I never heard of no one else as was single an' had two names. That's why I was interested."

It was quite possible. Only Jenny's association with Meg and Joyce cropped up to tell her that a child who looks you straight in the face with eyes of angelic innocence and makes a statement may have more than one reason for doing so. Meg had rather a talent for doing that sort of thing, and Jenny was strongly reminded of Meg as she met Dicky's blue and innocent gaze. She thought of what he had said, "Then if there was a note with Miss Jenny Hill on it, would that be for you, or wouldn't it be?" She said,

"If you know anything about a note for me you had better tell me what it is."

The innocent blue gaze stayed on her face.

"I never said nothin' about a note for you. I couldn't, seein' as how there wasn't one, could I?"

Jenny would have laughed, only somehow she didn't feel like laughing. There was a feeling of pressure, of the importance of what was said. She spoke abruptly.

"You couldn't have said it if there *really* wasn't

one—I know that. But you said—you did say, 'Then if there was a note with Miss Jenny Hill on it, would that be for you, or wouldn't it be?' "

"I said that?"

"Yes, you said that. I want to know what you meant by it."

"I didn't mean anythin'. You're not angry, miss, are you? I didn't mean no harm."

"I don't say you did. I just want to know why you said it."

Dicky thought that this had gone on long enough. He had two accomplishments. The wide blue gaze was one of them. He thought the time had come for the other. He let his lids fall and squeezed them down upon his eyes, at the same time he clenched his hands. A gush of tears followed. It was a very useful trick. If the wide-eyed gaze did not prevail, the gush of tears could be relied upon. But Jenny was once again reminded of Meg.

"I didn't mean no harm," said Dicky with a most effective catch in his breath.

"I want to know why you said it."

Dicky stood rubbing his eyes.

"I didn't mean no harm. I dunno why I said it. I dunno anythin'."

And as Jenny advanced an ominous step in his direction he turned and ran from her through Mrs. Bishop's garden and out on to the common at the back. He thought he would keep clear of Miss Jenny Hill for the time being.

Jenny went on her way frowning.

CHAPTER 32

Richard had been in town.
He came back, and when Caroline Danesworth had gone to get the supper he got up and, standing on the hearthrug with his back to the fire which was so pleasant in the evenings, he said,

"Jenny—"

Something in his voice quickened her heart-beat. She turned round, brown startled eyes on him, and said,

"What is it?"

"Nothing. Don't look like that. I thought we ought to find out for certain, so I went to Somerset House today—"

"Somerset House?"

"That is where they keep the marriage certificates and all those sort of things. That is where Mac had got his information. What was open to him was open to me. It is quite true—your father and mother were married in January 1940. January the second to be exact. When were you born?"

She said, "August 31st, 1940. My father was killed at the end of May—I don't know which day. And my mother was hit in an air raid about the same time. I told you."

"Yes, you told me. She was struck on the head, wasn't she?"

"Yes, she was. And she never spoke. The blow did something to her. I don't know if she ever knew about my father being killed. I don't think she did from what Garsty said—I hope she didn't. And as soon as I was born she died. It's a very sad story, isn't it?"

Richard said, "I don't know—it seems sad to us because we only see one side of it. It wasn't so sad for them, you know. They weren't separated very long— not nearly as long as they might have been as the war went on. Don't grieve over them, Jenny."

"I'm not really. It just makes me cry a little, that's all."

"I can't bear to see you cry. If you go on, I shall come across and kiss you, and Caroline will take that moment to come in for something, and—well, don't try me too high."

Jenny looked up. Her eyes were swimming with tears. She blinked them away and they ran down and fell into her lap. She put up a hand to brush the traces away and smiled through her tears.

"Did you get the certificate?"

"I got a copy for you. Do you want to see it?"

"Please."

He took out a pocket-book, opened it, and extracted the certificate. When he came over to her with it he sat down on the sofa beside her.

"You're too young, you know, my dear," he said in a moved voice. "I didn't think of it like that until I looked at the date on this. Do you know that I was eight years old when you were born?"

Jenny said, "Why shouldn't you be?" Then she took up the certificate and looked at it long and earnestly. She said in a moved voice, "They had so little time together."

Richard put his arm round her.

"Please God we'll have more time."

She clung to him.

"Oh, yes—yes!"

It was a little later that he said, "Better give me the certificate. It'll be wanted."

"What are you going to do with it?"

"Mac and Mrs. Forbes must know that you have it. I think you ought to write to them."

Jenny stiffened up.

"I don't want to."

"I think you'll have to, darling."

"I don't see why."

"Well, it's this way. They probably guess that you know something, but they can't be sure, and they can't know. You'll have to tell them."

"Must I? I don't want to."

"It doesn't matter whether you want to or not. You are the legitimate child of your parents, and you've got to be acknowledged. There's no need to wash a lot of dirty linen in public unless you want to."

"Oh, I don't!"

"Well, short of that there's a perfectly easy way out. I can be the one who wrestled round and found out about the marriage certificate. Mrs. Forbes and Mac will be only too glad to fall in with what we propose, to save their faces. They don't deserve to be saved. They don't deserve anything except the utmost rigour of the law. Not that the law comes into it—fortunately for them. But there could be a good deal of local talk, and they'll be glad to be saved that."

Jenny was silent. She slipped her hand through Richard's arm and squeezed it.

"Richard, I don't think I want to tell them," she said.

He put his hand over hers.

"Why don't you want to?"

Her eyes looked up at him, very big and dark.

"I don't know. That is to say, I don't know exactly."

"Well, what do you know that isn't—exact?"

"It's just—there was a boy this morning and he said my name—the one I've never used here, Jenny Hill."

"Oh—"

"He said it over and over as if he was saying it to

himself. And when I asked him about it he said it was just a name that took his fancy and he wanted to know if I'd ever heard it before. I said yes, it used to be my name. And he wanted to know why I had changed it, and I said that you sometimes grow up with a name you think is really yours, and then you find out that it isn't yours at all. You've got another name, but everyone doesn't know it—not at first."

"My dear child!" said Richard half laughing.

"And he said, 'That's very interesting.' And then after a moment he said, 'If there was a note with Miss Jenny Hill on it, would that be for you, or wouldn't it be?' And I said it would be fore me, and I asked him why he wanted to know."

"Well, what did he say?"

"He said he was just wondering. Well, I pressed him—I felt I must. I asked how he knew that I'd ever been called Jenny Hill, and he said that everyone knew it. The woman who works for Mrs. Merridew, she'd got hold of it, I don't know how. And he said there was something exciting about having two names, and except for changing your name when you were married he'd never heard of anyone who had two names, and that was why he was interested."

"Well, that's quite a reasonable explanation."

"No. No, it isn't really. It didn't really fit in with what he'd said before—'And if there was a note with Jenny Hill on it, would that be for you, or wouldn't it?' So I said, 'If you know anything about a note for me you'd better tell me what it is.' And the little wretch said that he'd never said anything about a note for me. He said he couldn't have said anything, seeing that there wasn't one, could he?"

"Well—"

"He put on a very good act. He began to cry, and when I went on pressing him he ran away."

"There's not very much in that. I expect you frightened him."

She shook her head.

"I don't believe that boy's ever been frightened in his life."

"Which boy was it?"

"His name is Dicky Pratt."

Richard whistled.

"He's a young devil—I grant you that. But why are you so disturbed about the whole thing?"

She said under her breath, "A note for me—addressed to Miss Jenny Hill—who would that be from? I don't like it at all."

CHAPTER 33

Dicky Pratt went home.
He was in good time for his dinner, a most unusual circumstance. Not that there was much to eat. There were a couple of big old potatoes which Dicky had brought home about a month before. Mrs. Pratt wouldn't have taken them from anyone else herself, but she had learned not to ask questions about what Dicky brought home. In her muddled way, what she didn't know about left her conscience free—and what were two or three old potatoes anyhow? She cooked them in their jackets and served them on an uncleared table with the cold rabbit they had left over from yesterday. Dicky had no nerves about eating rabbit. "This here myxy,"* as he called it, which had reduced the rabbit population to almost nothing was to him a "black shame." Rabbits had been his main supply of meat since he had caught

*Myxomatosis.

his first when he was no more than six years old, and then just when he got really good at it there had come the "myxy" plague and all rabbits ceased for a time. Enforced abstinence had whetted his appetite. Birds weren't the same—there was no real meat on them, and his mother was no hand at cooking them neither. And then he had seen what were certainly traces of rabbit out back of the house, and a month later he had knocked one out down by Mr. Fulbrook's in the late evening. There weren't very many of them yet, and they were shy. He thought with reluctance that he'd have to make do with one a month.

He ate his cold rabbit and his hot potatoes with enjoyment but with a slightly distracted mind. When he had finished he went upstairs to his own room and shut the door. There was no key in the door, but when he had any private business he would pull the bed across it, which was quite satisfactory from his point of view. The room was bare enough, the bed a welter of untidy clothes roughly pulled together. Yet a millionaire might have envied the sweet sleep which Dicky enjoyed in it.

But today he was not bent on sleep. When he had secured the door he turned out his pockets on the bed. This, which was his grand account, took place as a rule only when the pockets were full to bursting. By putting it off as long as possible he not only saved time, but he enhanced the interest of the proceedings. If, for instance, some time had passed, it was possible that an added interest would have accrued to something that had merely been stuffed in as an afterthought. There was Mrs. Merridew's earring for example. He had found it just outside her front gate, and it had never occurred to him that there was anything special about it—not for a week. And then his mum had come in, in one of her talking moods. She didn't get them very often, and when she did he didn't always listen. Grown-up people—the things they worried about! But this time he had taken notice of what she said, and just as well he had, for it seemed that Mrs. Merridew had lost an earring.

"What's it like, Mum?" Dicky had said, only half interested, and out had come a whole lot of explanations—Mrs. Merridew had a pair of them, and they were worth a lot of money. Dicky pricked up his ears.

"What's a lot of money, Mum?"

"I don't know, I'm sure. Some people have all the luck whichever way it goes."

The affair of the earring stuck in his mind. He had put it in his pocket and forgotten about it, and if his mum hadn't come home in one of her talking moods, that might have been the end of it. It was bent, and muddy, and twisted. He'd seen something like it in a shop window in Collingdon, and the price was ten-and-six. He hadn't thought that one broken earring would be worth anything at all, but he'd kept it just on the chance, and the day after his mum had come back with her story he had gone over to Mrs. Merridew with his limpid smile and a "My mum says as how you lost an earring. Would this be it?" Mrs. Merridew was in a state, and when she was in a state she scolded all the time, but you didn't have to take any notice of that. When she had gone on for as long as seemed proper, he pulled out the earring and showed it. And the end of it was that she had given him half a sovereign and sent him away very much exalted in his mind.

But this was a different matter. This required deep thought. The letter to Jenny was in the bottom of his pocket. He got it out and he looked at it. More than a week in the welter of his pocket had not improved its appearance, but it was plainly legible. He read it:

Jenny, *don't say anything to anyone,* but come out and meet me up on the heath as soon as it is quite dark.

Mac

Bring this with you.

And in the top left-hand corner there was a date.

The date was that of last Saturday week, the same date that the note had been given to him. He was quite clear about that. He was quite clear about the whole thing. The note was dated last Saturday week. This was Monday—the second Monday since the murder. He'd got it quite clear in his mind. The question was, did he do anything about it, or didn't he? There were things he could do, he knew that very well. The question was, would it pay him to do them? He wasn't sure. And he'd got to be quite sure before he said anything to anyone. Not sure about what happened—he was perfectly sure about that, and no one would get him from it. Not if he decided that way. But he thought that he wouldn't decide yet. He'd got to be certain of other things besides the facts. It was the facts that he had to speak about and swear to. A tingle went all through him as he thought about that. He'd been in a court, but not for a murder trial of course. He had only had to hold the Book and swear to speak the truth, the whole truth, and nothing but the truth when there was a case about a motor accident in the village and as luck would have it he had been right there on the spot when it happened. He had enjoyed that case, but he wasn't so sure about a murder. They might want to know too much. Suppose they were to ask him why he hadn't spoken up at once—what was he going to say to that?

He shook his head. He didn't know what to think. On the one hand there was the exhilarating mental picture of himself in the witness-box as the only person who knew the truth. And if he was to get this young fellow, this Jimmy Mottingley off, what would he get out of it? They said his father was a rich man. Dicky hadn't seen him, but Bob Wilkins had. Bob was a softy. He wouldn't take his word about anyone, not if it was ever so. If he had seen Mr. Mottingley himself he would know. He began to devise ways of seeing him. Only he'd have to be very careful not to give anything away until he had really made up his mind. He wasn't going to do anything in a hurry. Once you'd got in with the law they'd see to it that you didn't get out again. He'd have to think it out very carefully. Very, very carefully.

His mind went back to his meeting with this Mac in the road. It was dark, and he couldn't see much of him, but that wouldn't matter as long as he'd got the note addressed to Miss Jenny Hill. It was signed Mac. The police would find him easy enough, but would it be safe for Dicky? That was the question. That was another thing that wanted a lot of thinking about. The note was to Miss Jenny Hill, but it wasn't Miss Jenny Hill who had been killed, it was the girl who had been visiting Mrs. Merridew—the same one as had been there in the summer. Now what had she got to do with it? It all went round and round in his head.

CHAPTER 34

Carter and the two little girls had gone into Langton for the afternoon. Joyce was rather quiet, but Meg was in a prancing mood. They went and came by bus, and she chattered all the time. Joyce sat very genteelly, as Carter put it, with her hands clasped in her lap, and her little serious face rather pale under a new blue felt hat. The children were always dressed alike, so Meg had on a twin hat and a twin coat, and showed them off with the full consciousness of their being new. They sat one on either side of Carter. They had new shoes on, too. Meg kicked her feet, one in, one out, and watched them complacently. She thought that she was going to have pretty feet. Her mother's feet were rather large, but she always wore such good shoes that it didn't matter. Meg thought that if she could keep her feet from growing they would be rather nice. They were much smaller than her mother's at present, but there were years of growing in front of them, and that made her feel rather sad. But she wasn't going to be sad today—not about her feet or about anything else. It was *very* exciting to be going on the bus to Langton. It was only the third time they had ever gone there, and they wouldn't be going now if their mother hadn't wanted some ribbon matched in a hurry. It was the ribbon she ran into her nightgowns, pink and blue. Meg thought that when she was grown up she would have yellow ribbon in hers, and she wouldn't let Joyce have the same colour. Joyce could have pink or blue or green if she liked, but *not* yellow. And Meg would have all the different shades of it, bright gold, and primrose, and pale cream colour. She would have lots and lots of yellow nightgowns, and a furry yellow dressing-gown as warm as warm, and furry yellow slippers. She kicked with her legs, and Carter said in a disapproving whisper, "Now, Meg, behave."

Joyce sat quite quiet on Carter's other side. She wouldn't confess it, but driving in the bus made her feel sick. Even riding in a car made her feel rather ill, and the bus was much worse. It would be too dreadful if she were sick with her new coat on for the first time. She kept her hands together in her lap. If they held on to each other as tight as tight she wouldn't be sick. She wished very much that Meg would sit quiet on Carter's other side and not jump about and kick with her legs. "Please, please don't let me be sick," she said to herself in her secret mind. "Please—*please*." And as if it had been an answer, she heard Carter say quite crossly,

"Now, Meg, if you don't stop flouncing about and going on like a demented thing, I'll tell your mother, and next time we go shopping you won't come with us!"

Meg stopped kicking.

"Won't I?" she said in tones of piercing interest. "Where will I stay, Carter?"

"I know where you'd deserve to stay," said Carter darkly.

"Where—where—oh, where, Carter?"

Two young men on the other side of the bus pricked up their ears and began to listen. Carter was silent. She knew Meg in this mood. Egg her on, and there was nothing she mightn't do or say. She looked so fierce that the young men rather withered away, though they kept an eye on Meg.

Meg was enjoying herself. She liked attracting attention, and she loved shocking Carter. If they had not arrived in the Market Square of Langton, there was no saying to what lengths she might not have proceeded. As it was, she was the only one of the three to be disappointed when the bus drew up. Joyce was thankful. She hadn't been sick, and going back she must sit with her eyes shut all the way, which was very dull. But she wouldn't be sick if she did that. She might even go to sleep.

They went across the Square to Moxton Street, and by the time they got there Joyce was feeling quite herself. Meg walked along discreetly, her right hand in Carter's left. She looked the very picture of a good little girl and would continue to do so while Carter had hold of her. But inside, in her own mind, things were very different. She was a Prisoner and Carter was the Wardress, and she was being taken to a Court of Law where she would be sentenced. Joyce was the humble attendant. Not in any danger.

They went into the biggest shop in Moxton Street. Its name was Jakers. That of course was a blind. And then quite suddenly with all the excitements of the shop round her Meg abandoned the drama of being a prisoner and gave herself up to the delights of the shop. She pulled at Carter's sleeve with her free hand.

"Carter—Carter!"

"Well, what is it?" said Carter crossly.

"I've stopped what I was doing—I really have! I'm sorry, and I'll be ever so good—I really will! But please don't hold my hand in the shop! And Joyce and me we've both got a half-crown to spend! Can we—"

"If you mean can you wander all over the shop like a wild animal, the answer is no!" said Carter.

"Oh, I didn't want to do that," said Meg in a shocked voice. "Only for Joyce and me to look round whilst you get Mother's ribbons."

Carter hesitated and was lost.

"You'll not get into trouble?"

"I'll keep tight hold of Joyce's hand—I promise you I will."

Carter turned to the counter where the ribbons waited for her choice, and Meg pounced on Joyce.

"There are some lovely things along here. Come and look!"

Meg was skilful. She kept near enough to Carter, but not too near. She examined with the deepest interest all the things that she would have liked to buy. Presently she was standing by the model of an exquisitely shaped female leg which set out the beauties of a superfine nylon stocking surmounted by a garter with a paste buckle.

"Ooh!" she said. "I like that!"

"Why is there only one leg?" said Joyce fretfully.

"It's to show the stocking, silly!" said Meg.

And then there were two ladies, not young, and they were talking together, and one of them said,

"That horrid murder on Hazeldon Heath—"

Joyce hadn't heard. She was looking at a little dog away on the far side of the shop. She pulled her hand out of Meg's and ran over to it.

Meg stood her ground. She knew that Jenny was at Hazeldon, because Miss Crampton had said so. And Mrs. Merridew who was Miss Crampton's cousin lived right next door to where Jenny was. Mary the housemaid had told her all about it, but not about the murder. It wasn't Jenny who was murdered—it couldn't be Jenny! Meg found she was shaking all over. It wasn't Jenny—it couldn't be Jenny! Why should anyone want to murder Jenny? She had missed something, but not much. She heard one of the ladies say,

"I used to know a Miss Danesworth. Such a very uncommon name. I wonder if it's the same. I think it must be, because I remember that she lived in a village not so very far away, and—yes, I'm sure it was Hazeldon. Well then, she was giving evidence at the inquest. This girl who was killed was at her house just before it happened. There was a girl staying with her too—Jenny Forbes I think the name was."

Meg stood with her eyes and ears wide open. Why was Jenny calling herself Forbes? She couldn't make it out at all. Mary the housemaid had blenched at repeating all the village gossip on the subject, so Meg had no clue.

She was very quiet all the way home. And she forgot to spend her half-crown.

CHAPTER 35

All the questions which Meg wanted to ask churned in her till the next morning. She managed, however, to run upstairs whilst Mary was making beds.

"Can I help you, Mary?" she said. "I've got a few minutes."

"Well, it's Carter's business really, but I suppose she thinks herself too grand for the making of beds."

"I'll help you. I'd like to," said Meg.

Mary gave her a sharp glance. What was the child up to, she'd like to know. Something, she'd be bound. Well, it would come out, good or bad.

They had half made Joyce's bed before anything came. Then Meg said,

"You know the big shop in Langton—the one where you can get everything—boots, and shoes, and boxes, and knives, and dresses, and hats—"

"Jakers," said Mary. "Of course I know it. It's a very good shop. What about it? Did you go there yesterday?"

Meg nodded as she turned down the sheet.

"Yes, we did. And when we were on the other side of the shop from Carter there was a little dog playing, and Joyce pulled her hand out of mine and ran to look at it, but I stayed where I was."

"You ought to have gone with Joyce," said Mary.

Meg straightened the eiderdown on her side of the bed.

"No," she said, "I wanted to listen. There were two ladies at the counter quite close to me, and they were talking. And what do you think they were talking about? You'll never guess."

Mary pricked up her ears. What in the world had the child got hold of now? She said, "Couldn't say, I'm sure," and waited for more.

It came, as she knew that it would.

"They were talking about Jenny—at least I think it must have been Jenny they meant, only they'd got her name wrong. They called her Jenny Forbes. Jenny Forbes—just think! As if she was our cousin!"

Mary said, "That's as may be," and flung the bed-spread over for Meg to catch and straighten out on her side.

They moved to the other bed, but before they got there Meg caught Mary by the wrist with a cold little hand and said,

"She's not our cousin, is she? I wish she was, but I don't see how she could be. Mary, do tell me! There's something going on—I know there is. About Jenny, I mean. Why did she run away in the night like she did? And why does she call herself Jenny Forbes? Oh, Mary, do tell me!"

"I can't, Meg—I really can't. Your mother would send me away as soon as look at me if I did."

"I won't tell—I won't ever tell. I promise I won't. If she's our cousin, we ought to know. Oughtn't we?"

"I'd have thought so," said Mary with a toss of the head.

"Well then, you can tell me," said Meg. She gave a little nod, let go of the hand that she was holding, and pranced round to the other side of her bed. "If you are nice and tell me all about it, I won't say a word. But if you're *not,* well then it'll be just too bad for you." She nodded her head and screwed up her mouth.

"Oh, you wicked child!" said Mary. Then as the roguish eyes met hers a little giggle escaped her. "My word, you are a one, Meg!" she said. "I don't know what children are coming to, I don't indeed. Well then, I can only tell you how the talk has gone, and from that it seems that Mr. Richard Alington Forbes was Jenny's father, but her mother had an accident the day he was killed in France, so she couldn't say they were married. And she came down here to Miss Garstone that had been her governess, and she died when her baby came. And no one knew they'd been married, so your father was the next heir, and he come in for the property, which was really Miss Jenny's. And somehow or another the truth come out and Miss Jenny run away."

Meg was deeply interested.

"Why did she do that?" she said.

"Oh well—" Mary had the grace to blush—"it was awkward for her being here. See?"

"No, I don't."

Mary had gone too far to draw back. She began to wish that she hadn't begun.

"Oh well, you're too young to understand, but it meant turning you out, and I dare say she'd feel awkward about that."

"Oh, she would. Jenny wouldn't like to turn anyone out—I know she wouldn't. I don't see why we couldn't all stay here together. Do you?"

Mary thought that that would be, of course, the sensible thing to do. But did she see Mrs. Forbes doing it? She did not, and that was the truth. She didn't know what Jenny knew, but with what she herself knew in her own mind she could very well imagine why Jenny had run away. She made some noncommittal answer, and was instantly met by further questions.

"I shall go to Mother and ask her why Jenny has gone away."

"Meg, you promised—"

"No, I didn't. I only said I wouldn't say anything that would get you into trouble. And I won't—truly. But I don't see at all why I couldn't go to my mother and say that I'd heard Jenny was staying at Hazeldon."

"Meg, you can't—you mustn't! Mrs. Forbes doesn't know that there's any talk about it. She'd be mad."

Meg considered this.

"Well then, I could write a secret letter to Jenny, and you could post it for me. I'll tell her I've heard where she is, and she can write back to me and put it in an envelope that is addressed to you at your home, so that no one will know anything about it except you and me and Jenny. There's a lovely plan for you!"

"But, Meg—I don't see—"

Meg waved her hands in the air.

"You haven't got to see anything. You've only got to take my letter to the post and put it in, and when the answer comes back you'll just have to put it in your pocket and bring it up here and give it to me when there's nobody looking. It'll be our own secret and ever so exciting. And it's quite easy, so there's nothing for you to fuss about."

Mary stood still on the far side of the bed. She was thinking. Suppose she did what Meg wanted her to do. She could do it quite easily. . . . Well, there would be an awful row if it ever came out. But how could it come out? It couldn't, really. Not unless Meg let it out—and why should she do that? She'd get into a most frightful row if she did. She considered Meg very seriously. Very good at escaping rows, that's what she was. And quite good at getting you into them if she wanted to. It seemed to Mary that it would be less dangerous to go along with Meg and do what she wanted. She could hold her tongue could Meg—she'd noticed that. The thoughts raced through her mind. If she went in with

Meg and Jenny got to know about it, there'd be a good wedding present to be got out of it perhaps. Jack Brent had a good job. She didn't want to get married yet, but she didn't want to lose him. He was getting a bit impatient, and there was that bold piece Florrie Hayling doing all she could to get him.

As these thoughts chased through Mary's mind, Meg stood watching her. She could manage Mary. She mustn't hurry her, not at this stage. She knew very well what she was thinking—could she do it without being found out? And the answer to that one was—easily. Only they two would know, and if neither of them spoke it was just too easy.

Would it pay her? Meg thought that one out too. She didn't know all the ins and outs, but she knew enough, and she had a very quick, sure instinct. She waited therefore with astonishing patience until Mary's mind was made up. She wasn't in any real doubt of the outcome. She knew all about Florrie and Jack, and took a passionate interest. She thought Mary would be very silly to let Florrie get him. She didn't like Florrie at all. A bold giggling piece, that was what Carter had called her. And Jack was nice. She liked him very much. He had a merry eye, and he could whistle beautifully.

At this point she began to think that Mary had had enough time to make up her mind. She said with an impatient ring in her voice,

"I *said* there was nothing for you to fuss over. What about it?"

Mary heard herself saying,

"Well, if you promise not to tell—"

CHAPTER 36

Mr. Mottingley was in his office. He had resumed his business habits, but his mind was elsewhere. Only by keeping it strictly on business was there any relief from the dreadful suspense that racked him.

There was a knock on the door, and he looked up frowning. His preoccupation was hard won and to be held on to at all costs. The girl who looked in was pretty and shy. She was quite dreadfully afraid of Mr. Mottingley, but she liked Jimmy. Everyone in the office liked him. She was hotly partisan, too. Whoever had killed that girl, it certainly wasn't Jimmy Mottingley. Anyone who knew him could tell that.

"What is it?" said Mr. Mottingley at his shortest.

"It's—it's Miss Lingbourne, sir. She—she wanted to see you."

"Miss Lingbourne?" He frowned. "What does she want?"

"She didn't say, sir."

"Tell her I don't see anyone without an appointment!" The words came sharp and hard.

And then as the girl turned away and was leaving the room his mind altered. Jimmy had been friendly with the family. It was just possible that the girl knew something that would help. Well then, why didn't she make an appointment? Her brother was there in the office. Girls didn't always tell their brothers everything. It was just a chance. He said,

"Wait a moment—show her in!"

He sat back in his chair and waited. When the door opened and Kathy Lingbourne came in he looked at her with attention. She was very quietly dressed, and she was pale. He did not know that he had ever seen her before. He might have passed her in the road, he might have seen her with her brother. She wasn't anything to write home about. And then she was looking him straight in the face and saying, "How do you do, Mr. Mottingley?" as if she had come on a social visit. He said rather grimly,

"What can I do for you, Miss Lingbourne?"

She took the chair on the opposite side of his table and looked at him. When she spoke he noticed her voice—a nice voice, quiet and sweet. She said,

"I've come to see you about your son—about Jimmy."

"Indeed? And what have you to say?"

Kathy paused. She was not afraid of Mr. Mottingley. Jimmy was—she knew that. She said,

"I thought I had better come and see you. Miss Silver asked me not to go and see Jimmy. She said it might do him harm. But I thought if I came to see you, that wouldn't matter."

Mr. Mottingley said harshly, "What have you to do with my son?"

A little colour came into Kathy's pale face.

"I'm his friend," she said. And whether it was the words, or her look, or the tone of her voice, Mr. Mottingley underwent a surprising change of consciousness. He believed her, and not only did he believe her, but he had a sudden and most amazing understanding of her motive in coming to him. He said quietly and gravely,

"He could do with a friend, poor lad."

Kathy's hands clasped one another tightly.

"Yes," she said. "Oh, Mr. Mottingley, you know he didn't harm her. You do know that, don't you?"

"Ay—I know it. He didn't harm her to her death—I

know that. But there are other ways of harming—I can't hold him clear of them."

Kathy looked at him.

"Was it all his fault?" she said.

"Maybe not. It's not for us to put the blame on one or on the other. Why did you come here?"

She gave him a straight answer.

"I wanted to see you for myself."

"And why did you want to do that?"

"I don't know. I felt that I needed to know you."

"Why?"

She spread out her hands.

"I don't really know. I just felt that I had to come."

Mr. Mottingley recovered himself with a jolt.

"Are you telling me that you are sweet on Jimmy?" he said sternly.

He was prepared for tears. He certainly expected that calm of hers to break. The curious thing was that when it remained impervious he felt, not frustration, but a secret triumph.

Kathy said, "Oh, no, Mr. Mottingley. It's not that. It's just that he has been like one of the family. I have two brothers and a sister, you know. He's a friend of Len's, so he has been at the house a good deal. And I wanted to see you. You see, I couldn't help knowing that Jimmy was quite desperately afraid of you."

Well, she had got it out. She had not known whether she would be able to say it, but she had got it out.

Mr. Mottingley felt as if a cold light had been turned on him. It was a very uncomfortable feeling. He frowned and said,

"You mean that he has a proper respect for me and for his mother?"

"Oh, yes! I know that he has—I didn't mean that. I meant—Oh, Mr. Mottingley, I meant that he is quite horribly frightened of you."

He stared at her.

"I don't understand."

Kathy's hands were clasped tightly together again.

"I know it's difficult for you. But won't you try? Please, *please* do! Jimmy is so afraid of you that he goes all to bits at the thought of telling you anything. Sometimes when I've said to him, 'But why don't you *tell* your father?' he has just wrung his hands and said, 'I can't do it—I just can't.' And that's true, you know—you can see it. He's just horribly afraid of you."

"He is the only one that lived," said Mr. Mottingley. "There were three that died one after the other. And then there was Jimmy. And we made a solemn promise that we wouldn't spoil him, but bring him up in the fear of God."

Kathy raised her eyes and fixed them upon him.

"It is better for children to love their parents than to be afraid of them," she said. "You see, if they're afraid, and they do something wrong, they don't come out with it. It just piles up inside them and goes on getting worse. I think that's what happened with Jimmy. At first he didn't mean any harm, and there wasn't any. And then he began telling lies about where he had been and what he had been doing. I found out quite by accident, and I didn't get a chance to speak to him because he stopped coming to our house about then. Miriam—I don't want to say anything about her that I needn't—but I've got to make you understand that it wasn't all Jimmy's fault. She—she was—I don't know how to put it, but I think that if she wanted something she would see to it that she got it. I don't want to be unkind, but I think that she was like that. And Jimmy was—I don't know how to put it—but he hadn't a chance. Len did speak to him, but it wasn't any use. He was—" she paused and said, "fascinated. But he didn't kill her. You do know that, don't you?"

"Yes, I know that." He got out a pocket-handkerchief and blew his nose. "Why are you telling me all this?" he said.

"I thought you ought to know. I'll go now, Mr. Mottingley."

CHAPTER 37

*Jenny came down to break-*fast to find a very peculiar letter propped up beside her place at table. That is to say, it would have appeared very peculiar to anyone with a different background, but to Jenny it simply said Meg. Meg had a passion for writing letters, and she had no one to send them to. They weren't popular with her brothers, who were away from home and might at least have pretended to be pleased when they got one, but they didn't trouble. Jenny would have thought more of them if they had, but they were not to know that. Mac wouldn't have cared, but Alan might have. So, in default of anyone else to whom she could write what she called a real letter, Jenny was the obvious person to practise on. But she had never had one through the post before. And it was addressed to Miss Jenny Forbes. That was strange. And the address was quite correct in Meg's big untidy writing.

She opened the envelope and read the letter inside. It said:

Darling darling Jenny, why did you go away? We miss you dreadfully. At least I do, and if Joyce has any sense she does too. You never know with Joyce, and I didn't want to make her cry which isn't good for her, so I didn't ask her. But I miss

you *quite dreadfully*. Why did you go away?
Please, *please* tell me. I don't want to be a bother,
and I won't tell anyone if you don't want me to,
but do just write to me. You can't have forgotten
about us all in such a short time. I will *never* forget you. I promise most faithfully that I won't,
and that I'll never tell anyone that you wrote. It's
quite horrid without you here, it really is. Mary
says you are called Jenny Forbes now. She didn't
want to tell me, but I made her, so you won't give
her away, will you? She said you are really our
cousin, which is very exciting and I am so glad.
She says the whole village is talking about it, so it
isn't a secret any more. She says it was a secret
that your father was married to your mother, and
that no one knew about their being married, because he was killed when his aeroplane crashed in
the war and she had an accident so that she
couldn't speak. And she died the day you were
born, so no one knew. It's a very sad story, isn't
it? I would have cried if I hadn't been so interested. When you are very interested you can't cry
somehow, but I feel as if I could cry now. Please,
Jenny, write and say that you haven't forgotten
me, and that you'll come back and let us be all
together again. I couldn't *bear* it if you didn't.

Your loving Meg

P.S. Please send the answer to Mary's house. I
think you had better put two envelopes, the one
inside to me and the outside one to Mary. Her
name in case you have forgotten is Miss Mary
Stebbins, Alingford. Good-bye. I do love you.
Please, *please* do write to me.

Richard, coming in, found Jenny crying.

"Darling, what is it?"

She put Meg's letter into his hand.

"She's such a dear, and she really does love me. What can I do?"

He read the letter and whistled.

"Well, it's out," he said. "You must write to Mrs. Forbes."

"I don't want to," said Jenny, looking up with drenched brown eyes.

"Darling, you really must. Caroline would say the same."

"I don't *want* to."

"Now, Jenny—"

She turned to him, clutching at his hand, his arm.

"Oh, Richard, no—no! I don't want to tell them where I am—I don't want them to know. It—it frightens me."

"My dear child—" He put his arms round her, and she sobbed and clung to him. When she was a little calmer he said,

"Can I see the child's letter?"

"Yes, yes. Oh, anything you like."

He read Meg's artless letter, and failed to see why Jenny should have been so much upset by it. He said so.

"She's a nice child and very fond of you. I don't know why it should upset you."

"I don't know why either, but it did—it does."

"I can't imagine why it should."

She took the letter from his hand and read it through. Then she turned a puzzled glance on him.

"Richard—"

"What is it, darling?"

"I don't know why it upset me so much. I don't *know* why."

"As long as it doesn't go on upsetting you—"

"No, it doesn't—not now. It was just one of those things. I opened the letter, and first of all I was pleased because Meg had written to me. And then quite suddenly I was most dreadfully afraid. It was just as if there was something shut up in the letter and I had opened the door for it to get out. I've never had a feeling like that before. It was quite dreadfully strong. It—it frightened me."

He was watching her intently.

"You're not frightened now, are you?"

"Not like I was. No, I'm not frightened—not any more. But I still don't want to write to Mrs. Forbes."

"You must," he said. And with that Caroline came into the room with the bacon.

They had breakfast without any more discussion, but when they had finished Richard said,

"Jenny has had a letter from one of the little girls. It's from Meg. She knows that Jenny is here."

Caroline looked up.

"That's due to Mrs. Merridew of course," she said. "You couldn't hope to keep it a private matter with her writing to her cousin at Alingford—and she'd be bound to do that. You say the letter is from the child?"

"Yes," said Jenny. "It's from Meg."

"Well, I think that you ought to write to Mrs. Forbes, Jenny. It won't be easy of course, but it hasn't been really right—" Her voice trailed away.

Jenny was looking at her.

"No," she said. "None of it's right, is it?"

She wrote to Mrs. Forbes after breakfast. She sat for a long time with the pen in her hand before she got going. In the end she dipped the pen again and wrote:

Dear Mrs. Forbes,

I heard what Mac said to you the night I went away. I couldn't stay after what I heard. I didn't mean to listen. I was in the window seat behind the curtain, and I thought that you would just look in and go away. But you didn't. When I heard what you had to say I couldn't get up and show myself. I suppose I ought to have done it, but I couldn't. I heard everything. You can't be surprised that I went away. I couldn't stay. I don't think you will want to see me. I am here with Richard's aunt, Miss Danesworth. I met Richard when I was running away, and he brought me here. He is Richard Alington Forbes, and he is a cousin. Richard went to Somerset House in London and got a copy of my father and mother's marriage certificate.

Jenny Forbes

When she had finished writing she put her letter in an envelope and addressed and stamped it. Just before she shut it up she went into the kitchen and showed it to Caroline and Richard.

"Is it all right?" she said. "I can't write it again—I really can't."

Caroline read it, kissed her without speaking, and went out of the room. Jenny was left with Richard. He, too, read the letter.

Jenny was watching him.

"There's nothing else to say, is there? Nothing at all?"

He put the letter back into her hand.

"No, there's nothing else," he said.

CHAPTER 38

Miss Silver had come down to Hazeldon. One or two points had arisen at the inquest, and she had a strong feeling that Hazeldon would bear to have a magnifying glass turned on it. For one thing, she believed Jimmy Mottingley's story. She found it impossible to do otherwise. Now, if Miriam Richardson had got up to go at seven o'clock, she must have been there on the Heath a few minutes later—a very few minutes. And Jimmy Mottingley was still in his mother's drawing-room listening impatiently to her conversation with old Mrs. Marsden at either six-fifteen or six-thirty. To have accomplished the drive in three-quarters of an hour would have been a clear impossibility. To have covered the same distance in a quarter of an hour's extra time would have been just barely possible. According to the evidence of the stranger, Mrs. Marsden, the time at which he left was just short of ten minutes past six, but his mother put it twenty minutes later. In the circumstances her evidence would be gravely suspect, and in view of Jimmy's statement that the clock was to say the least of it erratic, no reliance could be placed upon it. If he had really left at ten minutes past six and had driven as fast as possible, he might have been at the place where Miriam met her death by, say, ten past seven. That is, ten minutes after she left Miss Danesworth's house. Miss Silver thought that she might try and find out whether anyone in Hazeldon had noticed the arrival of Jimmy Mottingley's car. If they had, and if they had any idea at what time they noticed it, it would certainly be a help.

She went into Mrs. Dean's shop, and was quite

pleased to find it full and everyone talking. The first words she caught told her what they were talking about. She stood still in the corner of the shop looking earnestly at some rather damaged liquorice sweets and hoped that her attention would appear to be focussed on them.

A fair-haired young woman was saying, "That Jimmy Mottingley he've got a sort of look of my brother Bill, and I've sure Bill wouldn't lay a finger on a fly."

An older woman took her up.

"Well, I don't know about that," she said.

"You don't know about what, Mrs. Wilson?" The young woman had flushed up. She had a pretty skin and a clear colour. "You are not saying that our Bill 'ud do a thing like that, are you? Because if you are—"

"Well, I'm not, me dear, and that's that, and no need to get red about it either. And I'll have a quarter of the tea and a pot of that black currant jelly. My black currants were no good at all this year. I'll have to have the bushes out, that's what, and whether it's worth while I don't know. I don't ever remember those bushes having anything wrong with them when I was a girl, but nowadays they keep on getting that big bud they talk about."

A little pale-faced woman next to her broke in.

"I don't know what things are coming to, I'm sure. They find out new diseases every five minutes, that's what I say. You dunno where you are for them. There's that myxy that all those rabbits have gone for—" Her voice died away. She said in a nervous undertone, "I don't know, I'm sure. There's some thinks one way, and some thinks another."

Mrs. Dean leaned across the counter and addressed Miss Silver.

"Good-morning," she said.

"Oh, good-morning." Miss Silver looked in her bag

and drew out her purse. "I wonder if you have any peppermints."

By the time that the peppermints were bought she had established the most cordial relations. The shop had cleared a little, and she managed to bring the conversation round to Jimmy Mottingley.

"That was a strange case you had here. The week before last, was it?"

"Dreadful," said Mrs. Dean. "You read about things like that in the papers, but you don't expect to see them happening on your own doorstep so to speak."

"No indeed," said Miss Silver warmly.

"Though I don't say it was a right down surprise to me her being murdered. I suppose I oughtn't to say so now that she's dead, but if she wasn't the very type and moral of what gets into the papers one way or another, well, I don't know what I'm talking about." She tossed her head as much as to say she knew very well, and so did Miss Silver.

Miss Silver looked suitably shocked.

"This girl—you knew her?"

"I've seen her," said Mrs. Dean darkly. "You're not supposed to say things about people who are dead, but I can't see it that way myself. If you're flighty and domineering, then you *are* and there's no getting from it, and dead or alive it's all one. But that's my way of thinking and no call to press it on you."

Miss Silver had a good deal to think about when she finally came out of the shop. Miriam had not impressed the village favourably. Jenny had. Mrs. Dean was loud in her praise.

"As nice a young lady as ever stepped. And they say that she's got a fortune, too. But there, perhaps I shouldn't have said that. The fact is, Mr. Richard's a favourite here, and everyone 'ud be glad to see him fixed up with a nice young wife. That girl that was murdered, she was after him, you know. But there, least said soonest mended, and I shouldn't get talking."

Miss Silver smiled. She had a gift for drawing people out, and, as Frank Abbott had often said, it was not done of design. When she showed interest it was because she was genuinely interested. As she stepped into the street she became aware of Jenny Forbes. She was just coming out of the other shop, and at the sight of Miss Silver she stopped and said, "How do you do?" Miss Silver found the meeting a pleasant and, she hoped, a propitious one.

"I was on my way to see Miss Danesworth. Perhaps I might walk with you."

"Yes, do."

Jenny's quick smile flashed out and her colour rose. She was nervous. Now why? It was the same thing which Miss Silver had noticed at their first meeting. And yet Jenny was not a nervous type. She should have a confidence which was quite plainly lacking.

"You must be wondering why I have come here again," she said, turning to Jenny.

Jenny changed colour. One moment she was pale, the next all a bright blush.

"Oh, no—no," she said in confusion.

Miss Silver smiled.

"My dear, why are you embarrassed?"

"Oh, I'm not," said Jenny quickly.

"I think that you are. And I think that I should like to know why. It is possible that you know something that you have not told. If that is the case, I would beg you to think very carefully of what you may be doing."

"Of what I may be doing?" Jenny's voice was a startled one.

"Yes, my dear. That boy in prison at Colborough—if you know anything at all you owe it to him to be perfectly frank."

Jenny's heart was beating so fast that she stood still. She did not seem to have enough breath to carry her feet forward—not with her heart thumping like this. She said unevenly,

"To be perfectly frank? But I don't know anything— I don't indeed. It's only—only—"

"Yes, my dear?"

Jenny had turned round and was looking at her. They had both stopped. Before them lay the dip in the road. Then it rose again, and just beyond the dip were Miss Danesworth's cottage and Mrs. Merridew's small house.

Jenny raised her eyes to Miss Silver's face. What she saw there apparently reassured her. She felt steadier. Her mind cleared. All at once the only thing that mattered was that she should tell the exact truth. She said,

"I've been troubled."

"I can see that, my dear."

"If I tell you—you see, I don't know if it will hurt anyone—" She stood there with her lips parted looking at Miss Silver, who was very grave.

"I cannot tell you that. I can only say that if wrong has been done, the consequences should fall upon the wrong-doer, and not upon an innocent stranger."

Jenny said, "Yes—that's what I keep on saying to myself. If he hasn't got anything to do with it—and he can't, *he can't*—Oh!" She put up her hands to her face for a moment and covered her eyes as if to shut something out.

Miss Silver's gaze was full of compassion. She spoke very gently.

"I think that you must tell me what you are afraid of."

Jenny dropped her hands. The tears were running down. She said,

"I don't know—I don't know what I ought to do—I don't indeed—"

And then all at once she did know. She held her hands together tight, tight, and she said,

"That boy—he said there was a note. For me. He took it back afterwards and pretended that he hadn't said it. It was a note addressed to Miss Jenny Hill. That's what I was called before I came here. It was my mother's name, and they thought—everyone thought that my father hadn't married her, so I was called Jenny Hill, which was her name. And then I heard Mrs. Forbes and her son talking. I didn't mean to listen, but I'd been crying, and I was sitting behind the curtain in the schoolroom. There's a window seat with a curtain in front of it. I was there, and they came in, and Mac told his mother he had been to Somerset House and he had got a copy of the certificate—my father and mother's marriage certificate. And he said the place belonged to me, but there was no need to tell me anything. He would marry me, and if I ever found out, it wouldn't matter then. So I ran away in the night, and I met Richard who is a distant cousin, and he brought me here." Jenny's tears had dried. She felt drained and empty, but quite calm.

Miss Silver was looking at her very kindly. Her mind was turning over the things that might have happened, and she came very near to the truth. That Jenny was speaking honestly and sincerely she had no doubt at all. She said,

"Do you mean, my dear, that you actually heard Mrs. Forbes and her son discussing this matter?"

"Yes."

"And that they decided to keep you in the dark, persuade you to marry your cousin, and trust to your not finding out?"

"Mrs. Forbes didn't want him to marry me. She said so."

"And he? I don't want to ask what you would rather not answer, but I think you must see that it affects the question of whether he is to be trusted or not."

Jenny shook her head.

"No," she said, "he is not to be trusted. That was why I came away. I didn't feel I could stay after I had heard them talk. They didn't pretend to each other, you know. And they didn't think of me at all—that was quite plain. They only thought about keeping the property. Mac said that it wouldn't matter so much if I found out after he had married me, but that it wouldn't be safe unless he did, because I might find out."

Miss Silver found herself shocked.

"You are quite sure about this?"

Jenny said simply, "I heard him say it. I wouldn't have ever thought of such a thing unless I had to."

All this time they had been standing in the road which led up to the two houses, Miss Danesworth's and Mrs. Merridew's. As if she had finished all that she had to say Jenny turned and began to walk towards the houses. Miss Silver followed her.

"And you met your cousin?" she said.

"Yes, I met Richard. Wasn't it a good thing?" The animation had returned to Jenny's voice. It was as if she had put away her old life with its pain and its disappointment and had turned back again into the new life with Richard.

"Had you known him before?"

"Oh, no. I didn't know that he existed. It was the middle of the night, you know, and I saw a car coming, so I stepped out into the road to stop it. And it was Richard. I made him get out, because I couldn't drive away with just anyone, and I wanted to see if I could trust him. And when I saw him—oh, it was wonderful, because he was the exact image of the Richard Forbes whom he is called after! I could see him quite plainly because there was a very bright moon, and when I saw him I did think that I was dreaming—just for a minute, you know. I asked him who he was, and he said, 'My name is Richard Forbes.' And I said, 'I've seen you before.' And when he said, 'Where?' I told him, 'All my life,' I said. 'You're the portrait in the hall—the picture of Richard Alington Forbes.' And he said, 'That's my name.' " She stopped speaking. All her colour had come back and her eyes shone. "It was a wonderful thing to have happened," she said.

"Yes, it was. How did he come to be there?"

"He was going to see them at Alington House, but he'd been delayed on the way, and he thought that he would drive a little nearer and then sleep in the car until the inn was open, and have breakfast, and then go round."

"Did they know he was coming?"

Jenny opened her eyes wide.

"Oh, I don't think so. No, I'm sure they didn't know. And he'd forgotten about it being Sunday, and of course they'd be going to church. It wasn't very clever of him—I told him so."

"And what did he say to that?"

"He just laughed," said Jenny. "And of course it didn't really matter, because he didn't go there after all. He took me to Miss Danesworth's instead."

They had arrived at the gate of the cottage. Miss Silver stood between Jenny and the gate.

"And what did Miss Danesworth say?"

"I don't know what she said to Richard. She was sweet to me."

"My dear, I must ask you one thing."

"Yes, Miss Silver?"

"It is this. Have you never heard from these Forbeses? Did they never try to trace you?"

"No, they didn't."

Miss Silver looked graver than ever.

"I find that a very singular thing. You did not leave a note, or tell them where you had gone?"

Jenny said, "No, I didn't. I didn't know where I was going." She wondered why Miss Silver was asking these things. A feeling of distress rose in her. "Why—why do you ask?"

"I am going to ask you something else. I am going to ask you how old you are."

Jenny answered her quite simply.

"I was seventeen in August."

"Then, my dear, do you not think that Mrs. Forbes should have taken some steps to find you?"

"I didn't want her to find me," said Jenny.

Miss Silver was very much shocked. She was accustomed to judging character, and she thought that Jenny was both truthful and innocent.

And then Jenny said, "I expect they knew where I was. Mrs. Merridew writes to her cousin who lives at Alingford. She must have told her, because Meg knew. She is one of the little girls. She wrote to me."

"When did you get the letter?" said Miss Silver quickly.

"It came yesterday morning, and when Richard and Caroline saw it they said that I ought to write to Mrs. Forbes. So I wrote to her—" Jenny paused, steadying herself. "I said that I had heard what Mac said to her the night I went away. I said that I didn't mean to listen. I said I had heard everything, and when I had heard it I couldn't get up and show myself. I said I was staying here with Richard's aunt Miss Danesworth. And I said that Richard had gone to Somerset House in London and got a copy of my father and mother's marriage certificate. And I signed the letter Jenny Forbes. It felt very strange, because I had never written it before, but I thought that I ought to. So you see, if everyone knew, then it wasn't a secret any more, was it? And if Meg could write to me, then Mrs. Forbes could have written, or—or Mac. That's what frightens me, Miss Silver. Why don't they say anything?"

Miss Silver said, "I don't know, my dear."

They went together into the house.

CHAPTER 39

Miss Silver had tea at Miss Danesworth's. Richard was not there. He had gone to London, and she had a very pleasant time with Miss Danesworth and Jenny. After tea she enquired the way to Mrs. Pratt's, and Jenny at once offered to go with her. Miss Silver thought for a while, and then accepted the offer.

It was bad luck for Dicky that things turned out as they did. On most afternoons he would not have been there at all. On this particular day he *was* there, because he had come in to wait for Stuffy Craddock who was going to pick him up when he had had his tea. Stuffy wouldn't miss his tea, not if it was ever so, and Mrs. Craddock wouldn't have let him miss it either. Dicky thought with assurance how much more fortunate he was himself. *His* mother never noticed whether he was in or not. And then quite suddenly he had a curious lonely feeling, and he set his chin and whistled quite loudly to keep up his spirits.

Mrs. Pratt was out. She wouldn't be home for another hour. She wasn't a good worker, but she managed to get enough work to keep her going. People were sorry for her, and she didn't do too badly under strict supervision.

Miss Silver and Jenny came to the door of Mrs. Pratt's cottage and heard Dicky whistling.

"He's there," said Jenny. "I was afraid he mightn't be. They don't have any regular times for meals."

Miss Silver looked shocked.

"Do you think that this boy's word is to be relied on?" she said.

"No, I don't," said Jenny frankly. "I think he'll twist and lie if he can. That's why I offered to come with you." She knocked on the door as she spoke, and the whistling stopped instantly.

After a moment steps could be heard descending the stairs. A pause, and the door was opened. An untidy, shabby boy stood there. He smiled and his face lit up. His very blue eyes beamed on them.

"My mother's out," he said. "Can I take a message?"

There was nothing to show that he recognized Jenny, yet he had done so at once. She said quite directly,

"Hullo, Dicky. It's you we want to see, not your mother. Can we come in? This is Miss Silver."

"How do you do, Dicky?" said Miss Silver.

Dicky gave back her "How do you do?" His mind was racing. He knew who Miss Silver was, and knowing that, he could guess why she had come to see him. The question was, did he tell what he knew, or didn't he? He wasn't at all sure. With a sense of the fitness of things he led the way, not into the dirty, crowded, and disordered kitchen, but into the front room, never used and dreadfully neat. Four chairs stood with their backs to the wall, and a hard unyielding sofa stood with its back to the window. The curtains were neither clean nor dirty. They had hung there since James Pratt had been carried home dead—untouched and disregarded over the years that had passed since then. To Dicky the room was a very fine one. He showed an immense pride in it. The stuffy atmosphere and the film of dust over everything merely marked it out as a place apart.

Having taken them into this room, he shut the door and leaned against it, his smile subdued by the importance of the occasion and by its setting. His blue eyes were soft and pensive. He was thinking very hard, and what he thought was, "They want something, else they wouldn't be here. What do they want? If I listen I shall find out."

He glanced up at Miss Silver. It was a look to melt the heart of any old lady, he knew that. But the look was met by a gaze so clear and so alarming that it was all he could do to hold on to the innocence of his smile. He would have backed away a little, but he was already against the door. In his mind he was saying, "What jer want? I've done nothing, I haven't. What jer want to come down on me for?" but he kept the words in.

Miss Silver spoke. She said his name.

"Dicky—"

Her tone steadied him. He smiled with an effect of shyness.

"Dicky, I have heard that you are a very intelligent boy. I wonder if you are intelligent enough to realize that it is better to keep on the right side of the law."

Dicky swallowed and said, "Is it?"

Miss Silver smiled.

"You will find that out for yourself," she said. "It is very easy to pull things crooked and to make an effect, and that is what starts a boy going wrong."

"Is it?" said Dicky in a tone of limpid innocence.

"Yes," said Miss Silver on an assured note. "Now you, Dicky, are at the parting of the ways. You can tell the truth and be praised for it, or you can tell lies which will be found out, and which will destroy your character."

Dicky hastened to put his best foot forward.

"I wouldn't tell no lies," he said. "Not if it was ever so."

Miss Silver nodded approvingly.

"I shall know if you do," she said.

And quite suddenly Dicky felt it in his bones that she would. It was a very alarming feeling. He had never had it with anyone before, and he didn't like it at all. If he had been outside the house he would have yielded to his instinct and have run away. He could have kept out of sight until the old lady had gone. He could—he couldn't do anything—not really. He was a fool to have got up against the door like he had. If he turned round to open it she'd have him, and the girl would come and help her.

All the while that he was thinking these things his smile remained limpidly innocent. It had only wavered for a moment. Miss Silver was saying,

"Now, Dicky, will you tell me truthfully about the note you had?"

"The note?" He might never have heard of such a thing.

"Yes. The note that was addressed to Miss Jenny Hill."

"Oh, that note—"

He was playing for time, but Miss Silver gave him no time. She said, "Yes," and then, "I want to know what you did with it. Who gave it to you and told you to give it to Miss Jenny Hill? Did you know who Miss Jenny Hill was?"

Dicky considered. If he put a foot wrong now it would be very difficult to recover. He could think of lots of lies to tell, but there was no doubt that the plain unvarnished truth would be safest. He immediately felt a strong glow of virtue.

"Course I knew!" he said in a tone of scorn. "Everyone in the village knowed as Miss Jenny Forbes had two names, and that her other name was Miss Jenny Hill. It was Mrs. Warrington as let it out. She's a talker she is. Everything as goes on at Mrs. Merridew's she talks about, and everyone in the village could know what she knowed."

"Then you meant to give the note to Miss Jenny?"

"Yes, I meant to. Only—" He came out with a burst of truth. "Only Roger Barton and Stuffy Craddock came up with me, and they had a smashing scheme on, and—and I went off with them. And I forgot all about the note until after the murder."

"And then did you not think that what you knew might be important?"

It was really astonishingly easy to tell the truth. You didn't have to think all round what you said. You could just go ahead and say it as it came. In a glow of virtue Dicky replied,

"Not at first I didn't."

"And why was that?"

Dicky wriggled.

"I don't know. It wasn't till I got to thinking about the number-plate being covered up."

Jenny had been standing over by the window. She felt terrified. Something was coming down on her—on all of them. She couldn't do anything to stop it. It was like standing in the path of an oncoming train. You could hear the whistle and you could see the smoke, and you couldn't move. She couldn't take her eyes off Dicky's face. She couldn't move, or speak, or do anything. The dreadful thing that was going to happen came nearer and nearer.

Miss Silver was speaking.

"How was the number-plate covered?"

"There was some sacking in the boot. It hung down behind and covered the number-plate."

"Then you couldn't see it?"

Dicky hesitated, but only for a moment. It was a smashing game telling the truth. And it was safe. You didn't have to stop and think about it, you could just go ahead. He went ahead.

"I'd some matches in my pocket. I struck one, and I looked at the number."

Jenny couldn't move. She had known that it was coming. Her hands were tightly clasped before her. When she looked at them afterwards she would see that her nails had cut the skin. At the time she saw nothing, felt nothing. Everything in her was keyed up to take what she knew was coming.

The questioning went on.

"Do you remember the number?"

"Acourse I do. It was 505." He gave the county letters too.

"You are quite sure about that?"

"Acourse I'm sure. I wouldn't make up a thing like that."

Jenny drew a long breath. The window seat was just behind her. She felt her way to it and sat down. She put her head in her hands and time went by her. So it *was* Mac. And Miriam had been killed instead of Jenny. She hadn't the slightest doubt about that. If Dicky hadn't met his friends, if he had delivered the letter, what would she have done? Would she have gone out to meet Mac? She couldn't tell. One moment it seemed to her as if she would have gone, and the next she recoiled with a shudder. She did not know what she would have done. She was never to know.

In upon her confusion and her hurrying thoughts there came Miss Silver's voice.

"Drink this, my dear. No, you must try. It is only water."

She managed a sip, and then another, and another. Her head cleared. She looked up at Miss Silver with piteous eyes.

"I'm all right."

"Yes, my dear, you are going to be quite all right. Stay still a little while."

Jenny opened her eyes. She had slid down from the window seat and was lying on the floor. The window above her head was wide open. It was the first time it had been open for years and years. Dicky disapproved very much. His mum never opened that window. His mum didn't hold with such-like, his mum didn't. These thoughts contended with the uplifting experience of having told the truth, the whole truth, and nothing but the truth. He remembered the words of the oath which he had taken in the case when he had had to give evidence, and repeated them to himself with the greatest satisfaction. There were no snags about telling the truth. You hadn't got to watch out for saying a thing one minute and contradicting yourself the next. You could just go straight on and tell it the way it happened, and nobody couldn't do nothing to you, not if it was ever so.

He ran upstairs and got Mac's letter. When he came down with it in his hand, Jenny had got up. She was sitting on the window seat and she looked very pale.

He came into the room with the letter in his hand and offered it to Miss Silver. It was indescribably dirty, creased, and stained, but it was still quite legible. Miss Silver took it, and read what Mac had written to Jenny nearly a fortnight before:

Jenny, *don't say anything to anyone,* but come out and meet me up on the heath as soon as it is quite dark.

Mac

Bring this with you.

And up in the top left-hand corner there was a date—the date of the murder.

CHAPTER 40

"*What will you do?*" said Jenny.

Miss Silver regarded her compassionately.

"I think you must know that, my dear," she said.

They were on their way back from the cottage. Jenny felt weak and tired, and as if a very long time had passed since she had got up that morning and Richard had gone off to catch his train to town. She said,

"Yes, I know. You'll tell the police."

"You know that I must tell them."

Jenny was silent for a moment. Then she said,

"It's a dreadful thing. It's too dreadful for one to take it in. Mac—he's always been so—so—" She paused for a word, and then said, "dominating. And for a long time I thought that he cared for me. When I found out that he didn't it was as if I was all alone. Do you know that feeling—as if everyone else in the world was gone away and there was nobody left but you? It's a dreadful feeling to have—like a nightmare."

Miss Silver looked at her very kindly.

"That is a very good comparison," she said. "There is no truth in the nightmare, and when you wake up it has no more power over you. You came out of the nightmare when you ran away from Alington House. You are not in it any longer, you know. You are quite free of it, with Miss Danesworth to care for you and Richard Forbes to protect you. You have nothing to be afraid of."

They came out of the side lane into the village. Jenny felt suddenly as if she had awakened from a bad dream. Up to now she had been taken up with Mac and what would happen to him, but now quite suddenly the other side of the picture came to her. There was Richard and Miss Danesworth. They were her family now. And she was safe. She wasn't alone and unprotected any longer. The consciousness slid in among her thoughts and steadied them. The next moment she was reproaching herself and thinking of the little girls and Alan, and even of Mrs. Forbes. She said,

"What will you do?"

"I must get into touch with Chief Inspector Abbott. He will want to take a statement. I think that I will leave you here, my dear, if you are quite sure that you will be all right."

"Yes, I'm quite sure," said Jenny. She wanted to be alone because she wanted to think. It is really not possible to think when there are people with you. She wanted to get right away by herself.

Miss Silver had very little time to think until she was in the London train. It had been a tiring day, but she was not thinking of herself. She was concerned with her coming interview with Frank Abbott. She had wired to him as soon as she reached Langton, and she hoped that he would not have left the office. She was not, however, prepared for him to meet her train, though she was very glad to see him.

"My dear Frank, you should not have troubled."

He smiled down at her.

"What have you been up to?"

"I will tell you, but let us get out of this first."

When he had put her into a taxi he got in himself and gave her address in Montague Mansions. Then he turned to her.

"Now, ma'am—what have you been doing?"

She said very gravely, "I have been finding a murderer, Frank. Let me tell you about it." And tell him she did, with all the scrupulous exactness which he had come to expect from her.

In conclusion she extracted from her bag the note which Mac had written to Jenny nearly a fortnight before, with its damning date in the top left-hand corner. He whistled as he looked at it.

"Where did you get this?" he said. And then, "It's had some rough treatment, hasn't it?"

"It has been in a boy's pocket. His name is Dicky Pratt, and he is a local boy at Hazeldon. He has no father, and I gather that he manages his mother. He was given this note on the date it was written, just before seven in the evening by a man who told him to give it to Miss Jenny Hill. He, as well as the whole village, knew that that was the name Miss Jenny Forbes had borne before she came there. They knew because Mrs. Mottingley who lives next door to Miss Danesworth has a cousin who lives at Alingford, which is where Jenny was brought up."

"My dear Miss Silver!"

"You must listen, Frank. You saw Jenny Forbes, and spoke to her. What you may not have known was her history."

He listened whilst she gave him the details. When she had done she went on,

"That letter was written by Mrs. Forbes' eldest son. He is, I think, about twenty-four years of age, and ever since he was six years old he has considered himself the heir of Alington. When Jenny heard him planning to marry her she ran away. Poor child—the whole affair was a most terrible shock. She ran away in the night, and she met her distant cousin Richard Forbes, who brought her to his aunt Miss Danesworth. It is an extraordinary story, but it is a true one. The letter which I have just shown you is terribly damning. There is no doubt that this Mac Forbes came down to Hazeldon with the intention of murdering his cousin Jenny. The girl who was murdered came from the house in which Jenny was staying. I do not wish to say anything against her. She paid very highly for what she did. But if, as seems likely, he mistook her for Jenny, she can have done nothing to undeceive him. He killed her supposing that he was killing Jenny. What he did not know was that the boy to whom he had given the note had crept round to the back of his car and had observed the number-plate. It was covered, my dear Frank, by a loose piece of sacking which hung down from the boot. This is clear evidence that the whole thing was planned. The number of the car was 505, and the county identification letters those of his home county."

Frank was putting away the stained letter in his pocketbook.

"And where is this young man to be found? Do you know that?"

Miss Silver said gravely, "I have his address." She gave it to him, and he wrote it down.

Jenny had gone home. She felt very, very tired, as if she could not think clearly. She did not know what to do, but with every moment she was realizing what she had already done. There was no future left for Mac—none at all. And it was she who had destroyed him. She stopped in the road and felt the mists close in on her again. She did not know what to do. She did not think that she could go through with it.

As she stood there it came over her that she ought to have died, then there would not have been any of this trouble. But she was strong and healthy—she had never even had a bad illness—and if she had died on the common it would have been murder. Mac was a murderer. The dreadfulness of what had happened was not hers, but his. Her mind went back to the scene in the court room, to Jimmy Mottingley's white face. How could she hold her tongue and let him suffer? The answer was plain. She couldn't. It just wasn't possible. The mist cleared from her, and she went on walking.

When she came to the door of the house and went in there was no one at home. Richard wasn't back yet, and she remembered that Miss Danesworth had said that she would go in and see Mrs. Merridew—"I don't want to in the least, but I think I ought to. I shan't stay unless she wants me."

Jenny went through to the sitting-room. She felt as if she had a great deal to think about. She sat down, and found that the telephone was straight in front of her. She changed her seat, and that was no better. She could not see it any longer, but she knew that it was there. She could give the number and ring him up. She could tell him what she had done. She could tell him that Miss Silver knew. That his dated letter was in her hands. That she had a statement from Dicky Pratt. She could tell him these things. And what was he to do when she had told him? Her mind shuddered away from that. She didn't know.

After a minute or two she got up, went to the telephone, and asked for Mac's number in London.

Mac was dressing. He was joining a party for *Whoops-a-Daisy,* the latest musical from the U.S.A. He whistled cheerfully to himself as he brushed his hair. He was quite at ease in his mind now. Whatever had happened to the note, it wouldn't turn up at this stage. On the whole he was well out of it. As for the young fool who had been arrested, he wasn't really likely to come to any harm, or if he did, well, it was just too bad.

The telephone bell rang, and he went into his outer room to answer it.

"Who is it?"

"It's Jenny. I've got something to tell you."

"Oh, have you?" his tone was short. What did the girl want?

She told him.

"Mac, something has happened—"

"What is it? I'm just going out."

"Listen, Mac. That boy you gave the note to—"

A crawling finger of fear touched his heart.

"What are you talking about?"

Jenny's voice came back strained and hurrying.

"I'm talking about you. That boy Dicky Pratt—he had your letter in his pocket."

"Oh, that old letter. What of it?"

Jenny's voice again. It sounded as if she was crying.

"It's dated, Mac. You dated it as you always do. Miss Silver—she's helping Jimmy Mottingley—Dicky gave her the letter, and she has gone up to town with it. And he can swear to the car. He came up the road and got behind it and lifted the sacking. He was just curious, but—" but her voice trailed away—"I thought I would let you know—" There was the click of the receiver as she hung it up, and that was all. That was all.

Mac stood with the receiver in his hand. He was very still, but his thoughts raced. He had time to get away. They could come and look for him, but they wouldn't find him. He would be gone. Where? And how? He saw at once with a desperate clarity that wherever he went and however he twisted there would be a price upon his head. The very suddenness of the blow shocked him past thought. He did not think these things. They were there, as an accomplished fact is there. They were not things that were going to happen. They were part of a chain of cause and effect which went on without wavering or hesitation to an appointed end. And there was only one end. He knew that.

He became aware that he was still holding the telephone up to his ear. A voice spoke through it. It asked him whether he had finished. He said, "Yes," and hung up. Then he opened the second drawer of his writing-table and took out the pistol.

Miss Silver was very glad to get home. It had been—she admitted it—a most tiring day. She had not ever been more glad of her comfortable room and of the thoughtful ministrations of her worthy Hannah.

It was when she was resting in front of the fire that her telephone rang. She got up and went across to it. At the first sound of Frank Abbott's voice she knew why he had rung her up.

"Is that you, Miss Silver?"

"Yes, Frank."

"We were too late. He had shot himself. The girl must have let him know."

Miss Silver said, "Poor Jenny!"

CHAPTER 41

Mrs. Forbes sat at her desk. She had sat there all night and had not moved. Only her thoughts moved, sliding from picture to picture, and when they had come to the end, the terrible remorseless end, they went back again and began at the beginning.

At the birth of her child—that was always how she thought of him, as *her* child. The little quiet man whom she had married didn't seem to come into it at all. The other children were his. She had borne them with impatience and without joy. But Mac was hers—hers only. He was like her people, the people from whom she herself derived her good looks, her pride, her independence. There was nothing in the other children that engaged her interest. As he grew, so her pride in him grew. When the war came he was between seven and eight years old. Her mind went back to a day in that first winter. They had just finished breakfast, and she had seen their name in the paper she had been turning over—Richard Alington Forbes. Her husband's second name was Alington. She said on a sudden impulse of curiosity, "Isn't that a relation of yours—Richard Alington Forbes?" Her husband said, "Yes," in his quiet absent way, and she had gone on to ask questions.

"Weren't they relations?"

"Oh, yes—some sort of second or third cousin—" He really wasn't sure which.

She remembered her own impatience.

"But good gracious me, one should keep up with one's relations!"

He was silent for a moment, and she thought he was not going to answer her, but in the end he said,

"What did you see about him?"

"Oh, nothing. I just saw his name. He was being posted to something or other. He's in the Air Force, isn't he?"

He said, "Yes, I believe he is."

That was the first time his name came up between them.

Then in the summer there came the landslide in Belgium—Dunkirk and all the excitement about that. Mrs. Forbes remembered that she had looked for news—not news of the battle, but news of Richard Alington Forbes. Her husband was the next of kin—she had made it her business to find out about that. Her husband was the next of kin, and Mac was the heir. Hope rose in her. It wasn't as if she had ever seen the man—and so many were being killed—Was it too much to expect that he wouldn't survive? She had so entirely made up her mind that he would die that when his name came out in the papers she accepted it as a foregone conclusion. It was perhaps as well for their future relationship that her husband was out of the country. She did not see him again while the war lasted, but she moved to Alington House, and Mac had been brought up there.

Her mind travelled slowly over the years. She remembered the first time she had seen Jenny. Miss Crampton had told her the story. "A very shocking thing," she had said. "But I feel I had better tell you about it. We all thought that Miss Garstone would get rid of the child to an orphanage or some institution of that kind. After all, it's not as if Jennifer Hill was a relation. I believe Miss Garstone had been her governess. Not anything to be proud of in the circumstances, I must say." The lift of Miss Crampton's chin came back with astonishing clearness, and the ring of her stentorian voice. She had thought the matter well over, and then she had gone to see Miss Garstone. She remembered that interview with bitterness, for, say what she would, nothing had had any effect. Miss Garstone owned her cottage, and quite politely but quite firmly Miss Garstone was not going to move.

With a kind of stunned bitterness Mrs. Forbes dwelt upon the obstinacy of Miss Garstone. If she had tried harder, if she had held out greater inducements, would Miss Garstone have yielded? If she had known at the time all that was involved? The answer to that stood out clearly. If she had known a thousand times, Miss Garstone wouldn't have given way. The house was her own. As long as she chose to stay there no one could shift her. She had been quite polite and agreeable about the whole thing, and quite adamant. There was nothing that Mrs. Forbes could do. So she had come away and left her.

After that nothing she did would have made any difference. When her husband came home he went to see Miss Garstone. He did not tell his wife what passed between them, and she did not ask. She determined on a certain course of action and she followed it. She didn't know, therefore, until her husband died that he had undertaken to pay for Jenny's schooling, and that he had left her enough to bring her in a hundred a year. This had caused Mrs. Forbes bitter resentment, but there was nothing she could do about it—nothing at all. She had known nothing until her husband was beyond her influence. She had known nothing until it was too late. The only thing that the discovery did for her was to bring into the light her hatred of her husband. She realized that when he was gone where it couldn't reach him. She had not admitted it even to herself until then.

She had shown nothing. The hurt went too deep for that. The money was paid over to Miss Garstone, and she tried to forget about it. The only person to whom she had spoken about it was Mac, and he had only laughed and told her not to worry. She wondered now what that had meant. Had he had any idea of marrying Jenny even then? She didn't know, and now she never would know.

Never is the most terrible word in the language. This thought came in upon her, flooding her mind with bitterness. She would never see Mac again. The word rang in her head like the ringing of a bell. Never—never—never—never. Her consciousness became deadened to it. It meant nothing. And then, like a curtain rising, consciousness came back and she saw in an awful perspective, as it were, endless mountain ranges of pain.

Her mind travelled on and on. She went through the last few weeks. Mac calm and sure, with his way out all planned, all ready, and that girl behind the curtain, listening to them. The cards had been stacked against them. Luck was on Jenny's side. You can't fight your luck. You can't fight it, you can't control it.

Her mind went back to last week-end, to Mac. . . . She hadn't known. . . . What was there to know? It was already too late. He wouldn't have killed himself if there was any other way out of it. There wasn't any other way. There was no other way for her. She did not even think of the children, or of Alan. They had never mattered to her in the way that Mac had. She opened the drawer and took out a loaded revolver.

No one in the house heard the shot.

CHAPTER 42

It was the next morning.
Jenny had not slept at all for the first part of the night, but towards morning she fell into a deep unconsciousness. As she came up from it she heard a bell ringing. It rang, and it ceased, and then it rang again, and ceased again. She dreamed that she was sailing on the sea. It was calm weather and the sun shone. And then suddenly the sun was gone and the day was dark, and above the crashing roar of the waves she could hear the sound of the bell. She was up on her elbow and half awake. And then she heard it again—the sound of the telephone bell in the room below.

She was out of bed in a moment and running down the stairs with her feet bare and her heart pounding. As she reached the telephone she heard Richard's step on the stair behind her. She heard her own voice, surprisingly steady.

"Yes—who is it?"

And then the ghost of Carter's voice.

"Miss Jenny, is that you?"

"Yes—yes. What is it?"

"Oh, Miss Jenny, I don't know what to do. I thought I'd better ring you."

Something clutched her heart. She heard herself say calmly and steadily, "What is it, Carter?"

"Oh, my dear! I didn't know what to do, but I thought you ought to know. It's Mrs. Forbes, my dear. I found her when I went down. Sitting at her table she was, and the pistol where it had dropped from her hand."

Jenny heard herself say, "Is she dead?"

"Oh, my dear, yes! And it's the little girls I'm thinking of. Mr. Alan's abroad, and we don't know where to get hold of him—and there's no one but you, my dear."

There was a question whose answer was a certainty, but she couldn't get it across her lips. Couldn't? She must. You can do anything if you've got to, she knew that. Her voice did not even tremble as she said, "Mac—" and listened for Carter's answer.

When it came it told her nothing which she did not already know, because only one thing would have made Mrs. Forbes take her life. She would never willingly have gone and left Mac behind her to face what must be faced. She knew the answer before it came with a burst of tears from Carter.

"Oh, my dear, he's gone too! That's what made her do it! I rang up straight away, and there was a policeman that answered! Mr. Mac, he shot himself last night, and she must have heard! I suppose the police would have told her! And she sat there all night, poor thing, and come the early morning, I suppose it got too much for her, and she took out that old revolver of the Colonel's and shot herself!"

Richard had come up close beside her. He had his arm round her and she leaned against it. His nearness helped her. It made her feel not quite so alone, not quite so friendless. She spoke into the receiver.

"I'll come, Carter. Tell the little girls I'll come this morning."

She hung up and turned to Richard.

"They're both dead—Mrs. Forbes and Mac! I can't take it in. But I must go to the little girls."

He said, "I'll drive you."

And then Caroline was there. Jenny turned and saw her standing by the door. She had waited to put on her dressing-gown. She looked calm, and she was a tower of strength.

"Yes, my dear, you shall go. And I think that Richard and I will come with you. We must dress and have breakfast, and then we will get off. Those poor little girls!"

Jenny said in a strange level voice,

"Alan ought to be there. He is the other son, you know. He is a year younger than Mac, and he's just left college. He's somewhere on the Continent, but they don't know where. We shall have to try and find him."

"Jenny dear, come and dress. We'll think of all the things we have to do, but not just now. The first thing to do is to get some clothes on."

Jenny looked down at her nightgown in a surprised sort of way. She had been quite unaware of it, and of her bare feet, but now she began to feel cold. She began to feel very cold. She held out her hands to Miss Danesworth, who put an arm round her and took her to the door. She said over her shoulder to Richard,

"Make some tea, there's a good boy, and when it's made bring it up."

Jenny went upstairs. She washed and dressed herself and drank some tea when it came. But it all seemed as if it was happening in a dream. Suppose she hadn't telephoned to Mac—they would both be alive now, he and his mother. And she had killed them? . . . No, it lay further back than that. She made herself look back, and she saw into Mac's mind. He had seen the whole thing quite simply. She knew that. His first choice had been to marry her, not because he loved her, but because that was the safe and certain way of getting the property. When she wouldn't—when she ran away—the only way he could think of was to kill her. He had planned it very carefully. If Dicky Pratt had been a reliable boy, his scheme would have come off. She would have gone to meet him, and she would have taken the note with her because he had asked her to. And then it would have been she that was killed, not Miriam. Not just there perhaps. He would have stopped the car, and she would have got in, and they would have driven off. He would not have gone very far, she thought—just a few hundred yards. And then he would have stopped the car, and she would be dead. Not Miriam. These thoughts went round and round in her head. Sometimes they were in the front of her mind, quite clear and distinct, and sometimes they were at the back of it, half hidden by a veil that was like mist.

When she had drunk some hot tea she was a little better, but she still felt as if she was in a dream. They had breakfast. Jenny choked hers down and drank two more cups of tea thirstily.

And then they were off. Jenny and Caroline sat behind, and Jenny was grateful because Caroline didn't talk to her. She sat with her face turned to the window and watched the side of the road. It meant nothing to her. She watched without seeing it. And all the time she saw Mac and Mrs. Forbes. Not dead but alive, dominant and aggressive. She couldn't think of them as dead.

When they came to the open gates she stiffened and sat up straight. And then they came to the drive, and up the drive to the front of the house, and with that the whole thing seemed to come to a head, because all the blinds were down. She said, "Oh!" and she caught Miss Danesworth by the arm very tight and hard. From the top of the house to the bottom all the blinds were down. It was a bright sunny day too, and that seemed to make it all much worse. A picture came up in her mind of the inside of the house, all dark, all closed up, all dead. She shuddered violently, and Miss Danesworth put her arm round her and said,

"You must think about the children, Jenny."

And with that Meg and Joyce came to her mind. And of course they were alive and they would need comforting. She said quite steadily,

"Thank you. I'm all right now."

And then Richard was opening the door and they got out and rang the bell. Jenny thought, "That's curious, to be ringing the bell," because it was such a long time since she had rung it. She couldn't really remember when she had rung it last. When Colonel Forbes was alive she had always gone round to the side door and in that way. She had been so fond of him. For the first time she was glad that he was dead. She hoped that he didn't know about his wife and about Mac. He had always been so kind to her—

As Jenny pulled the bell she thought of all the times that she had gone in and out by this door and by the little side door, and had never rung a bell at all. It seemed strange to be ringing it now when it all belonged to her. She couldn't realize that. She didn't realize it at all.

And then the door opened, and there was Carter, her eyes red and both hands out to her.

"Oh, Miss Jenny my dear! Oh, my dear—I'm so glad to see you!"

Jenny kissed her.

"And this is Miss Danesworth," she said. "And Richard. He is Richard Alington Forbes like my father was. And we're going to be married. Miss Danesworth is his aunt."

And with that there was a scurry of feet on the stairs and Meg was in Jenny's arms.

"She told us to stay upstairs! As if we could! Oh, Jenny, you won't go away again, will you? All the dreadful things have happened since you went away! And we don't know where Alan is, or anything!"

Step by step down the stairs Joyce came. She dragged her feet, and she looked so scared and miserable that Jenny ran to meet her.

"Poor child!" said Carter. "It comes very hard on the children, Miss Danesworth."

CHAPTER 43

Jenny found plenty to do.
The little girls clung to her, and it was difficult to get away from them. Sometimes it seemed as if she had never been away, and sometimes her short absence seemed to have lasted for years and years and years.

She went down into the kitchen and saw Mrs. Bolton, who began by being a total stranger receiving her new mistress, which was dreadful, and then suddenly burst into tears and addressed her as "Miss Jenny my dear," which was a great deal more comfortable.

"And they do say that everything belongs to you now, my dear."

"Yes, Mrs. Bolton, it does."

Jenny didn't cry, though she felt it was expected of her. She thought that if she could have cried she would have felt better. Tears would have been soft and comforting, but she couldn't make herself cry. One thing was spared her. She did not have to see Mrs. Forbes, for only half an hour before they had arrived her body had been removed to the mortuary. It was wrong to feel that this was a relief, but she did feel that it was.

Early in the afternoon Miss Crampton arrived, dressed in the funereal old black which was her habitual garb at funerals and visits of condolence. Mary opened the door to her, and was promptly buttonholed.

"This is dreadful news, Mary."

"Oh, yes, ma'am."

"Those poor children—I've come to see them. And Miss Jenny—she's come, I hear."

"Oh, yes. Carter rang her up at once."

"It is most improper that she should be here by herself. I cannot think how Miss Danesworth can have allowed it!"

Mary was beginning to enjoy herself.

"Oh, but she isn't alone," she said. "There's Mr. Richard—"

Miss Crampton interrupted her.

"Do you mean to tell me that she is here alone with that young man? How exceedingly improper!"

"No, miss, I never said so. Mr. Richard drove Miss Jenny here, and he drove his aunt too, Miss Danesworth. They are both here."

"Oh—" Miss Crampton stepped across the threshold. "Well, I'll come in. And I'll see Miss Jenny."

Mary lacked the assurance to stand up to her. She had attended Sunday School under Miss Crampton.

The habit of obedience persisted. She showed her into the drawing-room, where the flowers which Mrs. Forbes had picked yesterday were still fresh, and went running upstairs, where she met Carter and burst out,

"Oh, Carter, there's Miss Crampton in the drawing-room! She walked straight past me, and I couldn't stop her!"

Carter gave her a dark look.

"You could have said Miss Jenny was lying down."

Mary shook her head.

"Not to Miss Crampton, I couldn't."

Carter went along to the schoolroom, where the little girls sat painting superintended by Jenny, and Miss Danesworth was reading. Richard had gone out for a walk. Meg was engaged on a grand picture of the house. She had just discovered that she had got one window too few in the front, and was debating what she should do about it. Joyce, who was copying a Christmas card with a picture of a highly decorated tree on it, was most unsympathetic.

"I don't see that it matters," she said.

"Of *course* it matters," said Meg. "It's one of the windows of Alan's room. I can't leave him with one window."

"Lots of people have only one window," said Joyce.

"I shall tear it up and start all over again."

"Well, I think you're silly," said Joyce. Her voice was obstinate.

And then Carter came in.

"If you please, Miss Jenny, there's Miss Crampton downstairs."

"Horrid old thing," said Joyce in a fretful tone.

Meg tipped her chair up.

"Miss Crampton's a horrid old thing," she chanted. "And how did she know you were here, Jenny?"

"Will you see her, Miss Jenny?" said Carter.

"I suppose I'd better," said Jenny, rising reluctantly. Miss Danesworth laid down her book.

"Shall I come too?" she said.

"Oh, if you *would*," said Jenny. "She's Mrs. Merridew's cousin, you know, and she'll ask a lot of questions."

They went down together. Just outside the drawing-room door Jenny stopped, and Miss Danesworth turned to smile at her. It was such a loving smile that the tears rushed into Jenny's eyes and she had to wipe them away before she could go in. Her mind went to the change in her circumstances. Not that she was Miss Forbes of Alington House—that didn't matter. It was because she had Richard and Miss Danesworth that she wasn't alone and unprotected any longer. She squeezed the hand that was put out to her, and then she went into the drawing-room.

Miss Crampton sat facing the door in her mourning clothes. When she saw Jenny and Miss Danesworth she got up. She was disappointed, very much disappointed, but she couldn't say so. She had felt so deeply the impropriety of Jenny, a girl of seventeen, being there alone that she had come prepared to offer her own sustaining influence. And now, there was Miss Danesworth.

"You must not think," she said, "that Jenny would be alone here—oh dear me, no! We should have seen to that, I can assure you. I am quite prepared to come myself. Jenny knows that she can rely upon her old friends."

"I am sure she can. But it won't be necessary for you to put yourself out. I can stay as long as she needs me."

Miss Crampton plunged into a series of questions. Where was Alan? Had they heard from him? Did they know where to send a wire? Did they know why Mac had shot himself?

"I never was more shocked in my life. I was in the

post office, and Mrs. Boddles gave me the dreadful news. I could really hardly believe it. Such a fine young man. Ah well, it just shows that you can't ever tell, doesn't it? You must have come away in a great hurry, Jenny."

"We came as soon as we heard," said Jenny.

"Oh, yes, yes—of course."

"It was the little girls," said Jenny. "I had to come to them. And Miss Danesworth and Richard wouldn't let me come alone."

"Richard Forbes?" said Miss Crampton. "Ah, yes—he would be the son of those people who were killed in an air raid—oh, a long time ago. They were cousins or something."

"Mrs. Forbes was my sister," said Miss Danesworth.

"Oh, yes, I believe she was. He's your nephew then. He would have been very much shocked by Miriam's death, no doubt. I do not remember if I ever saw her, though of course I remember her mother. She was a sort of third cousin—you know how it was when families were so big. I wrote to her, but I have not had a reply. People are very careless about those sort of things nowadays. My dear father was most severe about it. 'It is the very least you can do to answer all letters of condolence promptly,' he used to say, and I have always done so. But Grace Richardson, I remember, was inclined to give way. It comes out at times like this."

At this point Richard opened the door and looked in. At the sight of Miss Crampton, very stiff and upright in her black clothes, he was visibly shaken, but seeing that there was no help for it, he advanced, was introduced, and shook hands. Miss Crampton looked him over, and exclaimed,

"What an extraordinary likeness!"

Miss Danesworth smiled.

"To the portrait in the hall?" she said. "Yes, he is

like it. He has the same name too—Richard Alington Forbes. Likenesses are strange things, are they not?"

"They are indeed," said Miss Crampton.

She seemed a little shaken by the likeness and kept on looking at Richard. When she got up to go she held his hand a little longer than was usual.

"I can't get over it," she said. "You're so like—so very like. I don't mean just the portrait in the hall, though you are like that too. But it is Jenny's father to whom the likeness is stronger. It is really very strong indeed—quite upsetting. Well, I must be going. You will let me know if there is anything I can do to help you."

She went out by the front door, and they saw her go. She walked with a lagging step and with less than her usual briskness.

"What did she mean?" said Jenny, looking after her with troubled eyes.

"I think perhaps she was fond of your father," said Miss Danesworth.

CHAPTER 44

Miss Silver sat in the train. She was on her way to Colborough. By her side sat Mrs. Pratt, a wan and tearful figure, and opposite them Dicky in a high state of excitement and good spirits.

"You be careful, Dicky—you be very careful," said Mrs. Pratt. She pressed a damp screwed-up handkerchief first into her right eye and then her left.

Miss Silver intervened.

"Now, Mrs. Pratt, there is no occasion for you to distress yourself."

"I'm so afraid," said Mrs. Pratt. "Suppose they was

to say that my Dicky was in need of care and attention and they sent him to one of them schools that are more like prisons than anything else—"

"I do not think that you need be under any apprehension, Mrs. Pratt," said Miss Silver. "Dicky is going to give evidence about the note which he forgot and which remained in his pocket. No one would dream of blaming you for that, and no one would dream of taking Dicky away from you."

"I'm so afraid," sobbed Mrs. Pratt.

Dicky had been whistling. The heart had gone out of it. Suppose his mother was right and the horrible danger of an approved school hung over his head—He cast an uneasy glance at Miss Silver, stopped whistling, and said,

"That's all nonsense, isn't it, Miss? They won't do nothing to me. I just got to give my evidence clear and truthful like you said—that's all, isn't it? Nobody's got any call to go sending me off to a home. Beastly old places homes. I knowed a boy as went to one, and he wasn't ever the same again, not by half he wasn't."

Miss Silver smiled at him.

"No one wants to put you into a home, Dicky," she said. "You will tell the truth, and that will set poor Mr. Mottingley free. No one will blame you for forgetting the note, I can assure you of that."

When they reached Colborough they took their way to the police court, which was quite near at hand. Frank Abbott was looking out for them. He smiled at Dicky, who wriggled rather uneasily under his eye, spoke to Mrs. Pratt, and smiled at Miss Silver.

"Punctual to the moment," he said. "And all complete. Now this young man will come in here"—he led the way to the waiting-room—"and Mrs. Pratt can either wait with him, or she can come into the court."

Dicky looked so dashed that Miss Silver hastened to

say, "I think that Mrs. Pratt had better come in with me. There might not be room later on, and she would like to hear Dicky giving his evidence. Would you not, Mrs. Pratt?"

Mrs. Pratt was understood to say something, but in so low and weepy a tone that no sense could be made of it.

Dicky was shut into the room with other witnesses, where he made himself quite at home, and Miss Silver and Mrs. Pratt followed Frank into the court room. He showed them to their places, and they settled down to waiting.

Mrs. Pratt was awed into silence for the first few minutes. Then she began in an awful whisper to detail all the troubles that had come upon her from the time of her marriage. At the most poignant part her voice sank into complete inaudibility.

"All in a moment he was dead. And we'd been so happy, and Dicky was only a baby. It's hard, it's very hard to know why such things are sent." There was a long inaudible piece here, and when next her voice reached Miss Silver she was saying, "Dicky's not a bad boy—reelly he isn't. Oh, do you think if I was to tell the magistrate that he was a good boy they'd not be too hard on him?"

Miss Silver said firmly, "Mrs. Pratt, there is no question of the magistrate being hard on Dicky. He is only giving evidence. He is not being tried—you know that."

"And I've always tried to keep him respectable," sobbed Mrs. Pratt. "And I never thought it would come to this."

"Mrs. Pratt, if you cannot control yourself you will have to leave the court. Nothing is going to happen to Dicky, I can assure you of that. If you do not sit quietly here you will be ordered from the court. Now pray control yourself."

Mrs. Pratt sat and wept silently—whilst the court filled up, whilst Jimmy Mottingley appeared in the dock, and whilst the magistrates came in, two men and a woman. At this point she raised her head a little and appeared to be taking some slight interest in the proceedings.

Miss Silver looked across at Jimmy and smiled. He was bearing himself well, and she was pleased to see it. His father and mother were both there. She had not seen Mrs. Mottingley before—a big fair woman with a controlled expression and hands that were twisted in her lap.

Jimmy's "Not guilty" rang out clearly. He looked down the court, and he saw Kathy Lingbourne. Her look encouraged him. It was full of faith and trust. Her brother Len was with her. After his time in prison it was good to see people who were free. He had undervalued freedom in the past. He thought that he would never undervalue it again.

Sir James Coghill, on the bench, was speaking.

"There has been a development in this case which will have the effect of changing the usual procedure. A witness will be called for the defence. Call Richard Pratt!"

There was a pause, and then Dicky Pratt appeared under the superintendence of an enormous policeman. He was quite composed. He wore his best suit, his golden hair shone, his blue eyes gazed trustfully at the court, and he took the oath with great decorum. Mrs. Pratt roused from her melancholy state to feel proud of him. He gave what may be called a perfect performance.

Mr. Carisbrooke rose from the table in the middle of the hall.

"Your name is Richard Pratt?"

"Yes, sir."

"You are—how old?"

"Eleven and a half, sir."

"You remember Saturday the thirtieth of September?"

"Oh, yes, sir."

"Will you describe what happened to you when it was getting dark."

"I was going along the road past Miss Danesworth's house, and when I'd got a little way past a gentleman stopped me."

"Was he on foot, or was he in a car?"

"He was on foot, but there was a car up the road. He came out of it. And he said to me, 'Hi, you boy—like to earn half-a-crown?' And I said, yes I would. So then he said as he'd a note he wanted taken to Miss Danesworth's house, and he arst me did I know it, and I said yes I did, so he said the note was for the young lady that lived there with Miss Danesworth, and he went away up the road towards the common where his car was."

"And what did you do?"

Dicky hesitated. Then he said,

"I thought as I'd find out what he was up to. It was dark, and I went after him."

"Did you catch him?"

Dicky shook his head.

"I didn't try to. I wanted to see where he went to. I hadn't ever seen him before, and it crossed my mind that he mightn't be up to any good, so I kept behind him."

"And what happened?"

"He went on up the road, and he come to where his car was standing—"

Sir James Coghill leaned forward and asked, "Whereabouts was this car? Was it beyond the place where the body was found?"

Dicky nodded.

"That's right. It was fifty yards beyond it."

"And how do you know that?"

"Because I paced it—see?"

"You paced it. Why?"

"Oh, not then, I didn't. I come back in the morning and did it. The murder was out by then."

"And how do you know that you'd got the right place to measure to?"

"There was oil on the road—that's why, sir."

Sir James leaned back again, and the questioning went on.

"Well, Richard, you came up the road and saw the gentleman get into the car. Is that right?"

"Yes, sir. And I went round without his seeing me to the back of his car."

"How do you know that he didn't see you?"

The blue eyes took on a dreamy gaze. They really were very beautiful eyes.

"I played Injuns with him, sir."

"How do you mean you played Indians?"

"It's a game we play, sir. I'm quite good at it. You must get to a place without anyone seeing you. It's difficult in the daytime, but it's dead easy at night. I got round to the back of the car, and there I see as how he'd got something hanging down over the back so that the number-plate was covered."

"You're sure of that? You're on oath, remember."

The blue eyes reproached him.

"Acourse I remember."

"What did you do?"

"I lifted the stuff that was hanging down. I'd some matches with me and I saw the number-plate."

He gave the county letters and the number of Mac's car.

"You are quite sure about that? Remember that you are on oath."

"I'm quite sure, sir."

"And then?"

"I was playing a game of cops and Injuns. The man in the car was a cop, and I was an Injun."

"Go on."

Dicky hesitated. There was something more to tell— something that he hadn't told to anyone, something that gave him a funny feeling when he remembered it. It gave him such a funny feeling that he didn't like talking about it. His voice fell.

"The man in the car was putting his moustache back on—"

There was a sensation in the court. Dicky, seeing the effect that he had produced, perked up a little. Mr. Carisbrooke came in quickly.

"He was putting his moustache back on?"

"Yes, he was."

"Let's get this quite clear. Do you mean that the man in the car had been wearing a false moustache?"

"Yes, sir. A big bushy one it was."

"And you're quite sure about this?"

"Yes, sir. He put on the light inside the car and he looked in the glass, and he was fixing it to get it straight. And I dunno why, but it kind of give me the creeps and I ran away."

"And then did you deliver the note?"

Dicky became noticeably deflated. He said, "N-no," and shuffled with his feet.

"Why didn't you?"

Dicky hesitated. To say that he had forgotten it would be the truth, the whole truth, and nothing but the truth, but he had found grown-ups singularly unreceptive to this kind of truth. And then with a glow of virtue it came over him that if he told the truth and they didn't believe him, that was their affair, he had nothing to do with it. He lifted his head, fixed his blue gaze on Mr. Carisbrooke's face and said,

"Please, sir, I forgot all about it."

"How was that?"

"Well, I met up with Stuffy Craddock and Roger Barton, and they'd got a wizard scheme on. . . . Must I tell you what it was, sir?"

"I think you had better." Mr. Carisbrooke's tone was affable.

Dicky brightened.

"They said there was a wheel sunk in the pond by Mr. Fulbrook's wall, and they said if we could get it out—" His voice rather trailed away.

"If they could get it out—"

Dicky's voice became small and miserable.

"They said as if we could get it out we could have a go at the apples on the other side of the wall."

"I see," said Mr. Carisbrooke cheerfully. "And did you get it out?"

"No, sir. And it was getting late and we was all wet through, so we went home, and my mother took off my wet clothes to dry them and I went to bed."

"And when did you think of the note again?"

"Not till next day, sir."

"And then?"

"I didn't think that I'd better do anything about it. It's—it's rather difficult, sir—"

Mr. Carisbrooke looked at him cheerfully.

"Let's have it," he said.

A faint angel smile trembled on Dicky's lips.

"It had got wet, sir, with us trying to get the wheel out of the pond. It was stuck in the mud and we got soaked, me and Stuffy Craddock and Roger Barton. Roger's father clouted him proper."

"Did your mother clout you?"

"*No!* My mother never clouts me."

"You are very fortunate," said Mr. Carisbrooke drily.

"Oh, yes, sir, I know that."

Beside Miss Silver Mrs. Pratt began to cry again. Her Dicky—to say that—in a court of justice! It was the moment of her life. She wept on silently.

The counsel for the defence was speaking.

"And what did you do about the note after that?"

"I didn't do anything, sir. I left it in my pocket."

"Until when?"

"Till Miss Silver come, she and Miss Jenny."

"When was that?"

"It was a week ago."

"And then?"

"Miss Silver she asked me about it, and I told her. I give her the letter."

"Is this the letter?" He was being offered it—the same dirty, creased note that Mac had written and that Jenny had never had.

"Yes, that's it!"

"Read it out."

"Do I read the date too?"

"You read everything."

He read the date aloud, and then went on, " 'Jenny, *don't say anything to anyone*'—that's underlined that is. And then it goes on, 'but come out and meet me up on the heath as soon as it is quite dark. Mac. Bring this with you.' "

CHAPTER 45

Dicky stepped down from the witness-box and made his way through the crowded court to where Miss Silver and his mother sat together.

Jimmy Mottingley had taken his place in the box. He spoke up well and clearly.

"You are James Mottingley?"

"Yes, sir."

"Will you describe what happened on the day of the murder."

He did so, and as he spoke it all came rushing back on him—his mother's drawing-room—his mother calm and placid—talking to Mrs. Marsden and delaying him when he wanted to get started. It all came back to him as if it had happened yesterday. He could hear the very tones of their voices. It was uncanny how the give and take of that conversation came back to him. It was only by an effort that he kept his voice loud enough to fill the court room. It was as if he was back in his mother's drawing-room with his eye upon the clock and counting out the time that it would take him to reach Hazeldon.

"I was very late in starting. The clock said half past six."

"You drove fast?"

"I drove as fast as I could. I had this appointment."

"With the dead girl?"

"With Miriam Richardson."

"Go on."

"When I got to Hazeldon I drove slowly up on to the Heath. I expected her to be near the road by the patch of gorse bushes, but I couldn't see her. So I drove on a bit, and then I got out and walked back. I thought perhaps she hadn't waited as I was so late."

"What time was it when you got there?"

"I don't know. I was in a hurry because I knew that I was late. I got straight out of the car and ran back to the clump of gorse. She wasn't there. Then I went round the bushes and I found her." His voice dropped to a horrified whisper, but it was a whisper that carried.

"Will you describe what you saw."

Jimmy went on in that strange carrying whisper.

"She was there—on the ground. When I touched her I knew—that she was dead—"

"How did you know that she was dead?"

"She was cold—she was quite cold."

"What did you do?"

"I went out on the road, and a bicycle was coming. I stood and waved, and it stopped. The man came with me, and I told him I had come there to meet a girl, and that I had found her dead. He took me to the police station, and we got the constable. That's all."

"Mr. Mottingley, you are on oath. Did you strike the blow which killed Miriam Richardson?"

"No, sir."

"Did you ever think of killing her?"

"No, sir."

"That is all. You can step down."

"Call James Fulbrook!"

Mr. Fulbrook stepped up into the witness-box and took the oath.

"Mr. Fulbrook, will you tell us what happened on your way back to Hazeldon on the day in question."

"I had been to see my daughter who was laid up with her first child, and as I was coming back—"

"What time would that be?"

"I should think it was a quarter or twenty to eight, but I can't be quite certain. I didn't look at my watch."

"That's near enough. Go on."

"I was coming down the road towards Hazeldon—"

"You were on a bicycle?"

"Yes."

"Go on, Mr. Fulbrook."

"Well, I was coming along, and all of a sudden there was someone in the road ahead of me holding up his hands and calling out. There'd been a car parked by the

260 • *Patricia Wentworth*

side of the road a little way back, and I thought someone had got into trouble, so I stopped. And when I
stopped, there was a young man in a great state of distress. He said the girl he'd come to meet had been murdered, and would I come and see her. So I came."

"And the girl was dead?"

"The girl was dead and cold."

"What did you do then?"

"I took the young man with me in his car to the police station, and we fetched the constable."

Dicky listened with all his ears. He was very glad that
Mr. Fulbrook hadn't been in the court when he was
giving his evidence. Not that they had touched his apples, but that was the reason they had had for trying to
get the cart wheel out of the pond. He wasn't going to
do that sort of thing any more—it wasn't worth while.

And then they had finished with Mr. Fulbrook, and
the Clerk said,

"Call Inspector Abbott!"

Frank stepped up into the witness-box. Dicky gazed
at him in reverence and determined in his own mind
that that would be a wizard career. If he were to study
good and proper from now on, why shouldn't he finish
up in the C.I.D.? That was what Inspector Frank Abbott was, and what he didn't know wasn't worth knowing. He listened with all his ears.

Inspector Abbott was asking for the discharge of the
prisoner. He was saying that the man who wrote that
note was the murderer, and the note was the one which
Dicky had had in his pocket until Miss Silver and Miss
Jenny had gone to see him. It was Miss Jenny that Mac
meant to kill, not the other girl at all. Coo! That must
have been a sell for him that must! And a let-off for
Miss Jenny. He liked Miss Jenny, and he hadn't liked
Miriam Richardson. If one of them had got to be killed
it was much better to be the Richardson girl. And what

a sell for this Mac when he found he'd killed the wrong girl! He wondered when he found out that he had made a mistake.

With all these thoughts in his mind the time passed. The Inspector was saying that Mr. Mac had committed suicide. That was a pity, that was. There'd have been a juicy big murder case if he hadn't. Dicky's imagination played lovingly with the thought of it.

And then it was all over. Sir James Coghill was telling Mr. Mottingley that he could go free. The lady whom he had discovered to be Mrs. Mottingley, the mother of the prisoner, was sitting very still and stiff. She was just in front of them. If he had been the accused his mother wouldn't have sat like that, she wouldn't. But Mrs. Mottingley she sat there stiff and straight, and as if she didn't feel anything at all. Or was it that way? He wasn't sure. He wished she would move or speak. It wasn't natural for her to sit so still. Her husband thought so too, because he stooped down and whispered to her. They were so close that Dicky could hear what he said. It was, "Marian—" That was her name, and he said it twice. And then he said, "My dear, are you all right?" and with that Mrs. Mottingley moved. Come to think of it, she hadn't moved until then—not all the time. But now she did move. She half turned towards her husband, and she gave a deep sigh and fell sideways. Coo! The excitement wasn't all over!

Dicky sat where he was and saw Miss Silver go round to the end of the row and down. She'd know what to do, she would. He felt an implicit trust in Miss Silver's ability to control any situation. There she was, as cool and as calm as anything.

"If you will all stand away and just leave her to me. Mr. Mottingley, will you kindly get me a glass of water? She will be all right in a minute. No, madam, she is not dead. She has merely fainted."

Dicky's bosom swelled with pride. She could manage them, she could! He was roused from his trance of admiration by his mother. She plucked him by his sleeve and said in a frightened whisper,

"Oh, what a dreadful thing! Oh, Dicky, is she dead?"

Dicky picked up the last word and said it loudly.

"Dead? What 'ud she be dead for? There's Miss Silver looking after her!"

Mrs. Mottingley drew a long breath. She was not back yet, but she was coming back. She felt weak, relaxed, and happy. She opened her eyes for a moment and saw Jimmy and her husband. They were her whole world, and they were safe. It was all right. The dreadful time was over. Jimmy was free. The little elderly lady who was kneeling beside her smiled at her and said,

"You are better now, Mrs. Mottingley? No, don't sit up just yet. Would you like a drink of water?"

Everything was relaxed and easy. She took a drink of the water and sat up.

"I'm all right now. I'd like to go home."

"My dear—" It was her husband. His arm was round her. She felt very safe and protected. And Jimmy was there too. He held her hand and said, "Mum—" She tried to think when he had last called her that. Not for years and years. There was something wrong about that. You oughtn't to lose the confidence of your child because he has grown up. There was something very wrong about that. She would try to do better. She pressed Jimmy's hand, and he said, "Mum—" in an odd shaken voice which took her back to the time when he had got out on the roof and she had thought he was going to fall. He was only seven years old. . . .

She shut her eyes again for a moment as she remembered the scene. She had been so dreadfully frightened, but she hadn't fainted—not then. And Jimmy hadn't been frightened—not a bit of it. She remembered the whole thing. Curious how it came back to her now— Jimmy dancing along on the edge of danger, and then her husband getting hold of him, and the piteous sobs of a hurt child. Jimmy had never been so confident and gay again after that. She held to his hand and pulled him down close while she whispered,

"You're safe, Jimmy—you're safe—"

And then the boy who was one of their clerks came up and said, "I've got a taxi outside, Mr. Mottingley," and her husband said, "Thank you, Lingbourne. We'll come."

Kathy, standing to one side, saw them go by. It had all turned out wonderfully. She felt so glad for Mrs. Mottingley, and for Jimmy. And then, as she turned to find her way out, Mr. Mottingley hurried up behind her.

"I've left my wife to her boy and to Miss Silver. I wanted to thank you, my dear."

The bright colour came into her cheeks.

"Oh, Mr. Mottingley!" she said.

"And I'd like you to know that we don't want you to stop being friends with Jimmy. A house like yours is just what he needs—young people's society and all that. And we hope you'll come to our house, too, you and Len. You will, won't you?"

"I shall be very pleased to, Mr. Mottingley."

"My wife would like you to come. We've brought the boy up too strict—I can see that now. If you pull the rein too tightly you've a nervous horse—" He broke off with half a laugh. "That sounds strange coming from me, but I grew up on a farm, and it comes back when you're moved. Good-bye, my dear."

He left her standing there and went off to join his wife and Jimmy.

CHAPTER 46

At Alington House Jenny sat and waited for the news. Miss Silver would ring up, she knew that, and she knew what the news would be. But supposing—just supposing— Her thought broke off. It broke off because she broke it off. She would not go on to suppose such failure of justice as would keep Jimmy Mottingley in any danger. All the same it would be nice to know that they could put away the unhappy past and go on into something better.

The last few days had been very trying. She did not know what she would have done without Richard and Miss Danesworth. She had stood between the little girls and all the worst of it, and Richard and Miss Danesworth had sheltered her as much as they could. It was lovely to have them. When she thought what it would have been like to have to stand alone her thoughts just blacked out. She could have done it, because you can do anything that you've got to do, but she was profoundly grateful that she did not have to stand alone. For one thing, Miss Crampton would have been very hard to deal with. She had faded away before Miss Danesworth's presence, and Richard coming in when he did had completed her discomfiture. Now that she had been routed Jenny could feel sorry for her. Once you have seen the softer side of anyone you can never go back to seeing them as they were. It was difficult to put into words, but it was in your mind.

Richard came into the room, and she put out a hand to him.

"It's so long waiting," she said with a little break in

her voice. "You don't think anything can have gone wrong, do you?"

"Of course nothing has gone wrong! Don't be silly, child! What could go wrong?"

"I don't know. Miss Silver said she would ring up when it was all over."

"Then she will. I like Miss Silver. She's bed-rock solid."

"Oh, Richard! That sounds as if she was one of those stout, hard people with bright red cheeks and the sort of eyes that pop out a little! Not the kind of person she is at all—neat, and old-fashioned, and governessy—only that I've never really come across a governess. People don't have them nowadays, but in Garsty's old books they did. But Miss Silver isn't really like anyone."

"No, I don't think she is," said Richard. He sat down with his arm round her. "Relax, darling. It's all right—it really is."

"I keep thinking of—of her," said Jenny.

"Not Mrs. Forbes? Don't, my dear!"

"I can't help it," said Jenny. "Oh, Richard, please let me talk about it. It all seems so dreadful. And the most dreadful part of it is that no one really misses her. Carter cried when she went down to the inquest. She admired her, but she didn't really love her. And her friends—I don't believe one of them really cared. They were shocked when she shot herself, but they didn't really care—not *really*."

Richard hesitated. Then he said,

"When something like this happens people either rush in and find they are not wanted, or they stay away and pretend that they haven't noticed. I think you would find that they don't know quite what to do. Don't get bitter about it, darling."

"I'm not. I just thought it would be rather lonely if it wasn't for you and Caroline."

"Well, you've got us," said Richard. "You've got us for keeps, and don't you forget it."

"Oh, Richard, you're such a comfort!" said Jenny with the tears in her eyes.

And then the telephone bell rang. Jenny was out of her seat in a moment, her breathing quickened and the colour in her cheeks coming and going. She heard Miss Silver say,

"Is that you, my dear?"

"Oh, yes. Yes—yes, it is. Oh, do tell me! What has happened?"

Miss Silver's voice came clear along the wire.

"It is all right, my dear. There is nothing for you to be worried about. Dicky Pratt gave his evidence very well indeed. I went over with him and Mrs. Pratt. He really could not have done better. And I think he enjoyed himself."

"He would," said Jenny.

"Yes, I remember that you said so. A boy of his age does not apprehend the seriousness of the position. Mr. Fulbrook gave evidence, and James Mottingley. He did very well indeed. I do not think that he could have failed to convince everyone in the court that he was quite innocent of that poor girl's death. And then Inspector Abbott came into the witness-box and gave his evidence. You know what that was. It cleared Mr. Mottingley completely, and he was discharged. And now, my dear, how is it with you? You have Miss Danesworth and Mr. Richard Forbes with you, have you not? I am afraid that this has been a sad and very trying time for you. You must look forward to the brighter days which lie ahead. Good-bye, my dear."

The click of the receiver sounded. Miss Silver was gone. One moment she was there, so much herself, so kind, so efficient, and so helpful, and the next she was gone. She was quite gone. It gave Jenny a curious feeling of unreality.

She hung up the receiver and turned to Richard. He put an arm about her.

"Yes, I heard," he said. "Mottingley has had a hard time."

Jenny was crying. She didn't know why. Everything was all right as far as it could be all right. She said, "Oh, Richard—" and they stood together for a moment or two. Then she drew herself away and dried her eyes.

"That's silly," she said. "And there's a letter from Alan. I didn't open it because—well, because I wanted you to be there. I didn't feel as if I wanted to read it alone."

"Well, I'm here, darling. Go on—open it."

The letter was in a foreign envelope. Jenny opened it and read:

Dear Jenny,

I don't know what to say. I feel quite bewildered with it all. Anyhow I don't see much good in my coming back until the unpleasantness has died away. The chaps that I am with say the same. I think I had better find a job. As a matter of fact I've practically got one. It's with a young Austrian. He's got to travel for his health. I've made great friends with him, and his people are very well off. His mother was Spanish, and the money comes from that side of the family. He is going to pay all the expenses, and I think we shall go to India first of all. He is supposed to be in a warm climate.

Yours affectionately,
Alan Forbes

As Jenny read on her colour rose. When she had finished it she put the letter into Richard's hand and said in a curious voice,

"He's going to India, and he doesn't leave us any address."

Richard read the letter.

"It's pretty calm," he said. "Nothing about the little girls, I see."

"There's nothing about anyone except himself," said Jenny. "But there's one thing—it does give me a free hand with Meg and Joyce."

"Oh, yes, it gives you a free hand," said Richard. "They are his sisters, and your second—or is it third cousins? But he gives you a perfectly free hand with them. You can pay their school bills, and have them in the holidays, and have all the burden and sweat of bringing them up, whilst he goes off into the blue and enjoys himself!"

But Jenny was laughing.

"Oh, Richard, I'll love it—I really will."

He said, "I'm angry," and he looked it.

"Oh, don't be, darling! Don't you see it'll be just perfect? Caroline was saying only this morning that she'd hate to give them up. And there would be room for them in her house—she said that too."

"Here, what have you been planning?"

"We're going to be a family," said Jenny. "Caroline agreed with me about it. The little girls can go to school, and we'll be all together in the holidays. At least—"

"And what happens to us?"

"I suppose we get married," said Jenny.

THE END